Praise for *The Measure (*

"An active, lucid, melancholy voice, telling unnatural world—J. Ashley-Smith's *The Measure of Sorrow* is half love, half fear, and all wonder."

—Kathe Koja, author of *Dark Factory* and *The Cipher*

"The impeccable and haunting stories in *The Measure of Sorrow* are filled with longing, frailty, and a most human sense of awe in the face of their horrors."

—Paul Tremblay, author of *The Cabin at the End of the World* and *A Head Full of Ghosts*

"*The Measure of Sorrow* could not bear a better title. This collection plumbs the depths of our darkest emotional states—grief, shame, madness, terror—and renders them with exquisite sensitivity and candor. There is both strength and vulnerability in these tales, and in the characters that find their way through them (or not), laced with a surreal strain of cosmic horror that J. Ashley-Smith truly makes his own. They are sure to linger with you for quite a while, these stories. If you're lucky, they may even leave a scar."

—Kirstyn McDermott, author of *Hard Places*

"J. Ashley-Smith writes stories like five course meals: rich, complex, satisfying. In his work, betrayal, grief, and sorrow bleed into and blend with situations ominous and surreal. There are echoes of Kafka, here, and Aickman, too, but the achievement is all J. Ashley-Smith's. *The Measure of Sorrow* gives measure of his talent, and that is considerable."

—John Langan, author of *Corpsemouth and Other Autobiographies*

"The exquisiteness and gentleness with which J. Ashley-Smith swathes his darkest stories, entangled in the cornerstones of serrated humanity, leave you fact checking everything you thought you believed. The theme story 'The Measure of Sorrow' is literary horror that taps on angst—a father's craving for his dead wife and pining to assuage his son's lostness—to spill out the guts of a luminescent magnetar in animated doom. The juxtaposition of opalescence and gloom in deeply-etched longing and need echo in ink until you forget, and forget, that what you're reading is horror, until—too late—it masticates you alive. For lovers of elegant literary horror."

—Eugen Bacon, World Fantasy Finalist and award-winning author of _Danged Black Thing, Mage of Fools_ and _Chasing Whispers_

"The soil of these stories is sown with the salt of night-sweat and grief-tears, and what it grows is resplendent in weird, wonderful riches. Bring home _The Measure of Sorrow_, let it take root in the grounds you walk alone, and cherish the bittersweet fruits of its seductive terrors for years to come."

—Matthew R. Davis, Shirley Jackson Award-nominated author of _Midnight in the Chapel of Love_

"_The Measure of Sorrow_ is a beautiful, deeply unsettling collection that explores the horror and the mystery of what it is to be human. Heartbreaking at times and raw, these stories always feel immensely true, no matter how fantastical they seem. Ashley-Smith has a talent for creating worlds that are hauntingly familiar, echoes of our own edged with a darkness that we can only hope isn't real."

—Joanne Anderton, author of _The Art of Broken Things_

Praise for _Ariadne, I Love You_

"_Ariadne, I Love You_, by J. Ashley-Smith, is my favorite kind of horror story: intimate, whip-smart, and relentless. The protagonist is in many ways a terrible human being: selfish, directionless, blind to the needs of others—and totally sympathetic, at least to this jaded reader. He is also doomed, which comes as no surprise. The mechanism of that doom is a surprise, though, and a delightfully awful one. More stories like this, please."

—Nathan Ballingrud, author of _North American Lake Monsters_ and _Wounds: Six Stories from the Border of Hell_

"A haunting tale of desire and madness and what might—or might not—be love. Ashley-Smith weaves a compelling story of music, bone, and nightmare."

—Angela Slatter, award-winning author of _All the Murmuring Bones_

"A nuanced and numinous rock 'n' roll Gothic about the distances—in time and space—that a broken heart will go to terrifyingly reassemble. You might begin J. Ashley-Smith's condensed riff on the abyss of student longing, artistic burnout and unresolved grief, on the train. You almost certainly will continue reading while stirring the pasta and eating it, and halfway through your meal you will look up from your second glass of wine and wonder where the hell you are."

—J.S. Breukelaar, award-winning author of *The Bridge*

"Ashley-Smith understands that ghost stories are, most importantly and at their core, about people, and with *Ariadne, I Love You*, he's crafted a haunting, ambiguous, confident and ghastly tale of eternal love."

—Keith Rosson, Shirley Jackson Award-winning author of *Folk Songs For Trauma Surgeons* and *Fever House*

Praise for *The Attic Tragedy*

"Ashley-Smith debuts with a gorgeous, melancholy coming-of-age novella about girlhood and ghosts. . . . This eerie, ethereal tale marks Ashley-Smith as a writer to watch."

—Publishers Weekly

"A beautifully written book about desire, pain, and loss, haunted by glimmerings of the supernatural. *The Attic Tragedy* manages to do more by intimation and suggestion with its fifty-three pages than most novels manage to accomplish over their several hundred."

—Brian Evenson, author of *Song for the Unraveling of the World*

"J.Ashley-Smith doesn't put a foot wrong in this chilling, devastating story. *The Attic Tragedy* is hard to read in the best possible way."

—Kaaron Warren, award-winning author of *Into Bones Like Oil* and *Tide of Stone* by J. Ashley-Smith

The Measure of Sorrow
Ariadne, I Love You
The Attic Tragedy

the measure of sorrow

stories

J. Ashley-Smith

Meerkat Press
Asheville

"The Further Shore," originally published in *Bourbon Penn* #15, March 2018.
"Old Growth," originally published in *SQ Mag* #31, June 2017.
"The Moth Tapes," originally published in *Aurealis Magazine* #117, February 2019.
"Our Last Meal," originally published in *In Sunshine Bright and Darkness Deep: An Anthology of Australian Horror*, edited by Cameron Trost, Australasian Horror Writers Association, 2015.
"The Black Massive," originally published in *Dimension6* #21, October 2020.
"The Face God Gave," originally published in *Gorgon: Stories of Emergence*, edited by Sarah Read, *Pantheon Magazine*, 2019.

Three lines of "I have many brothers in the south . . . ." from SELECTED POEMS OF RAINER MARIA RILKE: A Translation from the German and Commentary, by Robert Bly Copyright © 1981 by Robert Bly. Used by permission of HarperCollins Publishers.

ISBN-13 978-1-946154-77-4 (Paperback)
ISBN-13 978-1-946154-78-1 (eBook)

Cover and book design by Tricia Reeks

Author photo Copyright © Mick Tsikas

Printed in the United States of America

Published in the United States of America by
Meerkat Press, LLC, Asheville, North Carolina
www.meerkatpress.com

For Ben, Ben and Cormac, for all the reasons.

CONTENTS

The Further Shore 1

Old Growth...19

The Moth Tapes 31

The Family Madness 43

The Whatnot Shop.. 71

Our Last Meal 78

The Black Massive..91

The Face God Gave.. 118

The Boon 122

The Measure of Sorrow..134

Acknowledgments... 185

About the Author 187

For high above my own station, hovered a gleaming host of heavenly beings, surrounding the pillows of the dying children. And such beings sympathize equally with sorrow that grovels and with sorrow that soars. Such beings pity alike the children that are languishing in death, and the children that live only to languish in tears.

—*Thomas De Quincey, Suspiria De Profundis*

The Further Shore

Renault was out beyond the littoral when the fear bloomed.

Drifting with the currents, he bobbed above the reef. The sun warmed his back, cast a spangled net of iridescent white on the ocean floor. The only sound was the rasp of his breath in the snorkel, the faint pop pop of unseen creatures in the labyrinth of black coral below.

The black reef, with its oil-slick glimmer, stretched as far as he could see. Crooked spires. Towers that jutted and curled like obsidian fingers. Was it a trick of distance or movements of the water that made the coral writhe and sway? It was profoundly hypnotic, drew him out over ever-deeper waters, farther from the shore.

Renault had noticed the pattern two days before. It was madness to think there should be order out here, among these chaotic accretions; yet there it was. The deep grooves of shadow that drew together, converging like vast, curved spokes around a distant axis. It had been too late to explore that first afternoon, and yesterday had been overcast, the light too diffuse to make out any detail in the reef. This morning he had woken early, determined to swim out to the point where those dark channels met.

His excitement mounted as each stroke brought him closer to the center. The crevasse he was following narrowed, its arc tightening around smooth plates that resembled the petals of an obscene black flower. These segments overlapped uniformly, interlocking at the hub around something that glinted, that refracted light in soft, shimmering rainbows. It looked very much like a pearl. A pearl the size of a boulder.

Renault strained to make it out, unable to believe what he was seeing. But his mask had fogged and his sight was confined to a blurred rectangle. Just outside this frame of vision, he caught a movement.

He spun, scanning the water around, below.

There was nothing. He could see nothing. But his back tingled, his chest tightened. Something was there. *Something.*

Renault became suddenly aware of the depth of water beneath him, the distance to dry land, the darkening sky. The shadows within the black landscape were spreading, swallowing the reef. And within them—

Fear propelled him. He turned shoreward, beating at the waves with his arms, with his fins, battling the currents of the outward tide.

Though every muscle screamed, he did not stop thrashing until he felt the sand beneath him.

—

The reef obsessed Renault. For days now he had been coming here, following the water's edge to where the salt-and-pepper sand turned gritty black. To where he had first found the shells.

He thought of them as shells only because he had no better word to describe them—organic forms that twisted and coiled without order, without repetition, conforming to some other geometry. Some ribbed, some spurred, some perfectly smooth, the shells were all black when dry, but iridesced when submerged in water, revealing shifting patterns of color. All alluded to the familiar, yet all eluded classification. No two were alike.

He was quick to intuit the connection between the shells and the black sand, but the existence of the reef was a hypothesis he was unable to test without proper equipment. A search of the shack had revealed a mismatched pair of flippers left by a past occupant, but it took hours of scavenging along the coastline before he found a mask, and weeks before a snorkel washed onto the shore.

To stave off the madness of impatience, Renault killed time collecting shells. He studied them, took them back to his room in secret, always careful to hide his discoveries from the others. From Benson. And from Webb.

After weeks of frustrated speculation, he finally swam out beyond the breakers. When he dipped his head beneath the waves, caught sight of that landscape of black sculptures, it was the closest to pure joy Renault had felt since he first awoke in the shack.

—

The wind had picked up, blew the tang of saltwater and rotting kelp in from the sea. Renault's stomach growled.

He knew he did not need food, yet the old triggers persisted. Mealtimes were the worst.

He walked north with the sun low behind the mountain, with shadows reaching seaward across the wasteland of scrub and salt grass. The ocean was marbling blue and golden red, a web of light that danced toward the horizon and the chain of hulking black ships. His feet made impressions in the moist sand, a trail of prints that faded beneath the lapping tide. He had stayed out too long, left barely enough time to make it to the shack before dark.

Renault quickened his pace, muttering, cursing. He was raging at his irrational fear, elated at the discovery of the black flower and the pearl. And his excitement made him rage all over again, impatient to be back out over the reef.

Among the tangles of driftwood and seaweed that littered the shore, a framed picture was caught in the foam, a monochrome of a woman and child in shades of silvery gray. It was drawn back with each inhalation of the tide, rotated gently, washed forward again with each exhalation. The photograph was buckled and warped, but Renault could see it clearly, felt deeply the ache it gave him.

Those people. He—

But he did not know them. Knew nothing of his life before the shack. Whatever memories the picture suggested were gone—if they had ever existed.

Renault kicked the picture as he passed, back into the surf, where it tumbled and rolled beneath the curling waves.

—

Renault's first morning in the shack, he woke with no memory of falling asleep. When he thought back there was . . . nothing. He had no idea where he was. No idea *who* he was.

There was only this moment. The muffled swell of the ocean. The rusting tin ceiling. The gritty, unwashed feel of the sheets.

Benson had loomed in what passed for a kitchen. Another man, Stacks, was seated at the table. His head was completely bald, with a face that sagged above its ridiculous handlebar mustache. They stared as Renault lurched into the room, slumped on a tea-chest. The table wobbled when he leaned on it. Benson brought him coffee.

Both men stared. Their look was neither kind nor unkind, neither surprised nor interested. Renault sipped his coffee, avoided their eyes, struggled to remember.

That morning he had taken his first walk out along the shore. He had first seen Benson's armchair sunk in the wet sand, seen Benson staring out toward the dark ships that girded the horizon. That morning he had claimed his first piece of flotsam.

Stacks hadn't lasted long. Just a few days after Renault's appearance he announced that he was going to scale the mountain. He set off at dawn and never returned. In the morning, his bedroom door had opened and out stepped a stranger with a confused look on his face.

Since then, Renault had seen them come and go.

They were like devotees of some terrible god, one that nobody quite believed in. They stumbled up and down the beach gathering their combings from the surf, eyes alight with the promise of revelation, hoarding their half-eroded trinkets like sacred totems. Mostly they made it to the shack before night fell. Sometimes they did not.

All wore the same blank expression: a mask of vacancy, ecstasy, melancholy. All believed they would be first to discover the hidden meaning, to reassemble from those worthless treasures the puzzle pieces of who they had once been. All feared they would never remember.

No one dared speculate that there was no meaning.

—

The path to the shells, to the discovery of the reef, had been opened by the question of food.

The shack was exposed to a stretch of coast too vast to explore in a single day, and there was no question of staying out past nightfall. In all his excursions, Renault had come across no evidence of habitation. There were no buildings, no roads. He had found no path or animal track through the scrub, no footprints in the sand but his own. No one but the occupants came to the shack. There were no deliveries.

So where did the food come from?

Before turning in one night, he had checked the fridge—a monstrous, noisy machine that bore the scars of a past life on the ocean floor. Inside, there were just scraps: leftovers under clingfilm, desiccated condiments, half a tin of beer.

Yet when he opened the fridge next morning, it was full to bursting.

That night he sat up, played hand after hand of solitaire with the shack's one, incomplete deck of cards. He sat on a milk crate, watching the fridge, trying not to listen to the nighttime sounds: the slithering and sucking, the scratching and chattering, the groaning of the shutters beneath whatever moved over them.

He awoke in the same position, aching, numb, an unfinished game on the dusty floor. The night terrors had retreated, but it was not quite dawn and the gray half-light merely scratched at the shutters. Renault groaned, stretched, opened the fridge. It was full.

The next night he stayed up again, but this time left the fridge door open wide. He perked himself with the bitter tar Benson called coffee, patiently built and rebuilt a tower with the playing cards. He did not sleep, but nodded with prickling eyes, enduring the noises. He placed card upon card until they collapsed, then drew them together, began again.

At dawn the fridge door was still open, its shelves as disheveled and bare as the night before. Renault felt both excited and disappointed, not entirely certain what it meant. He rose and closed the fridge door, padded toward his room, to bed. He paused at the entrance to the living room, looked back toward the fridge. He strode back, flung open the door. It was completely full.

After that, he lost his appetite.

—

The sun was no longer visible behind the black mountain. Renault was jogging now, his feet slapping the wet sand, fins bouncing against his thigh.

When he saw Benson's armchair up ahead, he broke into a sprint. The shack was only minutes away.

Though Benson was tall, at least a head taller than Renault, he was dwarfed by the chair. It was an ugly thing, a huge reclining easy chair in beetroot maroon, half bleached by the sun, half darkened by the tide. Only Benson knew how long it had been there, rimed with salt, eternally moist.

As soon as the theater of the morning meal was complete, and he and Renault and Webb went their separate ways to pursue their separate obsessions, Benson, stooped and scrawny, in his sleeveless pullover and rolled-up trousers, would slump within the decaying mounds of his armchair. He sat motionless from sunup until late afternoon, staring out toward the distant ships.

Renault passed within meters of Benson, but neither one acknowledged the other. He was in sight of the shack when he heard the splash.

He turned back, but the chair was empty. Benson, still fully clothed, was swimming with confident, powerful strokes, away from the shore. Past the breakers, past the bar, and out into the darkening ocean.

—

Renault still came to meals. He still sat with the others around the rickety driftwood table, still picked at the food that Benson placed before him—the barbecued meats, the exotic salads with their unusual dressings—still drank tin after tin of the beer. How else could he sustain himself?

But then he noticed that, despite preparing the daily meals and sitting down to each with he and Webb, Benson did not eat.

The gangling cook served himself, pushed food round his plate, sometimes lifted it on his fork. But never once did Renault see a morsel pass Benson's lips.

Neither did he drink. He sat with the others, at the table, on the couch that smelled of rat dirt and brine, clutching a tin of beer, a cup of coffee, a glass of milk. But he did not so much as sip.

Benson kept up the vague pretense of subsistence, and for Renault and Webb—and who knew how many others before them—that was enough. They were too preoccupied with their own sustenance to notice, too immersed in their own worlds.

But once Renault had seen, it was impossible to unsee.

At every meal, as Webb shoveled forkfuls into his mouth and swilled them down with beer, Benson would feign interest in the other's jibber-jabber, move food from one place to another on his plate, raise and lower an empty fork. Before Webb had scraped his last mouthful, Benson would rise and scoop away the plates, mugs and bowls, emptying his untouched meal into the dustbin.

Renault watched him with increasing curiosity. If Benson did not eat, then he must know something about the food. If he could live without eating then he must have discovered some means of sustaining himself. Or learned that he did not need to sustain himself.

Renault had to acknowledge a grudging respect of Benson. He

longed to find out what went on beneath that shiny dome, with its wisps of hair like spiderwebs. What else did Benson know?

Benson was not open about his knowledge, clearly unwilling to share his hard-earned secrets. The few times Renault tried to steer the conversation toward these hidden insights, Benson changed the subject, or gave answers to an entirely different question. Renault dropped that line of inquiry, decided instead on his own empirical study.

It was painful, at first: the pit in his stomach, the weakness, the exhaustion; the agony of yearning, sitting out mealtimes in his room, trying not to notice the aroma of cooking meat that wafted under the door; the long nights clutching his belly, pillow pressed against his ears to shut out the slurping of the terrors. But after several days, Renault recognized that the pain was mostly in his mind. It was a pain of wanting rather than a pain of hunger. After a fortnight there was no pain at all. Only the triggers at the old mealtimes, echoes of habit rather than need.

This self-denial acted like a gateway, opening him up to a new view of their world, of this endless shore, and of his place within it. Following Benson's example, Renault overcame his obsession with the beachcombing that, up until then, had been his sole preoccupation. Instead, he posed questions, he framed and tested hypotheses. He ventured, by day, farther and farther from the shack.

He began looking for a way out.

—

In the twilight, the shack looked more dilapidated than ever. A simple structure of graying wood and rusting tin, it nestled against the shifting dunes, half buried at the back by sand.

A wooden sign hung from the roof by weathered chains, its forgotten message worn away by the moisture, salt and sand in the evening winds. The shack creaked as he approached, shook slightly as he opened and closed the door.

Webb was at the table, legs spread, scratching idly beneath luminous board shorts. He was poring over some new collection of flotsam.

They were childish things: a toy robot; a muscular doll in a battle stance; an abstract, plastic shape that might have been a bird. Webb held each one up to the light of the oil lamp, the puffy moon of his face transfixed with wonder, delight, confusion. It was an expression both ecstatic and anxious: intoxicated with the promise of meaning, afraid it might never be fulfilled.

Webb pulled a cord that dangled beneath the bird thing. It lengthened with a grating, ratcheting sound. When he released the cord, hidden chimes plinked a lullaby, not quite in tune. Webb looked up at Renault with foggy eyes, a maudlin half-smile.

"Still works," he said, choked with tears.

"Benson's gone."

Renault sat down across the table from Webb, making no effort to conceal his distaste.

From the moment Webb first appeared at the shack he had made Renault's skin crawl. Something about his doughy physicality, the way he spread himself like melting butter over every surface he covered, the way the roll of his gut overlapped his shorts, the way he was not disgusted by himself as Renault was disgusted by him.

What grated most was Webb's almost sociopathic extraversion. Withdrawn silence had always been the rule in the shack, with conversation kept to a terse, functional minimum. But, since Webb's arrival, there had been no escape from the torrent of banalities. Renault often imagined he would prefer the terrors of night to another second of Webb's overloud platitudes.

As long as Benson had been in the shack, he had acted as a fulcrum that kept Webb at a safe distance from Renault. Without Benson around, there was nothing to hold Webb's boorishness in check. Renault was not sure how he would get through the night without killing Webb, or himself.

For all the good that would do.

"Gone, where? It's almost dinner time."

"Benson's *gone* gone. He's not coming back."

Webb's face grayed. "You mean, *they* . . . ?"

"Look outside, Webb; it's hardly dark. No, he's gone off on his own. Swimming. I think he's trying to make it to the ships."

Webb looked sick. He rocked, rubbed his palms against his thighs. His eyes bulged.

"Why would he *do* that?" Webb moaned. "I mean, he'll never make it. And what'll we do about dinner? Why would he go out to the ships?"

"I don't know," said Renault. But he wondered.

Webb was right about one thing: there was no way Benson could make it to the ships before night fell. And who knew what horrors emerged from the water once the sun went down. It was possible Benson had discovered some secret about the ships, something that might justify his insane gambit.

But then perhaps it had nothing to do with the ships at all. Perhaps Benson just wanted to drown.

—

Renault never quite believed in Benson's whimsical suicide attempts. He had all but passed them off as a dream, choosing to ignore them rather than accept what they implied.

The first time, Renault had found him in the bath. The tap was still running, and the cracked enamel tub had overflowed. Red water gushed from the sides, pooled on the floorboards, dripped steadily through the cracks.

Benson had been fully clothed, submerged to the neck. His head was cocked to the right, eyes glazed, just cavities in his parchment face. One arm hung over the side of the bath. Dangling from the limp fingers was an ivory-handled razor.

His forearms, from wrist to elbow, were open, the edges curled back like sneering mouths. A provocative last gesture.

Or so Renault thought.

It was after dinner and the shack's third occupant—at that time, a man named Baker—had retired to his room. The terrors were out in force and, while Renault drained the tub, he could hear them pulsing and squelching against the outer walls, converging on the bathroom. Renault hefted Benson's limp, sodden body, out of the bath and over his shoulder. The head struck the wall, arms flapping against Renault's legs as he staggered toward the bedroom.

He toed open the door of Benson's room, dumped the sodden corpse onto the bed. The room was otherwise bare, just a driftwood desk with a small arrangement of treasures: a leaping fish made of smoky glass; a wooden cigar box; a silver pocket watch with no hands; a rusting sextant. Renault folded the razor and placed it with the other objects, flipped the lid of the cigar box. Inside were two large brown coins. They were old, thick and dented, greening at the edges, and covered with symbols he did not recognize.

Renault went back to the bed, pulled up the blanket, looked down into Benson's staring eyes. The pupils were so black and wide. Renault saw himself reflected as he leaned over, brushed down the eyelids, placed one coin, then the other.

Renault lay awake all that night, going over and over the scene. The red waterfall in the bathroom. The ancient pennies on the pinched, skeletal face. He had no idea what to do with the body. Perhaps he and Baker could bury it in the sand. Or throw it out to sea.

But when he rose, blear-eyed and aching from the night's exertions, he found Benson in the kitchen, making breakfast. There were no marks on his arms.

They did not speak about it.

Weeks later, when dinnertime came and Benson was not in the kitchen, Renault pushed open the bedroom door, found Benson dangling from the rafters by a length of sea-worn rope. Renault did not bother to cut down the body.

Next morning, Benson was at his place in the kitchen, frying bacon, making coffee for the new occupant—this time, the white-haired Ogilvie.

Benson could not die. At least, not of his own volition.

Renault grasped, without fully understanding, the possibility that this phenomenon might apply not only to Benson, that it might even be a condition of this in-between place, this limbo: the shack and the endless shore. But he did not quite dare test the hypothesis. After all, no one else had come back. But then no one else he knew had attempted suicide: they had ventured too far on their wanderings; or chosen deliberately to leave, to explore the mountain or the wasteland beyond the dunes; or they had gone cuckoo, run screaming into the night.

Renault assumed that all of them had failed, because every one of them had been replaced: Baker by Ogilvie, Ogilvie by Ng, Ng by Argento, Argento by Webb. The new occupant waking up the next morning in the bed of the old.

No matter how they tried to get away, not one of them lasted the night. Because night meant the terrors.

Benson *knew* that. So what was he doing?

—

". . . and now there'll be nothing to stop them."

Webb was spouting nonsense, delusional gibberish that went from brain to mouth without review. Renault wasn't listening, had his own thoughts to chase.

"All this time," Webb maundered, "they've been waiting for his signal. A lantern in the window. A secret radio. A spy, that's what he was. And now his mission's complete. They've called him back."

Webb sniffled, wiped his nose along the length of his arm.

"I never trusted him, always knew he was up to something. Standing there in the kitchen with his queer smile. Peering through cracks in the wall, taking notes, transcribing all we say or do. Now they've called him back, to tell them everything he knows."

Renault closed his eyes, tried to tune out Webb's ravings. Benson had been gone little more than an hour and things were already falling apart. Without the familiar routines, without Benson in the kitchen, dinner on the table, Webb was losing his mind.

"Black figures. Shadow people. On deck with their spyglasses, watching everything. Recording *everything*. But why? What do they want? It doesn't seem real. None of it. I just want to wake up, Frenchy. But the dream won't end. And if it's not a dream, then what? Some twisted game show? Then Benson's only gone and—"

Renault looked up. "What," he said, "is a game show?"

Webb stared back at Renault, bloodshot eyes ringed with painful red. His lip quivered, on the verge of tears.

"I . . ." he said. "I . . . I don't know."

They stared at each other across the table. Webb swallowed, rubbed at his thighs. The shutters rattled, and from behind them came the first slurps and gurgles of night.

Webb started, glanced up at the sound, as though whatever was out there might rip through the boards, slither over and digest him where he sat. Renault eyed him with disgust.

"Don't dwell on it, Webb," he said and stood, pushed back his chair.

"But what about dinner?" Webb called after him.

Renault paused at the door to his room.

"I think you'll survive," he said.

—

Renault sat on the bed with his back to the inner wall, farthest from the sounds of night.

His ears were plugged with pillow stuffing, but he could still hear Webb in the living room, talking to himself, tugging at the string of the bird toy, falling silent to moon over the lullaby. Renault could still hear the sobbing.

He stuffed the wadding deeper, continued to fondle, one after the other, each shell in his collection.

There was the ribbed black finger that made him think of a talon, only where the claw should have been was a sphere, like an eye. There was the spiral stack of cogs, its minaret crowned by splayed black tongues. There was the curved fetish, shaped like a rodent; only the insides were on the outside, the folds and striations so very like nerves, organs, entrails. Then there was the screaming mouth, the severed ear, the mechanical skull, the necrotic penis. All these *almost* shapes. All in the same cold, smooth coral. All as shiny black as hardened oil.

And these were just the handful he had kept. Back on the beach, where the salt-and-pepper sand turned gritty black, there were hundreds, thousands more just like these. Alike, and yet wholly not alike.

He thought again of what he had seen that afternoon at the reef, the abyssal grooves of shadow all curving toward the same central point. He tried to picture the vast structure from a vantage point far above. He imagined a great wheel, a black eye with the gleaming white pearl at its center. What did anything matter compared to this? Benson? The ships? The terrors of night? All were meaningless compared to this other world that he alone had discovered.

Overwhelmed with fatigue and with his mind adrift, Renault let slip his hold on consciousness and sank beneath dark waves of sleep.

He was woken by a bang. He fumbled the wadding from his ears and listened.

Silence. A complete absence of sound, as though even the terrors were holding their breath. Then the shushing of feet through sand. And sobbing.

Webb had snapped. He had run out the front door and was out behind the shack, trying to scale the dunes.

Renault sat up, straining to listen. He heard nothing of the terrors on the walls. Just the feet in sand, the sobs, and crazy muttering, some phrase repeated over and over. Then Webb began to wail.

Then he began to scream.

Renault lay back down, plugged the wadding deep into his ears, stuffed it in so far it hurt.

He closed his eyes, wrapped the pillow round his head. But he could not escape the sounds—the slurping, the guzzling, Webb's final, bubbling whimpers.

It was a long time before he fell asleep again.

—

Renault woke before dawn, pushed himself upright, pressed his feet against the cool boards. He listened. The shack was silent, just the whisper of sand on tin as the wind blew out to sea.

An indefinable sense of wrongness pervaded the shack, as though everything had been blown wide open, leaving nothing certain. The kitchen was dark and still, but the door to Benson's room was ajar. Renault listened at the crack, peered into the gloom. Nothing. He swung the door open and stepped in.

The bed was empty, neatly made. The desk was clear; all the mementos—the razor, the cigar box, the glass fish—all were gone. Benson had not returned.

But he had not been replaced.

Renault pulled the door to. There was a cough from Webb's bedroom, then a groan. Not Webb. Renault tiptoed through the living room, grabbed his fins, his snorkel and mask. He slipped out of the shack and down to the water's edge, turned south toward the reef.

Ahead of him, and behind, the endless shore merged with the horizon in a white haze of sea and sand. Renault wondered, not for the first time, if there might not be *something* out there in that indistinct distance; other shacks, other people. He imagined an infinite beach lined with dwellings of driftwood and tin, each little further than a day's walk, but too far to be reached or even sighted before nightfall. He pictured a multitude of amnesiac beachcombers, each blind to the other, scouring the interminable waterfront for some clue to their previous life. Might there not be others, too, just like himself, looking for a way out? Others, like Benson, who had perhaps found one? The thought was both dizzying and strangely comforting. More so than the gnawing suspicion that there was nothing, that the beach stretched indefinitely nowhere, serving no purpose. That they were entirely alone.

He saw Benson's armchair ahead, like a monument jutting from the surf. He half expected to see Benson's angular knees, his long pale feet, but the chair was empty. Renault sank into it and looked out to sea, out to where the ships—

The ships were gone.

Renault stared and stared. The absence made the skyline naked, vulnerable, as though only the ships had kept the sky and sea from collapsing into one another, swallowing the world in a swirling, bubbling deluge.

His heart raced. Benson had swum out to the ships, had not returned. And now the ships were gone. What did it mean?

An insane thought gripped him, made him panic. What if Benson's disappearance had begun a chain reaction? First Benson, then the ships, then . . .

Renault jumped down from the chair and sprinted along the beach, fins bashing against his thigh, not slowing until he reached the bar of black sand. He fell into the waves, tugged on his flippers, bit the snorkel, swam out past the breakers, scooping and kicking at the water with fearful urgency.

Once offshore, the shelf dropped away and he saw with relief the tangled spires of the reef below. It was still there. Of course it was still there; just as it had been the day before, and the day before that. He calmed his strokes, matched his rhythm to the rise and fall of the waves, steered himself in what he hoped was the direction of the great wheel. And the pearl.

His anxiety did not entirely ease until he reached the first of the reef's shadowed trenches. He swam above it, glancing ahead to the point where the dark furrows converged. The morning sun cast its net of white gold among the black sculptures; the coral seemed to move, an illusion caused by the purling iridescence. When he saw again the petals of the black flower, the hub of the vast coral wheel, his heart began to pound; but with excitement this time, with anticipation.

He let his arms hang behind him, flipping gently with the fins until he drifted above the black flower. It was larger than he remembered. The petal-like structures formed a jagged disc almost fifty meters across, and there in the absolute center, lustrous and opalescent, gripped by fingers of black coral, lay the pearl. *Renault's* pearl.

But it was so far down. Impossibly far. Renault sucked air deep into his lungs and dived. Down he went, two, three, almost four meters, before his lungs began to burn and his ears threatened to burst from the pressure of depth.

He jerked up, thrashed for the surface, broke free of the water gasping for air. At the lowest point of his dive, the pearl had seemed no closer than it was at the surface.

He trod water, letting his heart calm, his breath ease, then bit down on the snorkel and dived again.

This time he made it almost five meters before his flaming lungs drove him back to the surface. He dived and dived again, and though, with each successive dive, he got no closer to the pearl—in fact, made less and less progress—he kept diving until he was overcome by exhaustion.

Renault rolled onto his back and closed his eyes. He had to get down to it. But it was impossible; the water was just too deep. He felt imprisoned, shut out of the world beneath the waves as surely as a moth, hurling itself against a window to reach the lamp behind.

The sun was now at its highest point in the sky, and bright, even through closed eyelids. It was past noon. Lunchtime. Renault felt the old hunger grip him. Lightly, true, but it was still there; an echo of the habits of that other, forgotten life. The life before the shack. But, in spite of the hunger, he knew he did not need to eat. He was sustained. He *continued*.

Benson could not die, and yet Benson was gone. And with him the ships. Precisely what this meant, Renault did not understand. But he knew he did not need to hold on any more to that other life, whatever it had contained, whatever echoes still surrounded him.

He inhaled deep into his belly, felt the air lift his body, hold him at the surface of the water. He exhaled slowly, felt the air warm at the back of his nostrils, his body dipping below the water again as he lost buoyancy. When he breathed in once more—his last breath—he let the air fill him until he radiated. Then he dived.

As he swam down, he pulled the mask from his head and let it drop, saw it spiral, catching glints of sunlight as it descended. His eyes stung at first, vision blurred from the salt, from contact with the water, but they soon cleared, revealed a perspective on the reef that was wider, an almost one-hundred-and-eighty degree view.

He reached the five meter mark and his lungs began to broil, then to blister. He panicked, started thrashing. He could no longer hold his breath and now had no time to make it back up. He gasped.

And water filled his lungs.

Renault hung. Motionless. Suspended. His chest rose and fell, rose and fell.

He knew that water cycled through him, from his nostrils to his throat to his lungs and out again, yet he felt only . . . he had no word for it. The ocean, the reef, the mass of coral had its own breath, a gentle, measured inward–outward motion, and Renault felt himself breathed within it as he breathed without breathing. A sense of peace washed through him, from his chest outward to his feet, to his fingers, to the crown of his head.

He raised his hands, studied them, the lines of his palms, the creases at the joints and knuckles. He clenched his fists, checking their solidity. He was here, and yet—

He moved his hands through the water, kicking gently behind, swimming down without effort toward the ocean floor. Within the reef at last, he observed how the movements of the coral seen from the surface were no illusion. It was not just the refraction of light, or the patterns of iridescence. The reef was alive in a sense that the shells' dead matter could only hint at. It was dynamic, animate, ceaselessly creative.

He reached out a hand to touch one of the spires, surprised by its warmth, its smoothness, the way it yielded beneath his fingers. The coral reacted to the contact, rippling into new forms and patterns. Human body parts coiled to form reptilian tails. The obsidian cilia of jellyfish writhed into plaits, broke apart, became exoskeletons of implausible crustaceans. Dead eyes opened and shut. Mouths yawned, bit, drooled. Black saliva hardened and split, morphed into the carapaces of crawling beetles. Black teeth impaled black flesh. Black claws ripped at their own black bodies; the coral tore at itself in a destructive orgy of generation. It was grotesque, beautiful. Renault was mesmerized, in an ecstasy of horror.

He swam through the labyrinth of iridescent buttes, marveling at the half-creatures born from the reef. Unformed things that scurried, slithered or clung to its surface, feeding on it; only to be devoured by it, as some other, contiguous part of the whole drew them back into itself. He saw crabs with legs of human fingers, snakes with a gorgon's head of squirming blind rats. He saw organic machines, reptilian organs, the sex acts of impossible mechanisms, all bound to the writhing black coral. All *within* it. And *of* it. A super-organism in perpetual evolution.

He was so absorbed in the spectacle of transformation that he did not notice the shadows lengthen, the rainbow luster dim, the sun descend.

The light faded so gradually he was not aware of it, the water hazing from crystal blue to gray, until it was almost as black as the reef; until, looking upward, Renault could see nothing. Only darkness. No way to tell where the water ended and the air began. No way to tell what was up and what was down.

He panicked. Swam crazily toward what he thought was the surface, crashed instead into a coral stack, recoiled, thrashing, at the sickening movement like fingers, like tentacles, like the grasping claws of an invisible predator that clutched at his back.

He screamed. But, without air, there was no sound, only water expelled into water and the burning fear in his chest. He spun, twisting to his left, to his right, feeling again that sensation of being watched, of being reached for, of being hunted. But, in the dark, there was nowhere to hide. Whatever was down here could not be escaped.

Renault went limp, let himself drift, up or down it did not matter. He felt a pull in his chest, that sensation of being watched, but different somehow; as he let go, as the fear began to melt, the pull seemed less a feeling and more like . . . a song, a song without sound. It was a call. He was being beckoned. Renault drifted toward the source.

He became slowly aware of shapes ahead of him, rising from the gloom. Deep in the reef a light flickered, gray-white-silver-gray-white, streamers of incandescence that strobed behind silhouettes of gnarled coral. Renault moved toward it with gentle strokes, the tugging in his chest growing stronger as he drew nearer to the light. He saw beneath him the polished surface of the vast, petal-like forms, crackling silver-gray with the light bursting from their center. From the pearl.

He swam closer, the bioluminescence fizzing like electricity in the surrounding water. Almost upon it now, he reached out his hand, fingers outstretched, longing to feel it against his skin.

But he never made contact. For there was no surface.

Renault's hand sunk inside the pearl, tingling as though nibbled by tiny, electric fish. He laughed, delighted, only half-aware of the segmented, chitinous limbs that rose up around and behind him.

He reached out his other hand and plunged it into the snowstorm, entranced by the flickering speckles of light, by the prickling that rose up his arms, along his shoulders, up and down the length of his body.

He felt nothing as the limbs, like the jaws of a trap, snapped down upon him. Then wonder, as the brutally sharp, talon-like points pierced his chest, his shoulder, his thigh. And when the coarsely serrated edges tore at his flesh, stuffing him down into the crackling sphere, there was only rapture.

"I am reborn," thought Renault, as his head disappeared inside. "I am—"

But the thought was drowned within a swell of white noise.

Old Growth

"Look, Dad," says Mika from the back. "Look at the faces!"

Scott adjusts the rearview mirror. The last he checked, Mika was slumped in a chaos of Lego, two minifigures squabbling inches from his face. Now the boy is fully upright, forehead pressed to the window.

"What do you mean? What faces?"

"In the trees," says the boy. "Bubbly heads poking out of the bark. Look, Dad, can you see?"

"What're you talking about, retard?" Ashley is scooched way down in the passenger seat, semi-fetal with her toes on the glovebox. Scott would think she was asleep if it weren't for the dance of thumbs over the screen of her phone.

"They're probably galls," says Scott. "Some trees grow them in response to bacteria, insects, that sort of thing. It's a kind of symbiosis: the trees grow galls to protect themselves, but the galls also protect the wasps, or the greenfly or whatever, by drawing them in, growing around them."

"Ha," says Mika and smiles, stares out at the milky light strobing through the trees. "Galls."

The car climbs, clings to the narrow snake of highway, winding upward, out of the rainforest and the stop-motion fireworks of ancient tree ferns, up into the dry alpine region and the edge of the burn zone.

"Whaaaaat!" Ashley thrusts her phone up against the windscreen, holds it over by the window. She shakes it, thrusts it out again. "No . . . Don't do this to me!"

"Dad," says Mika, still hypnotized by the flickering trunks. "Dad, I'm starving. How long till we get there?"

"No reception?" Scott asks Ashley. To Mika, he says, "Not long, mate. Greenville's about ten minutes away. We can stop there and grab some bits for a picnic. Looks like there's a nice spot in the bush just outside town."

Ashley groans and rolls her eyes. "Great," she says. "More trees."

Scott breathes slow and deep, lets his daughter's sarcasm wash over him, trying not to bite. He hoped this holiday might bring them closer, heal some of those old wounds Ashley loves to keep scratching. But the gulf between them is wider now than ever. Next year she'll be eighteen: old enough to make her own decisions; old enough to turn down this yearly trip and sever all contact with her father.

"See how the trees are charred down one side?" Scott says. "There's some up there that've really burned. They should be dead, but they're putting out leaves; new shoots literally bursting from the trunk. Epicormic growth, it's called."

It hurts, Ashley's obvious distaste, the sense she genuinely *dislikes* him—although perhaps it's better than that other impression she gives, that she feels nothing toward him whatsoever. It hurts, but only so much. Their relationship has been complicated ever since he first held her wriggling and squawking in his arms. To think he might not see her again is painful, but it's a pain he's long grown accustomed to, one that brings with it a guilty sense of relief.

Perhaps it's not too late, though. Ashley might be a write-off, but Mika . . . Perhaps there's still a chance with Mika.

"Isn't it amazing?" he says. "This mechanism they've adapted for survival. They can be dead inside and still go on living."

———

Greenville is deserted. No one walks beneath the stands of gnarled, flesh-colored trees, through the dappled shadow and the drifts of leaves that rattle along the empty street. Lights are on in the shop windows. *Open* signs hang in the doors. Yet everywhere there is silence, as though the town has been abandoned.

"There's a café," says Mika, pointing across the street.

"Looks closed to me," says Scott without turning. All week they've eaten at cafés and diners, in pub family rooms and bistros, the kids choosing overpriced meals they don't finish, brother and sister bickering without cease. Not today. Today they'll buy picnic food and take it out of town; show these kids a corner of the *real* world—the world *outside*—before driving them back to Melbourne and Marion and their safe, suburban lifestyle.

He drives at a crawl, scanning the shop signs for a general store, but his attention is drawn by another of the huge, pink-skinned trees. So unusual. Like coastal angophora, with smooth, dimpled bark, but as vast and gnarled as a Moreton Bay fig, their great, fleshy boughs engulfed by the canopy. And, as Mika had said, the galls; or rather, the *faces*. He's never seen anything quite like them, organic gargoyles bubbling with deformity. Scott would love to stop the car, to get out and search among the leaf litter for seed pods, gum nuts, anything he could use to identify them later. But, mindful of the time and the children's mounting irritation, he turns off the high street, follows a sign to the supermarket.

Apart from a silver Toyota and a grubby white ute, the car park is deserted and gray, untouched by the afternoon's last light. Ashley zips the neck of her fleece as far as it will go, rubs her arms, shivers. Lego clatters to the asphalt and Mika tumbles out after. He's wearing only a t-shirt but seems unmoved by the temperature. Scott thinks about making him put on his hoodie, but he's not about to ruin their last day with a fight he can't win. From tomorrow, if the boy catches cold, it will be Marion's problem.

Scott fills a basket with tomatoes, sliced cheese, packet ham, lets the kids throw in any old crap without complaint: jelly snakes, lurid colored drinks, Doritos dusted with toxic waste. When he heads to the front to pay, Mika's on the floor by the counter, fondling a disposable plastic toy taped to a comic. The shutter-rolls of the cigarette display are papered with photocopies, black-and-white headshots of a man, an old woman, two girls that might be twins, and phone numbers. The woman behind the counter does not smile when Scott hands her the basket.

"Looks like you got lucky," Scott says and gestures with his thumb toward the car park.

The woman has a pinched, mean-looking face, and sucks a lozenge with odd little jerks of her chin. She stares at Scott as though he were drunk.

"The fires, I mean. Everything round here's burned, but you seem to have done alright."

The woman drags a pack of bread rolls across the scanner. The twitch of her jaw quickens.

Scott rummages for his credit card, pretends not to notice when Mika slips a comic into the basket. Ashley rests her head on his shoulder, takes his arm as though such gestures were common currency between them.

"Daddy," she says, drawing out the vowels in a wheedle that sets his teeth on edge. "You're looking so tired. Perhaps you'd like me to drive the next bit?"

Scott groans. "We've been through this, Ashley. You're not insured to drive the car. If anything were to happen—"

She roars in frustration. "*What* is going to happen? Troy would—"

Scott puts up his hand. "Enough. We're not going over this again."

It takes the eftpos machine forever to approve the sale. The woman makes no apology for the delay, just sucks and sucks and stares at some distant point beyond Scott's ear. It's an effort to stay calm, to pretend he's not anxious that his last card will max out in front of his kids, but at last the receipt chugs from the machine and he reaches for the bags.

"Your card," says the woman. The words drip spearmint.

Scott thanks her and reaches for the card, but the woman does not loosen her grip. Her fist is clenched, knuckles white. Scott feels Mika at his legs, rummaging for his comic in the bags. The woman glances at the noise and Scott tugs the card from her fingers.

As they turn to leave, Scott looks up at their reflection in the domed security mirror. The woman is staring after them. Her lips move like she's muttering under her breath.

The automatic doors whir behind them as they step out into the car park.

"Shotgun!" yells Mika, hopping and bounding around Scott like a spinning top knocked off its axis.

"Turd," says Ashley.

"It's about time Mika had a turn in the front," says Scott. He tries to sound impartial, but can't help feeling a small thrill putting Ashley in her place, bringing the boy up to sit with him.

Perhaps, on the way, they'll see more of those interesting trees.

—

Ashley misses nothing; he knows that. Knows too that it all goes straight back to her mother. Those endless frantic text messages, no doubt, a moment-by-moment account of the trip and its horrors, a mounting tally of Scott's shortcomings: the unsatisfactory living conditions; the inadequate personal hygiene; the dwindling financial resources. Not that Marion can take any more from him than she already has. These days even pride is in short supply.

Yet Scott had longed for the divorce, had fantasized the separation years before their marriage actually fell apart. What the world could not deliver, his imagination supplied: a picture of the life he wasn't living, a life that better suited his temperament, his need for simplicity, for solitude and the outdoors. Not the stifling restrictions of suburban family life, the daughter and the wife with their needs that he did not understand, the hidden grief, unending and unnamed. In these fantasies, he pictured himself in a small house on the outskirts of the city, a weatherboard cottage backing onto the forest. A slow-combustion stove. A rickety workshop. Silent hours working with his hands, caressing the grain of newly chopped wood. The crackle of flame. Orange sparks bursting into darkness.

In these fantasies he was always alone; alone except for the trees. The unmeasurable expanse of bushland became the landscape of his longed-for inner life. The Candlebark, Peppermint and River She Oak, Yellow Bloodwood, Yellow Box and Mountain Blue Gum became a pantheon of heretical gods, unknowable, inhuman and infinitely patient; waiting for that day when he would close his ears to the world of things and people and, at last, listen only to them.

His dreams for Marion were not so lofty.

Failure. Destitution. Charcoal and ashes. Fitting reward for the years of carping and bitterness, the neuroses, the shrewery.

But, five years on, Scott was no closer to that house of his dreams; further from it perhaps, because now the dream itself seemed distant and vague, the images sapped of the power they once held. He still lived in the same two-room apartment off Parramatta Road, still drove the same shitty old Holden Viva, still sat in the same gridlock each morning on his way to the same job at the same second-rate consultancy. The closest he came to the woodland of his imagination was his work, the fauna and flora reports he daily half-baked. Appendices to appendices, the reports were little more than technical footnotes to the development applications they justified, for dams, for railways, for open trench excavations, highway expansions, and mining sites on Aboriginal heritage areas. His youthful idealism had eroded many years before, along with any sense of value in his work. Or in himself.

Not so, Marion. Barely eighteen months after the divorce, she'd married an estate agent—nauseatingly wealthy—moved with the kids to a McMansion in suburban Melbourne. Each morning, she dropped them off at private school in her gleaming, silver Pajero, drove to the studio of her successful online business: designing boutique terraria for offices and corporate waiting rooms.

Worse than all of this, she seemed happy. Genuinely happy.

—

The picnic site is not what Scott imagined.

The map on Ashley's phone shows a picnic table icon surrounded by unbroken green. The reality is a browning grass verge bounded by charred logs. There are picnic tables—that much is true—one so badly burned that all that remains is the bent metal frame. Another is only half-devoured, with great black bites scorched from the boards.

Beyond and above the tangle of regrowth, the sloping mountainside is a graveyard of gray and black. The forest is devastated, hundreds, perhaps thousands of trees reduced to twisted wreckage, the half-cremated skeleton of a vast, unknowable life-form.

The engine idles. Scott grips the steering wheel, stares at the landscape. Unutterably desolate, it reminds him of his dad's old picture books of World War One, of the Somme. Maybe they *should* go back to town, see if that café is still open. It could hardly be worse than—

But Mika is already out of the car.

"Seriously?" says Ashley from the back. "This place is a shit-hole."

Scott doesn't answer, just pops the door and steps out, trying to see where Mika has gone. He leans back in for the shopping bags, carries them over to the half-burnt table. The crinkling of plastic seems overloud, an intrusion in that funereal silence.

The boy has found a gap in the trees and a creek running behind, is halfway across on a path of wobbly rocks and rotting timber.

"Look, Dad. Look at this!" Mika is teetering on a boulder in the middle of the creek. "This place is amazing! Look, it goes all the way up!"

The boy points along the creek, to some distant wonder Scott cannot see.

"Come on, Mika," says Scott. "Lunch is out. Let's go and eat."

"Okay okay," says the boy, arms out for balance as he pitches left then right. "But let's explore first. This place is amazing!"

Mika hops back to the bank in three steps. A wall of foliage obscures all but this narrow entrance to the creek, and he runs alongside, past the car, past the picnic table, disappears into a gap at the far end of the thicket.

Ashley hasn't moved from the back seat. Sulking, no doubt. The front doors are still open, the rental like a swollen beetle preparing for flight.

"Come on, Dad!" Mika's voice from the trees.

Scott follows the voice, but half-heartedly. Something about this place makes him uncomfortable leaving either child alone.

"Follow me, Dad. In here!"

An impenetrable understory has shot up since the fire, strangled by the shoots of an unfamiliar creeper. Mika has made just enough space to squeeze between the poles, carved a fairy path to the bole of an ancient, half-burnt tree. The unburned side has the same smooth, pink skin as the trees in town. The fire must have blazed through here faster, or with less ferocity than the slope above. The older trees are scorched up one side, but few have been gutted and fingers of new life are already bursting through the blackened shells. From every trunk, the epicormic sprouts seem to quiver.

"Come on, Dad. It's amazing in here! Look, I can see the creek!"

Stepping over a fallen tree, Scott parts the barricade of poles, draws his hand back in surprise at the scratches on his palms. The skin begins immediately to itch, some irritant released by the creeper.

A door slams. Ashley is out of the car, hugging her elbows.

"Come back now, Mika," says Scott. "It's time to eat. We can explore after."

———

Both kids ignore the sandwiches Scott makes, filling up instead on fluorescent sodas and bright-orange corn chips, jelly snakes for dessert. Scott isn't hungry, but eats anyway, picking at his sandwich and half of Mika's. They're all squeezed together on the one unburnt side of the picnic bench.

Scott is far away, his mind on the hilltop and what remains of the forest. Unlike this side of the creek, the fire up there must have raged and raged, burning the life out of every trunk until there was no hope for regrowth, until the once majestic wilderness was reduced to a plain of blackened stumps. Those charred wooden stalagmites are like gravestones, like tiny, forgotten burial markers. Something inside him aches, weighed down by the ravaged bushland and its eerie calm. With every bite of the unwanted sandwich, the lump in his throat tightens.

When their second child was born still, when no cry came from the tiny lungs and the nurse carried off that helpless, motionless body in its swaddle of striped terrycloth, Scott had felt it would never end. That germinal grief was so intense it transcended pain, became instead a landscape of exquisite, deadening absence. It blazed through him with all the intensity of a bushfire, leaving him scorched and empty as a husk. Only with time did the nerve endings reawaken, and despair crackle in his every fiber.

It was Marion that wanted to try again, wanted another child to dress the wound that would not heal. Scott accepted her decision, yielded to those months of joyless coupling, not because he believed that a living child could balance the vacuum left by the other, but because change of any kind was better than the unbounded wilderness of his grief.

She believed he had a lover, could see no other reason why, in the first months after Mika was born, Scott should routinely fail to come home. But it was nothing so complicated. He was stalled on roadsides in state forests and national parks, car parks and picnic sites so very much like this one, gripping the steering wheel and staring, just staring out at the trees, at the green, at the life that persisted whether he willed it or not.

Divorce by then was inevitable, though neither blamed the black emptiness that yawned between them. By then the reasons were so many, and so distinct, that the din of those thousand small certainties overwhelmed the whispers of buried silence.

Marion clung to her new baby boy. Ashley disappeared inside herself. Scott turned away.

"—and you come along the creek and find me."

Scott turns away from the hillside, from the corpse-shells of old growth, looks into the face of his son. Mika beams.

"Sorry, what?"

"A game. I'll go through the forest and you go along the creek and we'll meet up in the middle."

Scott smiles. And behind the smile there is an ache, the pressure of irreclaimable time. He stands.

Ashley rolls her eyes, bites the head off a jelly snake.

———

It was a nice idea, but it cannot work. There is no way he can get through.

Leaning out from the bank, Scott peers upriver, up toward the wall of unbroken green from which Mika, by the rules of the game, should appear at any moment. But he cannot go any further. Beyond this dirt promontory and the makeshift bridge of stones and deadfall that spans the creek, there is no path upstream. The steppingstones end at the edge of the bank, where the regrowth forms a barricade along the creekside, leaving no space for footholds. The flaming itch in his palm warns against searching for grip in the tangled foliage.

He attempts the passage anyway, not wanting reality to interfere with what may be the last chance to connect with Mika this trip. For his efforts, he is rewarded with more cuts to his hand, a foot submerged to the ankle in icy water.

He gives up, climbs the bank with his shoe squelching. He's almost back at the picnic bench when Mika starts to scream.

"Help, Daddy, help!" The boy's voice, shrill in the smothering quiet. "Daddy, quickly! I'm scared!"

Scott doesn't think, just runs. Past Ashley on the blackened bench, past the skeletal steel frame, over a fallen eucalypt and into the thicket of poles, tearing at the undergrowth.

"Daddy!"

"I'm coming, Mika. I'm coming," Scott yells. "Where are you?"

Scott forces his way between the staves. His face, his neck, the backs of his hands burn at the creepers' toxic scratches. Inside the underwood, what little remains of the afternoon sun is choked to a dusky gloom. He drags through snarls of vine, pushes against the unyielding brake, locating the boy by the sound of his voice.

"Daddy!" Desperate now, panicked, but the voice sounds close.

"Mika, where are you?"

"Daddy!"

Disorientation. The voice comes not from ahead of Scott as he'd expected, but from behind and to the left. He has pressed too far into the cage of scrub. He pauses, catching breath, hands and face flaming with welts.

"Daddy!"

The voice again, but farther this time, as though Mika is moving, as though he is being carried away.

Stifling panic, Scott doubles back, pushes on in the direction of Mika's last shouts. The understory is thicker here, the poles closer, the vines more deranged. There's no hint of a breeze, but epicormic shoots on every charred trunk are quivering.

He calls out his son's name again and again, but the sound is deadened, suffocated by the foliage.

—

Ashley looks down at her phone. Still no bars.

She sucks air noisily through her teeth. No phone means no escape, no alternative but to *be* here in this miserable nowhere carpark, trapped with her dipshit brother and their pointless biological dad.

They ran off to play their faggy little bush game. No one thought to ask her. Not that she'd have said yes. But still, it hurt not to be asked, to not have the chance to refuse. The little turd had started yelling about something-or-other—typical drama queen—and Scott ran off after him. She can still hear them shouting to each other from inside the forest.

She tugs the last of the jelly snakes from the bag, ties it in a knot and pops the whole thing in her mouth.

Worse by far than being with them, though, is being alone. The sun is gone now, the hillside a silhouette, the foliage leached of all color. Only the shadows have depth.

A cold gust makes the leaves rattle and Ashley shivers. Then something moves on the edge of the clearing.

"The fuck've you been?" says the girl.

"Oh, hey Ash," says Mika, brushing himself down. He limps over to the half-burnt table and drops onto the bench beside his sister.

"What's with all the yelling, retard?"

"I was afraid of snakes," he says, thrusts a grubby hand into the lolly packet. "You finish these?"

Ashley pokes out her tongue, shows him the half-sucked knot of goo. Mika scowls.

"You know, you were right," says Ashley and nods toward the trees. "They do look like faces."

—

Scott rips at the confusion of vines, hoping to find some small clearing where he can catch his breath, get his bearings, find his way to Mika. Through the murk, a semi-scorched trunk, the smooth flesh-like bark bursting with galls.

He remembers how he was going to look for gum nuts. But, in the gloom, he can hardly see his feet, let alone details in the leaf litter. Besides, he doesn't care anymore what species or variety of tree these are. He wants only to find his way back out, find his son.

"Mika!" Scott yells.

But there is no answer; he might as well be alone here in this wood. Only he is not alone.

In the wood to his right, poles rattle.

"Mika?"

Then a clattering, but from the left. Closer this time.

"Mika?" But he knows it is not Mika.

Scott backs toward the tree, hands trembling, half falls against the charred bark. Feet enmeshed by creepers. Legs snared by cords of vine. A wall of ancient roots. A trunk so vast it's engulfed by the darkening canopy.

His palm connects with something smooth—a patch of the tree's unburnt skin—and he recoils, nauseated by its warmth. But the vines are tightening, the understory pressing on him from all sides, forcing him up against the bark. He tastes charcoal.

The clatter of poles is all around him, louder now. Creepers snake up and around his thighs, wind between fingers, twine round and around his throat, lashing him to the trunk. Worse than the fear, the itch. His face is on fire where the vines have touched, the skin swollen and bubbling. The bark has a pulse.

The clattering crescendos—*takka-takka-takka-takka-tak*—a cacophony of bickering wood rising to a climax, to an unknowable, ceremonial peak.

Scott gasps as something moves beneath him. Something deep within the burned surface of the tree.

Sprouts burst from the charred bark, thrashing against his cheek, his chest. They convulse, searching like palsied fingers, whispering.

There is a stillness, a lacuna that expands between the mad fire of the itch, the seething of the shoots, the racket of the rattling wood, as though those vibrations, each insufferable alone, in unison harmonize. The pain is still there. And the fear. But beyond them is an emptiness both vast and ancient, an immeasurable landscape of silence.

He sighs. And something slips between the buttons of his shirt.

The Moth Tapes

So here we are, little one. Our new home sweet home.

Not that I've fixed up your bedroom yet, but there's still time. And it'll be lovely, Noodle, I promise. We'll go down to the shop tomorrow and look at colors. I'll paint you a mural, get one of those things that dangles over your bed. When you look out your window, you'll see the garden and the trees and the mountain behind. When you're big you can walk out the back gate and spend all day up there, among the shinglebacks and roos and galahs. I'll blow a whistle when dinner's ready and you'll come running back.

I found something out there today, out near the back gate where the veggie patch will go. It was poking out of the dirt and at first I thought it was a loose cable or something. When I looked closer though it wasn't anything like that.

It took a bit of wiggling to get out of the ground, but I'm glad I made the effort because it's just so unusual. I'll put it somewhere safe for when you're older; you can keep it in a box with all your other treasures. A sort of hollow leather cigar, all plump and shiny and rippled, the end's torn like something burst out from inside, and I guess that's exactly what happened. Perhaps it's some kind of cocoon. But of what, though?

I have no idea.

—

I was going to start unpacking today, had such a grand plan. I wanted books on the shelves and plates in the cupboard and quiet hours sorting through all that baby stuff we were given. At the very least, I wanted a cup of tea and to change out of these clothes I've been in since we got back. So I went down to the basement to bring up the first of the boxes.

Would you call it a basement? It's a funny sort of room under the house you can only get to through the carport. A kind of brick box, only full of holes peeking through to the foundations, to heaps of rubble and the slope of earth the house is built on. It's dingy as a cave. The only light's this fluorescent thing balanced on a shelf that takes forever to pop on and seems to cast more shadow than anything. This basement's where we stored everything—*all* our belongings—before we went away.

The door was swollen shut and I had to yank it so hard I almost broke the key. When I dragged it open, water sloshed onto the drive.

The basement is flooded, Noodle. There's stinky black water everywhere and all our stuff is ruined.

—

The plumber says it's groundwater. Whatever that means.

His name is David. He's tall and quiet and thoughtful and reminds me of my dad. I liked him right away, how awkward he was, and how capable.

I was afraid that a pipe had burst and we were going to have to pay through the roof to get it fixed. But David said it wasn't a pipe. He stood a long time at the basement door, looking down at the mess. Then he clomped around the outside of the house in his work boots, stood for a while in the middle of the garden, staring up at the mountain.

He said there's nothing to be done about it. Something about the water table and the mountain, about water under the ground, flowing down the mountain and into our basement. He said the best we can do is keep the door open until it all dries out. And not to worry. He said there won't be another rain like that for years.

I wanted to make us both a cup of tea. But I didn't know where to find the kettle, or the cups, or the teabags, and I wasn't ready to go back down into the basement to start pulling everything out. All those sodden boxes.

And the stream of black water running down the driveway.

—

I'm tired, Noodle, and achy. I've not slept well.

It's not that I'm blaming you, though it is sort of your fault. All my life I've slept on my front, right up until I started to show. Then I got worried I might squish you—even though I wouldn't have. And now you're really sticking out, all poky and bony.

Before we moved, I had so many pillows, I could make a sort of nest with you in the middle. I'd lay on one side with my leg stuck out and I slept so well it was like heaven, I'd do that here too, only our sheets and all our pillows are under the house, soaking in black water.

The best we can do is a bare mattress with an open sleeping bag and a pair of jeans rolled up under my head. I have to lay all twisted and it's so uncomfortable, and to top it off I had bad dreams last night. Well, a sort of dream.

It was one of those where you don't know if you're awake or asleep and everything seems so real, like it's happening right there in the room. There were noises coming from the cupboard, like an old boiler, whirring and fizzing and hissing, only softly and all at once; a kind of white noise that lived in the cupboard. I felt so scared, Noodle. There was a weight on my chest so I couldn't move and the noise in the cupboard was getting louder and in it I could hear voices, far away. Children's voices. The noise was like a tunnel behind the cupboard door and the voices echoed off the walls.

Got to sort out the basement today. Get out those boxes. Get everything dry.

I hope the pillows are alright.

———

It's worse than I thought, Noodle. So much worse. The water's got into everything.

Pretty well all the boxes are soaked. Only the ones up the far end are dry and even they have that smell. I dragged them all out into the carport. The ones by the door were the worst: wrecks of collapsing, rotten cardboard, the sides falling away like molten wax. The first one I picked up, the bottom fell out and all my clothes tumbled into the filthy water. I just stood there, staring down at that heap of clothes in the dirty puddle, like I'd sloughed some part of myself. Some old dead skin that would never fit me again.

But I kept going, dropping boxes in heaps on the carport, all burst and spilling their contents. Swollen books. Moldy sheets and pillows and towels. All my favorite clothes. I carried everything up and round to the back lawn and laid it all out like some ghoulish yard sale. It took forever, Noodle, draping the Hills Hoist with our stinking things, my heart heavy with all that ruin and waste. Then down again to slosh through that horrid pool.

I tried to clean it up, once the worst of the boxes were out. First with a mop, soaking up the black water and squeezing it into a bucket outside the basement door. But there was too much and I mopped and mopped and it didn't go down a bit. So I tried it with a broom. I swept and swept and out it poured in rank black sheets, a black waterfall sloshing over the basement step, a black river flowing down the driveway and into the gutter.

I thought I was all done, but when I stepped back in, the floor tiles sunk under me with a sucking noise and water gushed up from underground, rank and gritty and black. It squirted out and soaked my feet and something about the way it came out like that felt all wrong, made me have to not be there anymore. I had to be out, away from the shadows and water and that smell of moisture and invisible life. To be dry and warm and feel the sun on my skin.

That's why my only clothes are out on the line and I'm stretched on the couch in my birthday suit. I'm starving, but there's nothing in the fridge. Nothing good anyway. I think first a little nap, and then . . .

—

"A good drying day!" That's the sort of thing I say now I'm a suburban housewife.

It's only been a few hours and everything's crisp as cardboard. For all the good it does. Apart from the clothes I came in, everything's moldy and covered in spotty black stains. I should just put them all in the bin and start again. It's not like any of them fit me now anyway.

It's got me so down, I've left everything out there just as it is. The back yard looks deranged, with its patchwork of shapes and colors.

Which reminds me: We forgot to go and look at colors for your room! I'm still going to paint you that mural, I promise. We've just been so tied up with this flood business, I haven't had time to go and get food even. We'll go tomorrow. Definitely tomorrow.

—

It's so sad, Noodle. Life is so fragile and fleeting, without pity for small things.

We went out the back gate today. Finally. I could feel you turning over and over as I walked, getting your own kind of exercise. It's so beautiful out there. I can't believe we've been moved in almost a week and not been out back. From now on, we'll go every day.

I've told you about the mountain, Noodle. How you can see it when you look out the kitchen window. Or, from the garden, how it looms dark and impressive, a giant hump-backed creature, bristling with its pelt of distant trees. There's a dirt path that runs along the bottom and smaller paths leading up, away from the suburbs and into the shade of the rattling gums. Up to where the water runs beneath the ground, down into our basement.

We came out here once before, remember? The day we bought the house. It was so dry then. A cold day, but sunny and bright. And everything brown and brittle. You would have been tiny then, no bigger than a peach. We came to view the house and I walked out the back gate, followed the path with one hand on my belly, on the tiny bump that was all that showed then of you. I was so excited. I let you talk me into making an offer on the house, right then and there. I remember we saw a mob of roos resting in the shade, the color of the trees, of the parched grass.

Today, though, it was nothing like that. It could've been a different country. The wasteland of grass beyond the gate was boggy and waterlogged, the path half washed away by a creek where before there had been no creek. I remembered, from that other time, a wombat trail curling up into the bush, a groove of dust that twisted between tree roots. Today, that little track was a meter wide and flowed with water the color of milky tea. We followed it upward, you and me, into the dappled wood and the cicadas and the creaking of gang-gangs. It all seemed so lush, so *alive*. Young shoots sprouted from every tree. Among the clatter of brown and gray, newborn leaves burst, red and green. And the grass, so thick it was everywhere. In the moist earth by the creek, I found more of those leathery cocoons, too many to count, erupting from the ground like fungus.

The trees thinned then sputtered out beside a gravel service track draped with powerlines. Above, the mountain was a beacon of leaf and shadow, urging me upward, daring me to follow the creek to its source. But I was getting tired then, and hungry. You were heavy in me and my legs were aching, my pelvis sore. I just wanted to be home. The powerlines swayed above the track, suspended from repurposed eucalypts, parched and gray. I rested beneath one, leaned against the warm cracked wood, straining to hear the hum of electricity in the wires. Something twitched beside me and I started, but it was only a moth. It looked sick. Its wings trembled. It looked like it was dying.

I cupped my hands around the moth and felt it between my palms, like the flutter of a tiny heart, then held it close until it clung weakly to my jumper. We walked home like that, with me talking to it all the way, trying to soothe it, I suppose, or keep it company. Or something.

I'm not sure what I planned to do with it. Take it inside; nurse it back to health; keep it as a pet. I wasn't really thinking. I just wanted to make it better. But by the time we got back, the moth was dead.

I didn't know what else to do, so I emptied out a matchbox and put the body inside. It's up on the kitchen worktop now, next to the cocoon.

It's so sad, Noodle. It's always the smallest things.

—

I had that dream again, of the children in the cupboard.

It started the same, with that same eerie sound, coming from the whole ground, from deep, deep in the darkness of the cupboard. I heard it, but I felt it too, in my body; in you, Noodle. I felt you inside me like a vibration, a kind of liquid darkness that was also the sound. Then I was inside—*we* were inside—only it wasn't a cupboard at all but a tunnel, deep in the mountain.

It was wet in the tunnel and not a bit cold. At first, the water was up to my ankles, then it came to my calves and I knew we had to go further, that I'd only find what I was looking for at the mountain's deepest part. With each step down the water came higher, to my knees, to my thighs. And it was warm, Noodle, so deliciously warm it almost wasn't there, wasn't water at all but a kind of *holding*. It was holding me. And then it was up to my belly and it was holding you too.

The strangest thing about this dream, Noodle, was that I wasn't a bit scared. I knew I should be, knew it was wrong to go down into that place in the cupboard, into the tunnel beneath the mountain. But I wasn't frightened. I *wanted* to go down.

When the water was up to my boobs, I turned and looked back up the tunnel. Hanging above me in the darkness was a disc of light, a silvery full moon. And in and out of that light tiny bodies fluttered. Above the low rumble I could hear the patter of delicate wings, and all about me whispers like the voices of children.

The dark was spangled with silvery dust.

—

There's something wrong with the house, Noodle. The water, it's . . .

When I made my tea this morning, put the kettle down on the hob, black water oozed from under the glass.

And the kitchen's not the worst.

In the bathroom, the water is backing up the plughole, in the sink, in the bath. Black puddles; and they're rising. The water is pushing *up* the pipes. I went to the toilet, but it wouldn't flush. It was like there was nothing in the tank. When I pressed the lever, the bath bubbled. I called David and left a message, but he hasn't called back. I don't know what to do.

I was afraid to think what might be happening in the basement, but I made myself go down there and it's worse than ever. The floor is completely submerged and the back wall is dark and wet. There's a dirty tidemark up near the ceiling, where the walls have soaked up all the water from the ground. And the more the walls suck up, the more there is. It's streaming down the basement step, a little river running through the carport, down the driveway.

It makes me feel sick, Noodle. Sick to my stomach. I feel like the house is going to collapse around us and there's nothing I can do about it.

—

I tried to get some work done tonight. I thought it might distract me to focus on something else for a while, something I can control.

I was on the couch, with the pad up on my knees, working on a piece I should have finished weeks ago. It felt good to be drawing again, but I couldn't concentrate. I was worrying about the house, and you were kicking like billy-oh. I must have restarted that sketch a hundred times.

Then there was a thump on the patio doors.

We don't have curtains on them yet or anything, so the lounge and dining room is all one big wall of glass, with the sliding doors out to the garden. At night it feels so exposed, like all the light and warmth in the room gets sucked out through those black glass sheets. I put down the pad, stood by the doors and peered into the darkness.

There was another thump, then a sort of muffled thrashing and I saw, over by the standing lamp, a huge moth beating itself against the glass. It looked enormous, the size of my hand, but that might've been a trick of the light. The glass, where the moth had struck, was dusted with silver.

I think I must have laughed. It wasn't the moth, but relief that it was *only* a moth. I don't know what I'd imagined, but the thump, that exposed feeling, it frightened me. The house feels so unwelcoming, the spreading damp so hostile, that the thump on the glass was like something inevitable; something I'd been expecting and dreading all at the same time. Then to find out it was only a moth—

I turned back to the couch and the sketch I couldn't finish and was about to sit down when there was another thump. Then another. And another. Then a pounding on the glass like muffled rain.

I ran.

Out of the room, away from the wall of windows and the high echoing ceiling; away from the pounding of bodies against the glass, the fluttering of delicately patterned wings; away from the shower of dust that danced as it fell, copper and silver and gold; ran up into the closed and quiet darkness of the bedroom. Before I reached the stairs, I turned once and saw the window, a writhing curtain lit starkly and askew by the corner lamp, a tapestry of artificial eyes that twitched and blinked with every wingbeat. I couldn't see the garden, only the madly thrashing wall of moths.

Now I'm huddled in the darkness of the bedroom, wrapped in the sleeping bag, curled around you. The room is cold and moist, the sleeping bag clammy. The air smells of damp.

And downstairs the moths are still beating on the glass.

—

I slept terribly again last night, haunted by the moon and its jagged beams. You were wriggling like mad, doing flip-flops in my belly, and my pelvis ached so badly I thought it would split. And the moths, all night the sound of the moths.

There was a dream too. Something so terrible it woke me with a gasp, though I don't remember it now.

When I came down in the morning, looked out the patio doors at the fence and the hedge and the lawn, at the mosaic of sodden books and clothes, when I pressed my hands against the door's cool glass and looked down, I saw in heaps and drifts the bodies of the moths. I thought I noticed, here and there, a fluttering wing, a trembling body. But nothing was alive in those terrible dunes. It could only have been the wind.

I couldn't bear it. It was so futile, so . . . pathetic. I felt I just had to do something, find some way to honor them so it wouldn't all be for nothing. But first I had to eat, to make myself a cup of tea. And the moment I stepped into the kitchen, there was the slick of black water stretching wall to wall.

I called David and got through this time, but he was out of town and said he couldn't come until tomorrow. I tried to mop it up myself, but only managed to swill it round and round, spreading the pool wider. Now it's spilled from the linoleum onto the polished wood floor and is spreading to the lounge.

The bath upstairs is half-full of bubbling black water and the toilet keeps hacking and gurgling. The stains, Noodle. The stains! Everywhere they are growing darker. Everywhere the floodmark is higher.

The walls are glistening and wet and blooming with mold, gray and brown and black. In among the fungal coils, I imagine I can almost see a pattern, a fractal motif that is sometimes like an eye, sometimes like a leaf or perhaps feathers, but everywhere repeated and everywhere the same. Almost like—

But that would be absurd.

—

I remembered my dream.

It's so awful, I can barely bring myself to speak it.

I was cramping and there was blood and the pain was so bad I knew it was happening, that you were coming out of me. You were coming too soon and there was nothing I could do to stop it.

And when I reached down between my legs to pull you up to me, to lay you against my breast for the first time, you weren't *you*. You were . . .

You were . . .

—

They're back, Noodle. Can you hear them?

Can you? Hear their wings like whispering silk, the drumming of their bodies on the glass? Oh you are *active* tonight. I know you can hear. Shall we go down and meet them?

Shall we?

There are so many! Even this close to the glass, there are so many and crowded so tight. Their bellies aglow in the lamplight, their wings a blur in clouds of silvery dust. Even this close I can't see through them. It's like there's no world outside, like there is *nothing* beyond this murmuring wall. Nothing but them, Noodle. And us.

Don't kick so. I know what you're wanting. See, I'm pressing my hand to the glass. See how they react! When I move my hand, see how they ripple! See how they respond!

You knew, didn't you, how they mean us no harm. You knew they only wish us well.

And I know what you're wanting. I'm going to let them in.

I'm–

—

Still here, Noodle. Still here. It's all okay. Everything's going to be okay.

When I dragged at the door, the moths poured in. They were louder inside. As the moths streamed through the crack, those muffled bumps and whispers behind the glass became a flickering, everywhere purr. I never knew there could be so many. When they came in like that, swirling and coiling like a whirlwind, I ran up here to the bedroom. But they followed, thrashing and spiraling, filling the air with wing-beats and dust.

But now here we are, my darling, my little one. Here we all are.

They've settled now. And I have too. Can you feel them, Noodle, feel their touch through my skin? It makes me shiver, so I know you feel it too. Their touch is so gentle, so kind, I wanted it all over me. Now they swaddle me, trembling—so soft, so gently warm. I've never felt so held.

But there is a pull, isn't there? I know you feel it too. An *inclination*. The moths have come with a message, but they speak so quietly I can barely hear. But you can, can't you, Noodle. You know what they're telling us to do, where they're wanting us to go.

Be still, they say. *Still unto the dawn.*

—

They're getting weak. I can feel them quiver against my skin. Some of the moths who clung to the walls have already dropped and are dusting the floor with their bodies. It will have to be soon.

You're more active than ever though aren't you, Noodle? You've been pressing against me all night, jabbing your feet into my ribs like you're ready to be born. Not yet, little one. Not for a long while yet. But something *will* happen this morning. And I know you feel it too.

Dawn, the moths whisper. *Dawn. Dawn.* And they're right. The condensation on the window glistens with gray half-light. It's time for us to go.

All night I've felt that subtle pull. I know where you want me to take you. But when I open the door to the bedroom cupboard, with all those shivering moths clung like an overcoat to my nakedness, there's nothing there but shadows and mold. It's just an empty cupboard.

Up, whisper the moths. *Up. Up.*

Through the window, through baubles of dew. The shadow of the mountain.

That's right, isn't it Noodle? You kicked as soon as I saw it. As soon as I knew.

Yes. The moths against me flutter. *Yes. Yes.*

Then that is where we shall go. Up, up, among the gums that rattle their leaves like tiny bones. Up, beside the tumbling creek, the murky flow that will not be there tomorrow. Up, until we find the source, the way down into the belly of the mountain.

All the way our sisters will dance about us in shimmering clouds, leading, tugging, drawing us ever up, even as they drop from exhaustion and cold and the sacrifice they have made to bring us home. And when we find the opening, then we shall descend into those blood-warm waters, the moist tunnel walls glistening with the dawn we are leaving behind.

And perhaps we shall turn, Noodle, take one last look at that floating disc of light above us. Not the moon—no, not the silvery moon—but our last glimpse of the cold and separate daylight world.

And we shall descend, my darling, my little one, my hands under my belly, holding you, as we are held by that everywhere warmth, by that loving dark.

And in the darkness, we shall become—

—

REQUEST RECEIVED: 20-09-2009
CLASSIFICATION: -PROTECTED-
SUBJECT: Maria Galen, Disappearance of. Also Galen M, "Moth Queen"

In response to your request for a check of the files of this Division concerning the captioned individual, you are advised that no investigation has been conducted since December 1998, at which time the case was shelved pending further evidence.

The collection agency's 1995 report is too far redacted to be of value, though you may find some interest in the attached photographs. These were captured *in situ* by the reporting agent assigned to Ms. Galen when her loan defaulted, following an extended period (some nine months) of delinquency. The more notable images you may remember from the coverage of the time: the infamous "stain wall," for instance; that expanse of mold in which the more credulous speculators perceived the form of a giant moth. Other shots are less well-known and verify at least some of Galen's recorded claims: the marks on the driveway; the rime of soot in the sinks and bath; the husks in the lounge and bedroom of several-hundred *Agrotis Infusa*–bogong moths.

The testimony of David Pembleton, Galen's "plumber," may yield further corroboration, though most of his statements have since been discredited. Many seem to be simple hallucinations, inspired by press coverage of the events and his (tenuous) association with the missing woman. Access to the transcript will require additional clearance, however, as the interviews were conducted in the psychiatric hospital where he was later committed.

You will find enclosed herewith transcribed in its entirety one copy of Maria Galen's audio journal–the three Dictaphone cassettes found in the bedroom by the reporting agent. Some thirty-four additional cassettes were also found among the garden debris, but were from an earlier period and not pertinent to the investigation.

The photographs and transcript summarize the full extent of the information in our files concerning the captioned individual as of that time.

ENCLOSURES
Photographs (27) MLG#101 – 127
Unexpurgated transcript, "The Moth Tapes"

The Family Madness

Uncle Nathan was already missing by the time the children returned from school. The old house was still and silent, the door to Nathan's workshop closed.

The house was the only property this far out along the ridgeline, four kilometers from the nearest school bus stop. Leo and Cam were always the first to be picked up each morning and they were always the last to be dropped off. By the end of the school week, Cam was feral with exhaustion and Leo was lucky to get her home at all without carrying her there himself.

That Friday, the walk back from the bus stop seemed to take forever. The sun had baked the unpaved road hard and orangey-red, and heat rose from the ground in dusty swirls. The cicadas were louder than usual, their shrill orchestral stabs drowned out even Cam's incessant whining. From the moment they stepped down off the bus, she had oscillated between extremes of manic energy and melodramatic collapse. Less than halfway along that endless road, she exploded, flung her bag in the dust and herself down after it, refusing to move even one step farther. Leo threatened and cajoled, but only the promise of carrying her bag and of making her favorite dinner when they got home could get her to keep dragging one foot in front of the other.

The sun was drooping by the time they arrived at Nathan's, their shadows long in the dust. In sight of the fading weatherboard, with its leaf-stuffed gutters and slumped tin roof, Cam forgot her exhaustion and sprinted to the edge of the woods. There she clambered in the gums and swung from the spider's web of ropes that Nathan had erected when the children first moved in.

Leo approached the house more cautiously, scanning the treeline for the mob of roos that often lounged there. He had stumbled among them one evening, calling Cam in from the forest for dinner, and been threatened by the leader of the mob: an enormous bull roo. It had towered over Leo, chest puffed, biceps and neck swollen with hostility. Leo had run, made it back to the house without incident, but had ever since been cautious, terrified of encountering that monster unprepared again.

The screen door banged behind Leo and he dropped both of their bags against the umbrella stand in the hall. He inhaled the musty air with its odd mélange of teak oil, dust and sulfur, stood a moment to listen to the dull, deadened ticks of the grandfather clock, the creaks of the old house settling as it cooled.

The kitchen was dim and just as Leo had left it that morning, the mugs and bowls still in the sink, the cereal box still open on the counter. He folded down the lid of the box, put it away in the cupboard, opened the freezer and blinked at the glare. From among the packs of fruit pies and frozen pizza, the bags of sausages and chicken nuggets, Leo took a half pack of fish fingers, the oven chips and a bag of frozen mixed veggies. Cam would complain about the veggies, but she could suck it up; someone had to make sure she grew up big and strong. Leo turned on the oven, shook the chips and fish fingers out onto a baking tray and slid it onto the middle shelf, closed the oven door. While the oven softly groaned, Leo put away the washing up from the night before, leaving out two plates and two knives and forks, filling a pan from the tap and putting it on the rings to heat. He shook the bag and frozen veg rained into the pan—sweetcorn, peas, tiny cubes of carrot. He set two places at the breakfast bar, filled two glasses with milk, drained one, filled it again, wiped the mustache from his upper lip.

Cam burst in just as the timer on the oven dinged—conveniently too late to help. She hopped up onto her stool at the breakfast bar and shook tomato sauce all over her chips. Her face was bright red and she was panting, like she'd run twenty times round the house. She stuffed sauce-drenched chips and fish into her mouth with mucky fingers, chugged at the glass of milk between swallows, drummed at the bar with dangling feet. She wiped her lip with the back of her hand, leaned back and let rip a belch so loud it made her laugh. She lunged for the sauce, but Leo pulled it out of her reach.

"Eat your veggies," he said.

Cam's brows furrowed and she snarled at her brother. "Sauce!"

"If you want more sauce, you've got to eat your veggies."

Cam growled, forked veggies into her mouth until it was bursting. "*Mmnnf*!" she said, her hand outstretched toward the bottle.

Leo slid it toward her, shaking his head. He was still eating his dinner, steadily and with care, when Cam pushed herself back from the counter and clomped toward the bedroom. She left her cutlery, plate and empty glass.

He called after her. "Hands!" But even as he said it, he knew she would ignore him.

Leo finished his meal with methodical formality, brought the knife and fork together on his plate. He sighed, stacked Cam's plate on his own, wincing at the sauce that smeared against his thumb. Gathering up the cutlery and the glasses, he placed them in neat groups beside the sink. As he plugged the drain, turned on the taps and squirted in the dishwashing liquid, some detail registered faintly, some absence he could not put his finger on, but which, as he cleaned first the glasses, then the plates and at last the cutlery, left him with a vague sense of unease.

It wasn't until after he had washed up and he and Cam were in the living room together that he realized what had been missing. Cam was kneeling on the floor beside the footstool, drawing intricately detailed plans for an underground hideaway. Leo was curled up in the worn leather armchair, struggling to concentrate on the copy of *To Kill a Mockingbird* he was supposed to have finished by Monday. He read the same sentence over and over five times before finally lowering the book to his knee. It was the coffee mug. Uncle Nathan's coffee mug had not been in the sink.

This minor revelation drained the last of Leo's energy. He closed the book, put it down on the footstool beside Cam's sprawl of loose pages, the scrappy bubble-diagrams of secret rooms and tunnels.

"Come on," he told his sister. "Bedtime."

He was too tired to register her complaints, too tired to harass her to brush her teeth. He was so tired he didn't even notice, as he stumbled to bed, that the door to Nathan's workshop was not limned with its usual yellowish light.

Behind the door, the darkness and the silence pressed; as though shadow and the lack of sound had substance, weight, and a longing to burst free of their constraints and engulf the house with absence.

—

Leo and Cam would have disappeared into the foster system if it weren't for Uncle Nathan. When their mother was sent away, he came to collect them, drove them and their two suitcases, out beyond the city, up and over the mountains to his home at the edge of the woods. On the way they stopped at a roadside café for milkshakes and toasted salad sandwiches. There, Nathan told them the rules.

The rules were few: tidy up after yourselves; don't disturb your uncle; and keep out of the workshop. Beyond that, Nathan didn't seem to care what they did. They had no bedtime, no foods off limits. They could have lain around all day eating lollies and watching TV, if only Nathan had one. But he didn't trust it. "That's their apparatus of control," he told them on that first day, when Cam was whining about her favorite show. "That's how they get inside your head. Trust me, you don't need that shit knocking around up there."

Nathan didn't take much stock in school either, called it "their indoctrination machine." It made no difference to Nathan whether they were home in the days or not, so long as they didn't disturb his work. But he humored Leo, let the boy enroll himself and his sister on the condition that he, Nathan, was not expected to get involved in any way, that he would never have to meet a teacher or discuss their "so-called education," and that the children would make the journey there and back by themselves. He teased Leo about it whenever he could. Cam always joined in, though with more ferocity than her uncle, resenting her brother's insistence that they both attend 'the machine.'

Nathan never explained who exactly "they" were, though he referred to them often. It seemed to be a catch-all expression for everything wrong with the world—vaccination; big pharma; rigged elections; contrails; electromagnetic energy and the 5G wireless service. "They" were always seeking out new ways to restrict his personal freedoms. He was eccentric, certainly, very likely a little cracked, but at least he wasn't mad. As long as the children stuck to the rules, he was a benevolent, albeit distant, influence, and Leo was grateful to him for taking them in.

It wasn't at all clear to Leo exactly what it was that Nathan actually *did*. He seemed to be an inventor, or scientist of some description, though Leo had yet to glimpse any output from all those hours shut away. Nathan spent so long in his workshop, or over on the other side of the property tinkering with his 'instruments,' that the children often went to bed without seeing or hearing from him at all. Then, out of the blue, he would appear the next morning, brimming with energy and excitement, urging them all to be up and out and doing something together. On one of those days, he dragged them down to the river and set up a rope swing with Cam, was the first to leap, yelping, into those brisk waters. On another, he drove them out along a road even more dusty and rutted than his own, out to a plummeting ridge, where they scrambled down rocky paths into the silence and splendor of the valley blue gum forest. On still another, they journeyed to the ruins of an iron smeltery, where he let them clamber through labyrinths of collapsed brick. Nathan marveled at the obelisks of once molten iron, rambling about alchemy and the proper process by which to attain the albedo.

Perhaps Leo imagined that tomorrow, Saturday, would be one of those days; one of those delirious joyful days where he could let down his guard, if only a little. Just enough to allow himself a moment's enjoyment.

—

Leo was woken, deep in the night, by the storm. Thunder grumbled and growled and lightning flashes cast eerie shadows on the wall of his bedroom.

There was no rain, only the rolling, rumbling boom as of great beings awakening in the sky, stretching down enormous limbs to shake the earth. The sounds were vast and alive and so close Leo could almost taste ozone. When lightning struck a tree at the edge of the wood, the crack was so loud it startled him out of bed and over to the curtain. On the other side of the bedroom, Cam snored, unruffled by the noise.

Leo peered out the window and into the dark of the yard. The storm continued to move, the thunder receding, though lightning still flickered, illuminating the yard in sheer blue-white bursts. With each flash, Leo caught details: a heap of rusty oil drums, the skeleton of the shed, Nathan's tumbledown Holden Special. In one brilliant silvery flare, so long and slow it seemed frozen in time, Leo saw, over by the wreck of the lightning-struck tree, a figure.

The flash burned in Leo's eyes, filling the dark with dancing spots of color. He strained to make out the shapes of the tree, the person—if that is what it had been—but there were only the blue and red and pink fireworks dancing across his vision. Then the lightning flashed again and he saw it. The bull kangaroo.

The distance and the darkness and the silent bursts of light made the bull seem bigger than he remembered.

It was . . . watching.

Again there was darkness and, when his eyes at last adjusted, all Leo could see was a ring of embers glowing among the trees on the other side of the yard.

Then the glow was obscured. The roo was moving.

Leo ducked away from the window, his heart clobbering against his ribcage. His throat was parched, aching. The thunder rolled, more distant now, and resonant, describing the contour and depth of the valley beyond the forest. Flicks of lightning pulsed. He squeezed his eyes shut. Cam snored.

When, at last, the thunder receded and Leo's heart had slowed to a mere pounding, he forced himself back up to a crouch. He listened, but Cam's loud and oblivious breathing eclipsed all other sound. Careful to part the curtain as little as possible, Leo peered out into the flickering dark.

Nothing. Even the glow from the tree was gone. Had it ever been there?

Another silent flash illuminated the yard and Leo yelled. The roo was there, only meters away, and moving.

Leo dived beneath his bed, dragged the cover down after him. He clutched the blanket to his face, pressed it hard against his eyes to mask the sobbing.

What frightened him most was not the size nor the closeness of the roo. Despite the dark and the drama of the storm, Leo's reason was intact—he knew it could not get inside. It was the *way* it moved. Perhaps it was a trick of the dark, or the way the lightning flickers resounded in his eyes long after they had ended, but something about the movement of the roo was *wrong*. The great bull had seemed . . . empty. An enormous, deflated balloon dragging itself toward him across the yard. No, not dragging itself. Being dragged.

And behind it, blocking out the ember-glow of the lightning-struck tree and the faint illuminations of the moon on the shed, on the car, masking even the pinpricks of silver-blue stars, a vast and pernicious blackness. Closing in around the house.

———

"What you doing down there?"

Leo startled, banged his temple on the wooden slats beneath the bed. Cam peered in at him, her face upside down and flushed, her hair dangling in dirty twists of gold and brown. He would have to make sure she washed it, he thought, before the weekend was out.

"You playing hide and seek or something?"

"Something like that," said Leo. He coughed, lungs filled with grit and dust from under the bed. There was something stuck to his lip. He peeled it off. A ball of lint.

He shooed his sister with a hand, pulled himself out and stretched, popping joints. The night seemed distant and mad, the storm a wild dream. He couldn't remember going to sleep. Had he fallen off the bed?

Leo padded through to the kitchen with Cam walking backward ahead of him, babbling on about some rubbish. He opened the fridge, pulled out juice, a box of eggs. He touched the kettle. It was cold. Nathan's cup still hung on the mug tree; the weird chicory powder he drank every morning still sat on the shelf.

Leo turned to Cam. She was chugging orange juice straight from the carton. He pulled it away from her lips, gestured vaguely toward a glass. "You seen Nathan?" he asked.

Cam pouted, grabbed for the juice, but Leo held it behind his back.

"You seen him?" he asked again. "This morning?"

Cam growled, shook her head.

Leo stood for a moment, half staring, seeing not his sister but his own tumbling thoughts. Cam snatched the juice and scurried round to the other side of the breakfast bar.

Still preoccupied, Leo rummaged around the dish rack for a pan. He placed four eggs in the bottom, ran enough cold water to cover them, put the pan on the stove. While the water came to the boil, he went out the front. The screen door banged behind him.

He walked the perimeter of the old weatherboard house, his feet kicking up dust. It was already baking and the air was jagged with the shrill of cicadas. There were the oil drums, the shed, Nathan's Special. Leo scanned the treeline, looking for a sign, some clue that might point to his uncle's whereabouts. But it was just as it always was. Though maybe not quite. One of the old gums at the edge of the wood had lost a limb. There was the fresh black of charcoal down its side, like after a bushfire, and Leo remembered the glow, the lightning. He shuddered.

In the kitchen, the water in the pan was bubbling over. Cam was curled on the floor in the corner, playing with a wooden ark and animals, two by two.

"Has this been boiling long?" asked Leo.

Cam shrugged without looking up. Leo sighed and took the pan off the heat.

They ate hard-boiled eggs with bread and butter. Leo made tea and they sat in silence at the counter. When they had finished, Leo piled everything in the sink but did not wash up.

"I'm going to look for him," he said. "In the workshop."

"Nathan said not to."

"We've got to. He might've had an accident or something."

"We're not allowed," said Cam.

Now it was Leo's turn to shrug. He was acting brave, but it was only for Cam's benefit. He didn't want her to get scared.

The truth was Leo had already begun to spin theories about what had happened to their uncle. None of them were good. All the accidents, the falls, the fatalities. He always did this, always had. Whenever their mother was late even ten minutes Leo imagined the worst, his mind spiraling to the phone call, to the funeral, to the desolate years beyond. Though he was anxious to find Nathan, and though he feared getting in trouble for breaking one of the only rules, that rational fear was overwhelmed by the other terrible possibilities. Better to get in trouble and Nathan be alright than . . . than what exactly?

They stood outside the door to the workshop. Leo bent his ear toward it, straining to hear through the wood to the uncharted space beyond. He knocked, tentatively at first, but then louder. The sound reverberated dully in the empty corridor.

"Uncle Nathan?" he said. "Uncle Nathan? It's me. Leo."

He turned to Cam, swallowed. Her eyes were wide.

He knocked again. "Uncle Nathan?"

His hand closed around the brass doorknob. It was loose and rattled when he gripped it. He turned the knob, pulled the door open toward them.

"Oh no," said Leo. "No."

Behind the door was a broom cupboard. Except for the lightbulb that dangled by a wire from the ceiling, and the dust-bunnies and cobwebs and the crumpled-up piece of paper in the corner, it was entirely bare. Bare, but for the writing.

The side walls were unpainted gyprock, the back raw weatherboard. Leo could see, exposed, the frame of the house, the skeleton of splintery wooden beams. The walls did not reach all the way to the back, but ended at a gap on either side, a crawlspace of about six inches between the outer wall and the inner. The cupboard was less a room than a gateway to the inside-out spaces of the house. And writing covered every surface.

From floor to ceiling, every wall was close to black with tightly packed, barely legible scribbles. The words, the strange drawings, seemed to have been burned into the wood. The hieroglyphs covered walls, beams, even the wire from which the bare lightbulb dangled. Writing disappeared round the corners of the boxish room and into the bowels of the crawlspace. When Cam flicked on the harsh bare bulb, she and Leo stood there dumbly, staring.

Leo's heart dropped to his belly. There was no workshop.

Uncle Nathan was completely mad.

—

Leo's mother had never been truly well. She'd always had that streak of insanity, even on the good days.

Cam was younger, so had seen less of the dark side of Cassandra's madness than Leo. She saw only their mother's 'quirks,' the energy and excitement, remembered only those precious few times Cassandra had given them all of her attention, lavished them with gifts and treats and adventures. Cam remembered only the good, because Leo had always been there to protect her from the rest.

For Leo, the good days were the worst. What Cassandra saw as recompense, the guilt payment for her fragmentary lapses, to Leo was a time bomb. All the hugs and smiles and lollies in the world couldn't dull the suspense as he remained alert, every sense heightened, scanning every cue in the hope of warding off her next explosion.

Like the time before Cam was born, when Cassandra was maybe seven- or eight-months pregnant. They were at home together, the cupboards bare, and five-year-old Leo was starving. She had been wracked with guilt, set him in front of the TV, told him she'd be back in five minutes. She left, locking the door to their apartment behind her. She was gone so long that Leo fell asleep where he sat.

He was woken by a commotion in the kitchen. The living room was dark but for the flicker of a cooking show on TV. He heard onions frying in a pan. The pictures of the TV chef searing a steak made his stomach tumble. He could almost smell the delicious food. From down the corridor, the clatter of pots and pans, the clink of glass. Leo rose, knees creaking, followed the unlit hall to the source of the noise. The kitchen lights were so bright they hurt his eyes. But though the sounds continued he could not see his mother. It wasn't until he rounded the small island bench that he found her, sat on the floor with her legs in a half lotus, surrounded by plastic supermarket bags. The floor was covered with mason jars, some empty, some half-filled with red lentils. Cassandra heard him come in, turned, smiled a strained, agonized smile. She patted the floor beside her.

"Come on over, sweetheart," she said. "You can help your mama."

Leo sat, leaned into her, pressing his cheek against the belly so full and firm.

"What are you doing, mummy?" he asked.

"We have to check them. You see?" Smiling, she held up a single orangey lentil between her thumb and forefinger. She brought the lentil toward her face until it was only a hand's width away, furrowed her brows, narrowed her eyes, turned the lentil this way and that. "You see?" she said again and dropped the lentil into a jar beside her knee.

Leo's stomach growled and he looked with longing at the shopping bags. Cassandra reached for a bag. "Here. You can have your own."

Leo took the bag, heavy with shopping and opened it in his lap. The bag was full of unopened packets of red lentils.

Cassandra handed him an empty metal pan and a jar. When Leo did nothing, when he just sat there clutching the bag, looking up at his mother with confusion in his eyes, she said, "Let me show you." She cut the top off the bag of lentils, poured them into the pan, reenacted the pantomime of selecting a lentil, bringing it up to her eyes for scrutiny, then dropping it into the jar.

Leo imitated her actions, though he had no idea what he was supposed to be looking for. He picked a lentil, wiggled it back and forth in his line of sight, plopped it into the jar. The process made no sense. Why couldn't they just tip the bags straight into the jar? Or, better still, put the pan on the stove and make dinner? Leo hated the tasteless, porridgy dahl Cassandra made, though at that moment he would have eaten anything. But he knew better than to correct her, or to point out the obvious, so instead he picked lentil after lentil, pretended to assess them for whatever mysterious characteristics his mother was checking for. Slowly, so slowly, the jar began to fill. But there were still so many bags.

How long did they sit on the floor that way? How many lentils had he 'checked' before his head began to droop? He didn't mean to do it. He was just so hungry, so tired. He didn't even realize that he was pulling out handfuls of the tiny red dots, sprinkling them into the jar without looking. He was almost asleep when his mother screamed.

"YOU. HAVE. TO. *CHECK*. THEM."

She roared and flailed her arms, sending pans and jars and lentils flying. The two fullest jars hit the wall, bouncing one into the other, exploding instantly. Shards of glass and dry pulses sprayed across the linoleum.

Cassandra tore at her hair, shrieking. She ran out of the kitchen, her bare feet leaving smears of blood in the chaos of lentils and jagged glass.

Leo had a lump in his throat as hard and painful as a stone, a weight in his belly so heavy it smothered his hunger. His eyes twitched but there came no tears; he had learned it was best not to cry, to always push down his own feelings for the sake of his mother. He sat there a long time after she left, the mess on the floor and the night silence like echoes of her departure. He strained with every sense to hear her. Would she return? What would she do if she found him sitting there still? Whatever he did, he knew, would be the wrong thing.

The next morning, Cassandra found Leo curled in a ball on the kitchen floor. Beside him, the dustpan brimmed with glass and lentils streaked with blood. A supermarket bag was propped open against the wall, filled with bloody litter. His hands, one still clutching the sweeping brush, were covered in tiny cuts.

That had been her first truly dreadful episode, and the agony of guilt she had shown on finding him, on remembering only flashes from the night before, had driven her to the first of the great extravagant apologies. Over the years, those make-up treats became to Leo more frightening than the manias that preceded them, but that day he welcomed her fawning, her tenderness. He almost allowed himself to relax, spooning down mouthfuls of ricotta hotcakes with strawberries, syrup and ice cream, swallowing gulp after gulp of hot chocolate and marshmallows. He almost believed, too, in her contrition—her apology was so sincere, so alive with remorse, he could almost imagine that the shadows had truly passed, that it would never happen again. He wanted so badly to believe her, wanted so badly for her to be happy.

Perhaps, when his sister came, things would be different. Perhaps then the madness would ease and they would be happy all together. A happy, normal family.

—

Leo grabbed their hats. He rubbed sunscreen on his arms and face and neck, then did his best to cover the squirming Cam. He pulled her hat down onto her head. It was squint. She pulled a face.

They ventured into the baking heat of the day. It was only ten past ten by the old grandfather clock in the corridor, but already the air shimmered. Their feet kicked up dust as they walked.

Cam was immediately distracted, scrambling up into the trees by her network of ropes. Leo paused at the edge of the forest to confront the lightning-struck tree. He reached out a hand to touch the ring of charcoal, half expecting it to burn. It was gritty and warm, but no longer smoldered. He wiped the smut on his jeans, toed the fallen limb on the ground, stepped past it and into the relative cool of the wood.

The shade was a relief and Leo took off his hat to wipe sweat from his brow. There were paths here beneath the trees, dusty tracks where leaf litter had been cleared and dirt packed down. There must be one that Nathan followed, disappearing into the forest to work on his 'instruments.' But which? They all looked equally unpromising.

Leo picked a path and set off. "Wait," yelled Cam from above.

But the trail he had chosen fizzled before she caught up with him, fading to nothing beside a pool of stagnant blackish water, filmed with shimmering oil. Cam poked it with a stick. Bubbles broke the surface, releasing a stench so foul they both recoiled.

"Let's go," said Leo, and they retraced their steps to where the paths had forked.

The second path led them deep into the wood, past thickets of new-growth gum trees jostling for space between their old established relatives. There was a slight but definite incline to the path and, as they descended, it widened, the landscape changing subtly around them. The trees were older here, colossal, with great twisted boughs and snaking roots so massive the children had to clamber to get over them. Beneath the monumental gums were explosions of green—tree ferns and ancient cycads—and the moist fresh smell of life in abundance commingled with decay. Down and to their left, the muffled trickling of a hidden creek.

"I'm thirsty," said Cam.

"You should've drunk something before we left."

"I'm tired."

"You'll be alright."

"I'm *bored*."

Leo shrugged.

"Where we going, anyway?"

"To find Nathan." He said it with certainty but did not look up for fear his expression would betray him.

"It's too *far*."

"Not much farther now."

In truth, he had no idea how far it might be, or even the extent of their uncle's property. They could be walking for days and never find the end of it. They could wander unknowing into the national park and starve to death searching for a way out of that infinite expanse. They could be lost in the bush forever searching for some instrument that didn't exist, a phantom machine which, like the 'workshop,' would turn out to be nothing but an expression of Uncle Nathan's garbled imagination.

"What's that?" said Cam.

Leo looked to where she was pointing. At the edge of the path, something protruded from the drifts of gum leaves. An image flashed in his mind of a pair of boots, toes pointing skyward. And attached to the boots, Uncle Nathan, stiff and cold and dead. He shuddered.

Cam ran over to investigate, her lethargy sloughed in an instant by curiosity. Leo followed, but cautiously. "Cam," he called. "Don't touch it."

But she had already picked it up, one of them anyway. It was a piece of black metal, strangely shaped—a clasp, or a clip of some kind. There was a heap of them, half covered by the crisp gray-green leaves. Bored with her examination, Cam tossed the clip, bounded over to sweep the forest scurf from a stack of two-by-fours. Leo's stomach tightened.

"Come on," he said. "Let's keep moving."

Up ahead the trees were thinning. Leaf litter made way to tufts of grass. The spots and dapples of patchy light grew brighter, the shade withdrawing. The air, now hot and dry, carried a faint smell of burnt wood. The path around them faded to nothing at the outskirts of a clearing.

"Bloody hell," said Leo.

"What *is* it?" said Cam.

"It's the instrument," Leo said as he stared at the charred monstrosity. "It's Uncle Nathan's machine."

He had no other words to describe it. The construct in the clearing was not like anything he had ever seen or read about or learned of in school. Even in dreams, Leo could not have conjured an assembly so strange, with a purpose so opaque. It dominated the open space between the trees, like a partially flattened crown built entirely from narrow wooden beams. The tips were scorched, and it was not clear if this blackening were part of the design or a product of its use. It seemed . . . intentional somehow and reminded Leo of the burned writing in the cupboard. Just looking at it gave him a queer feeling, a sense of wrongness and dread that hinted of things beyond what he could see.

His first thought was that Cam would want to climb it and he turned to tell her not to. But she was cowering at the treeline, shaking her head.

"Let's go, Leo. I don't like it." Her voice had a tremble in it he'd never heard. Cam was always the fearless one.

"We've got to find Nathan," he said. "Don't worry. There's nothing to be afraid of. It can't hurt us or anything."

But it was a lie and he knew it. The more he looked, struggling to comprehend that incomprehensible structure, the more he was gripped by a coldness from within. It seemed to warn of plenty to fear and a certainty of pain. And yet, they *had* to look, had to try and understand it. What else did they have to go on?

Leaving Cam at the edge of the wood, he stepped into the baking heat, willing himself forward to examine it more closely. She ran to catch up, pressed against him, gripping his hand.

Holding each other close, they made their way slowly, falteringly around the edge of the instrument.

It was bigger than it appeared from the treeline. The prongs of the scorched wooden crown towered above them, as tall as the roof of their uncle's house. Taller. And where it met the ground, the struts were buried crudely beneath the dirt. As they drew nearer, Leo realized it was not so much a crown as a flower, with great blackened petals and a second construct at the center, like a burned and broken tepee. The wood was most charred at this middle point, black and distorted, reminding Leo of the lightning-struck tree and the embers glowing red in the night. It seemed a conflagration had burst from this central hub and encircled the structure, lapping at the flower's petals like a flaming, sightless insect.

They were so close now that, had Leo dared to reach out, his fingers would have brushed the splintery outer struts. The smell was stronger too: burnt wood and sulfur; the faint tang of ozone. Each two-by-four they passed was connected to its neighbor by the black metal clasps.

At the center of the instrument, flowing outward from beneath the conical structure, there were . . . what could he call them? Drawings? Designs? Patterns etched in the orangey dirt. Some were lined with small round stones. Others capped by obscure symbols, eucalypt sticks bound with twine. There was a grim symmetry to the design, as though it somehow mirrored or revealed the construct of burnt wood and metal that loomed over him and Cam. Leo could not explain the intuition, but the markings on the ground, he knew, were a part of this machine, its expression in another, somehow *vaster* form. They were the engine, the purpose, the source of power. Looking down on them felt like falling: a fall without end through infinite space. A fall with neither up nor down. Only cold blackness forever and ever.

It seemed they had been walking the circumference of the instrument for an eternity. The uniform design of the outer structure and the hypnotic arrangement of the central markings together lulled both Leo and Cam into a kind of trance, a waking daze in which only they, the instrument and the baking heat of the sun were real. They were perhaps halfway around the outside of the clearing when Cam moaned.

"What is it?" Leo glanced down at her, surprised as though woken.

She shook her head, gripped his arm so tight it hurt.

The instrument was more badly burned on this side. Two of the petals had collapsed, exploded outward by some pressure from the center. Scattered across the ground ahead of the children were heaps of charred wood and slag. Even the dirt was scorched. A trail of blackened earth led through the debris to the edge of the forest, where the trunks of the trees and the overhanging leaves were all seared.

"You're right," said Leo. "We should go."

He picked up his pace, almost pulling Cam along, trying to shake his lethargy. He had the strong urge to run, to be away, as far as he could get them from that infernal structure. Wrongness pervaded every corner of the clearing. It crackled with a weird electricity that jangled deep in his bones. The urge overwhelmed him and he ran, dragging his sister behind him.

They fled the clearing by the nearest opening, half sprinting, half tumbling along the leaf-strewn path.

It was only when the stitch beneath his ribs grew too painful to ignore that Leo slackened his pace, came falteringly to a stop. Cam collapsed onto the ground beside him. She made no show of her exhaustion, merely lay half curled among the leaves, sobbing quietly.

As his breathing slowed and the pounding of his heart subsided, Leo looked around them, realizing only then that this was not the same way they had come. He had no idea where this other path might lead, only that they could not go back, that they must never again lay eyes on Uncle Nathan's monstrous, purposeless creation.

The awareness of being lost sunk to his belly like a stone. All around them was unfamiliar. He had no sense of the direction they were pointing, only that the light seemed wrong and the path devoid of any landmark he recognized. Cam still lay on her side, her eyes fixed on some faraway point. She was quiet now, having abandoned her sobs for a silence Leo found more disturbing. The only sound in the dead, still wood was their breathing and the drone of flies.

"Come on," said Leo. He tugged at his sister's arm. "We've got to keep moving."

She let him pull her up and drag her behind him, as lifeless and empty as a puppet. But she didn't complain, continued to put one foot down in front of the other.

They came upon the body round the next corner. Even before they saw it, the smell assaulted them, rich and rank and inescapable. Leo gagged, covered his mouth with his t-shirt.

The corpse lay across the full width of the path. Its enormous size made the space seem cramped, as though the forest were closing in around them. Flies covered every surface. Leo recognized it immediately. The bull kangaroo.

The discovery seemed to wake Cam from her stupor. While Leo hung back, his arm across mouth and nose, she stepped toward the stinking heap. She picked up a stick and poked at the body. Flies panicked, swirled and landed again, disappearing into the mass of black that seethed over every inch of the roo.

Cam swiped at the flies, exposing ever-larger sections of the roo's flank and midsection. It was entirely without fur, and scored into the red rawness was a uniform pattern of coils that made Leo think of a bottle cap. He was thinking, too, of the bull he had seen in the depths of night, the weightless body with its strange fluttering movements.

Cam whacked the ground with her stick, discharging an explosion of flies. Bared yellow teeth. Taut knots of muscle. Lidless eyes staring, frozen in surprise.

Leo turned and ran for the edge of the path, vomiting egg and orange juice until there was nothing left in his stomach.

———

The trip to the museum was another of Cassandra's apology specials. Another morning of pancakes and strawberries and ice cream. More promises that Leo could have whatever he wanted. That it would never happen again. Not ever.

Leo couldn't even remember what triggered it—another wild over-reaction to some untraceable slight. Cam was a baby then, old enough to sit up, but still too young to crawl. She mostly slept as Cassandra pushed her in the stroller through the museum.

The museum was, for Leo, an extraordinary treat. He loved especially the airy mezzanine floors, with their wood-framed cases displaying row upon row of bugs and beetles, butterflies and moths. He was awed by their number and variety and would pore over the contents of each glass case with meticulous care, examining every specimen in detail. He marveled at their colors and shapes, how similar they seemed, and yet how different. All the hand-typed paper labels and the words he could not read, the pins inserted with exquisite care through the bodies of each tiny creature. The wonder and diversity of life, only frozen in time; so much easier to fathom than life as it was lived, always in motion, always unpredictable.

That day, though, their time in the insect gallery was tense and unsatisfying. Cassandra's earlier remorse made way to a mounting irritation. She quickly tired of Leo's silent contemplation of the static, miniature world within the glass cases. The walkways of the mezzanine were too narrow for the stroller and, though it was quiet, the few people that tried to pass them did so with a grudging politeness that rankled. Leo sensed all this through invisible antennae, forever scanning for shifts in his mother's mood. His back was tense, almost crackling with discomfort at her restlessness. He was too aware of her anxiety to concentrate on the butterflies.

Leo relented to her suggestion that they head down to the café, allowed her to lead him from the gallery and into the dim corridors of the museum. They must have taken a wrong turn—or, more likely, Cassandra had never known which way she was heading—for they found themselves in an older section of the building, a dark wing lined with glass cabinets illumined from within. Leo wanted very much to hold his mother's hand, but he knew better than to reach for it. The exhibit stretched on into darkness, with only the oozing glow from the cabinets to light the way.

Inside the cabinets dangled costumes from other lands and other times. They hung behind the glass, shadowy and strange. All of them empty, like bodies deflated.

Leo could still remember Cassandra's sharp intake of breath, the pain as she gripped his shoulder, the strange moan that escaped her throat. In dreams, he still heard the echo of her footsteps on parquet as she ran back down the corridor and out of the museum, her strangled cries reverberating off the glass.

It seemed an eternity before the museum guard found him there, alone with the baby in the stroller, surrounded by shadows and silence and the creepily suspended clothing.

—

"So what was it then? A monster?"

"I don't know," said Leo. "I'm only telling you what I saw. It was so dark. But whatever was behind the roo was darker—blacker than night. It blocked out the stars."

Cam went quiet, brow furrowed.

They were almost back at the house, walking a familiar path through dappled afternoon light. Leo had thought them lost, but the path from the roo led them by twists and turns to the stagnant, stinking pool. The weirdness of the morning was lifting now they knew where they were, knew that home was only moments away.

Cam's spirits seemed greatly restored by each step they took toward her own stomping ground. It was as though her essential Cam-ness had been drained by Nathan's diabolical instrument—by the mere sight of it. The further she got from that construction of wood and metal and stone, the more like her noisy and hyperactive self she became.

Leo had brooded on whether to tell Cam what he had seen the night before. He'd been protecting her for so many years, shielding her from the full brunt of Cassandra's madness, that it had become a habit. He didn't want to expose her now to the horror building inside him. But Nathan was gone and in a few hours it would be dark again. And then what? Whatever it was, he couldn't face it alone. And, if they were to be prepared, Cam needed to know.

At last, she looked up. "It's alright, Leo," she said. "We can get it, whatever it is."

—

"Uncle Nathan? Uncle Nathan?"

Leo's voice rose as he called out into the empty house. The sound was strange and hollow and seemed to hang there in the silence as he paused, listening, in the entryway. He closed the front door behind him with a soft click.

Cam had stayed outside at the edge of the wood. She was clambering in her network of ropes, making "preparations." When Leo left her, she was hauling sticks and largish rocks up into the treetops, tinkering with imaginary traps.

It made him anxious leaving her alone there, but the climbing soothed her. The familiar space—*her* space—helped her let go of whatever malaise had gripped her that morning. Besides, it was full daylight outside. Whatever he thought he had seen in the depths of last night would surely not come out in the afternoon sun? And who knew what the evening might bring? Nathan might be back. Anything.

Leo gave the workshop a wide berth as he made his way to the kitchen. Anger bubbled in him at the thought of it: the empty cupboard with its web of scribbles. Madness. Everywhere, the madness of grownups. And he and Cam paying the price, over and over. He thought of forgetting the search, abandoning Nathan and his insane projects, just packing their bags, running away to start a new life, just the two of them. But he knew that idea, itself, was madness, that he and Cam could not survive alone out there. At best, they'd be living on the streets, never knowing where the next meal was coming from. At worst, they'd be found, packed off to foster homes or an institution. They'd be separated. It was unimaginable.

No, whatever happened, they would stay here as long as they could. Together.

Opening the freezer drawer, Leo appraised the contents with a new eye. There was enough food to last them a few weeks, more if they eked it out. Then there were the tins. They'd be right for a while. And when they weren't . . . ? He'd just have to work that out when the time came. He took out two frozen pizzas, placed them on a baking tray and set the timer on the oven.

The emptiness of the house pressed in on him. The dead, still air, the creaking of the tin roof in the afternoon heat. Outside there was a commotion in the trees, cockatoos and their grievances. He went to the window and looked out at the bare yard, the woods, the far peak of the mountain. It all seemed alien to him now, hostile. Even the house did not feel safe. He tried to spot Cam, up in the treetops, but the angle was wrong; she was round the other side of the house where he couldn't see her.

Leo went back to the kitchen, pulled out drawer after drawer. He found the flashlight in the cupboard under the sink—heavy and black, as long as his arm. A disc of light appeared at his feet when he clicked the button; at least some things of Nathan's were just as expected. He stood for a moment outside the workshop cupboard door, then tugged it open and stepped inside.

The light was still on from before, the air in the cupboard close and dusty. Leo breathed slow and deep, willing his pulse to calm. Uncle Nathan's graphomania pressed in from every wall.

It was madness, every word of it. Leo struggled to make sense of what he was reading, but it was all over the place, a hotchpotch of staccato journal entries tumbled together with arcane symbols, incantations and some sort of primitive bestiary. There were diagrams, too, shapes Leo recognized as early sketches of the structure in the clearing. He followed his uncle's scattered trains of thought out of the cupboard and into the crawlspace, reading by the flashlight gripped awkwardly against his shoulder.

Perhaps he hoped the notes would make things clear, that all would be explained: Nathan's disappearance; the storm in the night; the queer emanations that seemed to pulse from the vast wooden instrument; even the corpse of the bull kangaroo. But it was impenetrable. The scribbles were barely legible and many were written in a language Leo did not understand—Latin, maybe, or Greek. The bits that Nathan had scribbled in English made no sense either. He referred often to "The Opus," wrote as frequently of "The Opening" or "The Breach," and peppered every note with magic-sounding hokum words like "The Beyond," "The Umbral Prince," or "The Wasting Shade." It was gibberish, the ravings of a madman convinced of some inscrutable higher purpose.

The more Leo read, the less sense it made. With each baffling sentence he struggled to comprehend, his anxiety mounted—a black fear that bloomed inside him, cold and vast and dark, devouring joy and hope. There wasn't enough air in the crawlspace. The walls were too close. And still the writing stretched on and on, far into the shadows beyond his flashlight beam.

When the oven timer dinged on the other side of the wall, Leo startled, banged his head on a beam and dropped the flashlight. Spots burned in his eyes, everything black but the strip of brilliance at his feet. He struggled to tamp down his panic, his urge to pound at the walls until he burst through, back into openness, clean air and daylight. Instead, he crouched, contorting his body to fit that narrow space, snatched the flashlight from the mess of shredded insulation, dust and rat turds. Just having it in his hand was comfort enough to regain control of himself. He shuffled back the way he had come, toward the bare cupboard and the relative sanity of the house.

—

"Nathan's not coming back," he told Cam. "We have to forget about him."

Leo had expected tears, or a scene, but she simply pursed her lips and nodded. Ropes dangled above them from her favorite tree. Its limbs groaned faintly, leaves rattling.

"But what about the monster?" she said.

Leo thought for a moment. He wanted to tell Cam that there was no monster, that they had nothing to be afraid of. He wanted to reassure her—and himself. But as the afternoon wore on and the sky reddened, the memory of what he'd seen the night before pressed ever more urgently upon him. The hollow puppet of the kangaroo. The vast black shape that blotted out the stars. He felt the approach of night as a loosening in his bowels, a cold that gripped him from a place so deep it could not be warmed by sunlight.

"I don't know." He turned to her, put on his bravest face. "We'll think of something. The important thing is that it's just us. There's no grownup coming to help. We've got to look out for each other."

Cam stared at her feet, screwed up her mouth. She looked up at her brother and smiled. "It's alright, Leo," she said. "We'll be alright. I have a plan."

She put down her plate of cold pizza crusts and scampered up the ropes into the boughs of the towering angophora. Her face appeared above him, a distant moon beaming down.

"Come on," she said.

Leo sighed, put down his plate and followed her up into the tree. It took him five times as long to get up as it had his sister. He was no fan of heights and the wavering ropes, the distance to the ground, made his head spin, his belly tumble. When at last he hauled himself up to her level, he debarked onto the thickest branch and clung to the trunk with his eyes closed, willing the seasick feeling to subside.

Cam sat beside him, holding on to nothing. Her feet dangled on either side of the bough, jiggling restlessly forward and back.

"Welcome to The Hideaway," she said proudly, gesturing around the treetops with a grand sweep of her arm.

Leo forced a smile, trying hard not to look down. He had never joined her up here before, never seen the world as she saw it. "It's great," he said, his grip on the trunk tightening. "I love it."

Cam beamed and Leo felt a twist of guilt. How happy it made her, him being here. Why had he never done this before?

"So, tell me your plan."

Cam's excitement bubbled over. Her feet waggled crazily. "Right. Yes. The plan. So, we hide up here and wait for the monster."

"We *wait* for it?"

"Yes, up here. And we keep watch, see. And when the monster comes," and here she paused and gestured below them toward the path, "when the monster comes from down there, we pull this."

She held a rope out toward Leo. When he didn't take it, she shook it at him. "Go on," she said. "Pull it."

Leo hugged the trunk so tightly he felt the scaly bark press into his cheek. He reached for the rope and tugged. There was resistance, so he pulled it again. The rope went suddenly slack and there was a whispering in the leaves as it snickered down from above them and pooled on the ground below.

"That wasn't it," said Cam. She covered her embarrassment with close scrutiny of two other ropes. "Pull this one."

Leo shook his head, unwilling to release his grip on the trunk.

Cam shrugged. "So we wait up here for the monster, and when it comes, we pull this." She tugged hard at the rope in her left hand.

There was a sound from behind Leo, like a cartoon spring, and a mad rustling as something hurtled through the forest toward them. A rope above Cam's head stretched taut and swung in a ponderous arc. Below them, the sound of crashing. Cam grinned proudly.

Without slackening his hold on the trunk, Leo peered out and down. A rock the size of a melon swung like a pendulum across the path. It was lashed on every side with knotted rope, and sharp sticks jutted from the knots. It looked like an enormous, primitive mace.

Leo stared at the rock swinging slowly back and forth across the path in receding arcs.

"Wow," said Leo, genuinely impressed. "You made that? Yourself? This afternoon?"

Cam beamed, reddening. She shrugged as if it were no big deal.

"Not *all* today," she said. "The Hideout's always had defenses. Me and Nathan . . ." She trailed off and her brows furrowed.

Leo looked down at the spiked rock dangling above the path, still gently swaying. For a long moment neither he nor Cam said anything. They just sat there on that high bough, as the shadows merged and color drained from the leaves. The cicadas had long ceased their shrilling. From somewhere overhead, the *kee-ow* of a black cockatoo was engulfed by the descending quiet of twilight.

"We should—" Leo gestured toward the rock.

They climbed down. Leo: tentative, shaking, every muscle taut. Cam: darting, impatient, performing feats of minor acrobatics as she waited for her brother. When Leo's feet at last made contact with the ground, his knees were trembling. His relief was so intense he almost wept.

He let her take charge, directing him to pull the rock back from the path—careful not to snag his forearms on the jagged spikes—and raise it high enough above the ground for her to loop the guide rope. From there, they could haul it into the treetops. While Leo gripped the rope, Cam scampered back up to tie the slipknot. By the time she came down, the trap charged, the last of the light had faded.

Cam shivered. It wasn't cold, but Leo understood. It was the dark. Night changed everything.

There was a sound from deep in the forest, a loud crack and a commotion of leaves.

"We should go inside," said Leo. "Just for now."

"It's probably dinner time," said Cam, and her small sweaty hand found his.

More noises from the among the trees—leaves rustling and a thumping on the earth. Roos, Leo told himself. Just a mob of roos. But his heart was thundering, his whole body tense. Hand in hand, he and Cam turned their backs on the forest and began to walk toward the house.

At first their steps were measured, as though willed to be slow. But Leo's foot caught on a rock and he tripped, almost spilling them both. That tumble broke the spell and they sprinted for the cottage.

They turned the lights on all through the house, everywhere but in the bedroom, where they closed the door, peered from the corners of the window at the shadowed yard. Oil drums. Shed. Nathan's Special. The dark mass of the forest. They couldn't see anything. No movement. Nothing. Cam fidgeted restlessly.

"Can we eat now?" she said.

Leo nodded but continued to strain his eyes, trying to make out shapes in the blackness.

A grim mood enveloped him, something like despair. As long as the sun was shining and they distracted themselves with the search for their uncle, he and Cam could pretend they were independent and free, old enough to make decisions, have adventures. Defeat monsters. But now it was night and Nathan had not returned—would not, Leo was convinced, *ever* return. Now it was night and all he could think of was the sagging puppet of the bull kangaroo, the vast black emptiness behind it. The kangaroo skin would be stinking by now, crawling with things, like the hideous lump of meat it was torn from. Again and again, Leo winced as the image flashed through his mind. He and Cam. Would it hurt?

He squeezed his eyes shut, wiped with his palm at the wetness there. "OK," he said. "Yes. Let's eat. Whatever you want. I'll make you whatever you want the most."

"Even pudding?"

"Only pudding, if that's what you want."

"I want pancakes, the fat ones. With syrup and ice cream and—"

"We don't have any strawberries."

"Then just pancakes and syrup and ice cream. Just like the ones that—"

"I know," said Leo. "I know the ones."

—

They sat at the breakfast bar in the kitchen, stooped over stacks of pancakes that dripped with ice cream and sweet syrup. The pancakes hadn't risen the way Leo wanted, and the syrup was the cheap kind—maple *flavored*—but still it felt like a victory. And Cam seemed happy enough. But, when it came to eating, they found that neither of them was hungry.

On the plate, the pancakes steamed deliciously, their odor nostalgic and filled with comfort. But in the mouth . . . Leo found he could not swallow. Even the soft, white vanilla ice cream seemed to stick in his throat, the sickly syrup tasted bitter and wrong. He lay down his fork and stared at the empty sink.

Cam was bent over her plate, fork hovering, eyes fixed on golden swirls of syrup in the melting ice cream. She had the air of a seer, of one seeking in those arcane patterns secrets of the future and the past. She sighed and her shoulders slumped.

"Do you remember that time Mum took us for pancakes? She had a bad morning, broke something and shouted. I cried, but you didn't. She felt so sorry, she took us out for breakfast."

"I don't know," said Leo. "There were so many times."

"It was the time she bought the frisbee. After, anyway. She took us for pancakes with strawberries and ice cream and said we could go anywhere, do anything. And I said I wanted to go the beach and play frisbee and that's what we did. Do you remember?"

"Yes," said Leo. "I do remember. It was one of those sport-shop frisbees, red and yellow and a bit spongy. And she threw it too hard and it ended up in the surf and got lost."

"Yes, but before that. When we were on the beach and Mum was playing with us, and even you were smiling, you were running around too, after the frisbee. You forgot to be so serious. In the café, Mum had looked so beautiful and sad, but that afternoon we were all happy. And even after we lost the frisbee it was still a good day because then we swam in our undies and I caught a wave. Then we all walked together on the wet sand and Mum had her arms around us both. Do you remember?"

"Yes," said Leo and his head hung. He remembered it now clearly, the memory pressing down on him like a great weight—Cassandra, her absence. Where was she now? In some faraway room, talking to herself, babbling insanities and thrashing against her constraints? Or drugged to the eyeballs, aware of nothing but the mad movies looping in her head? Either way, it was worse than death. Sometimes, Leo wished she *were* dead. That would be better than this in-between place, this tangle of hope and despair. All this endless longing. While she was alive, there was always the possibility she would return, that he and Cam would once again have her back—their 'old' mother—looking sad and beautiful, chasing a frisbee across the sand. Happy memories were the worst. Perhaps that was why he seemed only to remember the bad times. Broken glass. Lentils. And the constant, unwavering vigilance.

Grim silence had descended over the kitchen. Leo and Cam leaned over their plates, ice cream pooling, pancakes untouched. The room was heavy with the memory of Cassandra, her presence, her absence. From outside, beyond the wood, thunder rolled, deep and long and filled with menace. Leo swallowed.

He took their plates to the sink, caught his reflection in the dark window. With the lights on, he could see nothing beyond the glass. Only the room behind him, Cam at the breakfast bar, and himself in the foreground, looking anxious and tired. He could see nothing outside. But anything outside could see them—could see *everything*.

Thunder rumbled again, closer this time. Leo's reflection in the window was splintered by a blue-white crack of lightning.

"Turn off the light," he said to Cam, his voice a croak. "We need to turn off *all* the lights."

"Why—" Cam started, but Leo cut her off.

"Just turn off the lights!"

She hopped down from the stool and over to the switch. Leo ran into the corridor, flicking off lights as he passed. Cam called from the darkness behind him. "Leo? What is it? Don't leave me alone!"

He felt his way back toward her. Even before his eyes had adjusted to the darkness, her hand found his. Lightning burst again like a camera flash, illuminating the breakfast bar, the stools, the dining table and chairs. Leo pulled her from the room.

"What, Leo? What is it?"

Leo's throat was so constricted he could barely speak. "It's coming."

"What, Leo? What's coming?"

Fumbling along the wall with his hand, he tugged her along the corridor, past the workshop, toward the bedroom. He almost fell through the open door, dragging Cam after him. The curtains were open, as they had left them, and the room was lit brief and stark by another flash of lightning. A shadow passed before the window.

Without a word they both dived to the floor, crawled beneath the bed. Side by side, they squeezed together as far under as they could fit, hidden but for the glint of their black eyes peeping from the shadows. It was dusty under the bed, and airless. The little gasps of Cam's breath were hot against Leo's face. His heart beat so hard he could feel it in his ears. Then came the scraping, and brother and sister inhaled sharply as one, neither daring to breathe out.

It was a rasping, scratching sound, like a claw, a talon, a knife. Something hard and horribly sharp dragging over the boards outside the cottage.

"Leo," Cam sobbed. "Leo, *what*—"

Leo shushed, brought a finger to his lips, rolled his eyes toward the window. The scraping was coming closer, almost outside the bedroom.

Then came the voice. It was just outside and yet far away, a whisper from some cold place beyond the silvery stars. Or was the voice inside his head? A voice of madness and despair, of command and betrayal.

"Chil-dren," it half spoke, half sang. "O *chil*-dren." *Scrape. Scrawp.*

The voice was tinny and high-pitched, a mosquito-whine played half-speed through a detuned radio. Whispers of distortion and TV static.

"*Chil*-dren . . ."

Lightning cracked and the boom of thunder was immediate. The storm was right above them. Beside Leo, Cam was weeping. In the blue-white flash, the figure at the window was illumined.

"Uncle Nathan!" Cam's voice cracked with relief.

But Leo knew what he had seen. The face was Nathan's, but the eyes were hollow and black. The body moved, yet took no steps. It floated like an empty suit—fluttered rather. And behind it . . .

The blackness. So deep and dark it obscured the stars.

Leo shuddered.

"I don't think that's Uncle Nathan."

The shadow passed out of sight of the window. The scraping moved away toward the front of the house.

The door, Leo remembered. *We didn't lock the door.*

The thunder growled, low and deep and bottomless, a belch without end from the cold of the heavens. Cam shuffled farther under the bed, as far back as she could go in what little space they had left.

Leo felt her fumbling against his leg and reached back. He took her hand and squeezed.

The whatnot shop

Nobody remembers when the Whatnot Shop first appeared in our suburb, only that it wasn't always there. Though most of us have, by now, made use of its indefinable services, we're none of us the wiser as to what the Whatnot Shop actually sells—if it can be said to sell anything at all.

Our local shopping center is entirely unremarkable. A sixties block of yellowish brick with a supermarket, a bottle-o, a bicycle repair shop, and a fluorescent-lit family bistro that runs a Friday-night meat raffle, looping sport on a big-screen TV. Round the other side, we have a hairdresser, a tolerably good coffee shop, and a Vietnamese bakery celebrated for its iced apple scrolls and banh mi.

The corner-most shop in the block was always changing hands. It seemed a magnet for dreamers with poor business acumen, fleeing the public service to "live their passion"—at least for the month or two before their capital withered and the laneway was again cluttered with the inevitable closing down sale. For the longest time it was a boutique florist, specializing in novelty terraria. Then it was a curtained treatment room, shared by a homeopath and a maggot debridement therapist. It had a brief stint as the office of a well-intentioned—but, sadly, doomed—sand-play financial advisor, before reopening as a Christmas decoration shop: in April. There was a running joke within our small community that the shop would only be leased to someone with a less marketable idea than their predecessor.

After the Christmas shop, the store was vacant for many months. We grew used to passing its darkened windows on our way to the supermarket, barely registering the accumulation of dust and debris on its floor of bare concrete, or the bright yellow *To Let* sign that hung in the door. We grew used to its look of barrenness and dereliction, perhaps imagining that the punchline to our neighborhood joke had at last been told and the cursed shop would never again be leased.

Nobody remembers when the Whatnot Shop first appeared, because it opened without fanfare. There was no bustle of preparation; no renovations, no tradespeople. There were no *Notification of Development* papers in the window for the nosier neighbors to scrutinize. There was . . . nothing. One day, the shop was a derelict void behind unwashed glass. The next, it was in every way the same but for two small details. In the doorway, the *To Let* sign had been removed, replaced by a small piece of cardboard—apparently torn from the side of a box—on which was scrawled the one word, OPEN. And, in the bare strip of wood above the shop front, someone had written, carelessly and in lurid purple paint, WUTNUT SHOPE.

It might have been weeks—maybe months—before we noticed these minute changes. It might have been the next day. The one thing for certain is that none of us took it seriously. It seemed, at worst, a kind of childish prank, at best an act of neighborhood altruism. Could the lessor have loaned the derelict space to the nearby halfway house? Could we then expect, until the shop was once again *properly* leased, poorly curated exhibitions of moribund primitive artwork? Group therapy sessions by candlelight? There was a good deal of speculation on the unchanging shopfront—which, though otherwise quite bare, persistently displayed the grubby 'open' sign—before one of us, at last, went in.

It was Nanette Toliver, the neighborhood busybody, who first stepped through that unwashed glass door to peruse the wares of the "Wutnut Shope." Did a bell tinkle as she entered? Was she greeted by a sales assistant—elderly, youthful, female, male? She cannot remember. Mrs. Toliver remembered nothing of her encounter, though we all grilled her that afternoon, desperate as we were for any scrap of information about the strange new premises. It was most unlike Mrs. Toliver to be lost for words. About every previous tenant of the corner property, she had been our font of knowledge, the source of all the gossip, both good and bad, on which the longevity of the new establishment would depend. She was the same with residents new to the area—always first to go around in quest of seed, which she would then scatter far and free among the community. This time, though, she was stumped. Who ran the shop? What were they like? What, oh *what*, did they sell?

Mrs. Toliver was quite out of sorts. The unbidden lacuna in her usually formidable memory caused her no small amount of disquiet. Had she bought anything? No. And on this she was most emphatic. She remembered clearly stepping down from the shop into the cool gray of morning, remembered the door to the shop wheezing shut behind her—and her without a wrapped parcel or a laden bag to show for her visit. In fact, bearing no evidence at all. Almost. When Nanette Toliver stumbled from the shop and down the laneway, she opened her hand to find a twenty and a five-dollar note, a two-dollar coin and a fifty-cent piece. She was twenty-seven dollars fifty richer than she had been when she entered.

Mrs. Toliver swears blind that there was no exchange. There was nothing missing from her bag or from about her person that she might have sold for so modest a sum. The small handful of notes and shrapnel seemed entirely philanthropic. A benefaction.

That afternoon, we noticed a change in the Whatnot Shop's display. In the center of its bare concrete floor lay a mattress. It was filthy and sodden, with a scorched and blackened hole the size of a tea tray at its heart.

Undeterred by Mrs. Toliver's story or the appearance of the mattress, and spurred on by curiosity and the promise of remuneration, other members of our fair community made their own surreptitious visits to the shop. It is possible that we all, every one of us in the neighborhood, at one time or another made our pilgrimage to that strange establishment. We all have in common the memory of stepping up to the door, of pressing our hands to the wood beside the scrappy "open" sign, of pushing to enter. We all have an empty space where what happens next should be. All any of us remember is the moment later—a minute? an hour?—when we step back outside to find our palms laced with $27.50 in legal tender, all in the same denominations: a twenty, a five, a two and a fifty-cent piece. Stranger still, though many of us remember seeing friends and neighbors preparing themselves to go in, and though we have seen others in the moments after they just stepped out, standing in a daze, staring at the money in their open palm, no one has ever seen anyone actually *inside* the shop. Neither neighbor nor proprietor.

Our only clue to the mysterious occurrences that may (or may not) take place inside the Whatnot Shop is the changing window display. There have been an odd assortment of objects—obscure in their randomness, alike in their shabbiness. After the mattress, there was a broom with a broken handle. Then came a conical mound of what looked like common garden dirt. Then there was the drift of empty chip packets. There was once a heap of filthy blankets—which led some of us to question whether a vagrant had moved in to the finally abandoned store—before this arrangement too was replaced by an empty ice cream tub brimming with disembodied doll parts. There was a limbless mannequin, its blank unblinking stare directed toward the window. There was a pile of half-torched Beanie Boos. There was a microwave oven trailing bare wires, its glass charred and cracked from inside. Once there was what appeared to be a first edition hardback of Melville's *Moby Dick*. This last was identified by a local antiquarian named Gauss, who entered the shop with the intention of bartering for ownership, only to find himself standing again out the front an indeterminate length of time later, $27.50 richer. In the window was displayed the body of a brown rat—*rattus norvegicus*—as dead and desiccated as a strip of furred biltong.

The procession of noxious, broken, dirty, useless objects on display in the window of the Whatnot Shop was dizzying in its variety and perplexing in its consistency. Each time one of us left the shop, the window display had changed, though no one ever saw it happen. Did the displays in some way relate to the customer who last entered the shop? We speculated wildly and at length. Was the display the physical manifestation of that transaction which had taken place for all of us, but which was remembered by none of us? It was a mystery. What happened to us inside the shop? What, if anything, had we sold? And why was it then represented—if indeed represented it was—by a display of common, albeit unusual, rubbish in the shop window?

One thing was certain. While curiosity led each of us into the shop at one time or another, the cost of those lost memories, of the questions unanswered, was greater by far than the sum reimbursed.

No one went back to the shop a second time. Well, almost no one. A man named Privett went in on at least three separate occasions.

Privett was already a strange fellow, a longtime resident of the halfway house and a high-function schizophrenic. He was often seen in the small community square outside the supermarket, chewing broodingly on a jelly snake while feeding the neighborhood birds—the lorikeets and magpies and the ubiquitous Indian mynahs that gathered near the bus stop. Privett, it seemed, went back for the money, each time spending the full allowance on a jumbo bag of party mix for himself and seven loaves of Tip Top sandwich bread for the birds. Fueled on lollies and good will, he patrolled the suburb with surrealistic purpose, decorating the bushes and front yards with hunks and tatters of white sliced bread, much to the chagrin of the garden owners.

The changes in display after Privett had visited the shop were odd to say the least—though perhaps "unique" would be a better word, considering that the unusual and mutable exhibition in the Whatnot Shop window was never *not* odd. After his first visit, the window displayed a clockwork toy carousel, with miniature tin horses and a key to wind it up. After the second, it was an antique Remington typewriter. The artifact left on display after his third and final visit was the copy of *Moby Dick*, previously described. Privett's multiple visits to the shop seemed to have no discernible effect on his person— though it would have been hard to detect a change in so enigmatic and impenetrable a character. We, all of us, scrutinized him closely (though, of course, from a distance), for any sign of ill effect. Our opportunities for prolonged observation were cut short, however, as, after his third visit to the Whatnot Shop, Privett vanished from the neighborhood. No one saw him leave. He was simply no longer there.

Absent, too, were the birds that twittered, fluted and squawked from bushes, treetops and gutters. The neighborhood went strangely silent.

Was that the watershed? Was Privett's disappearance the fulcrum, on either side of which the happy memories of our colorful and convivial suburb hung in fragile balance with its decline into entropy and decay? No one can say for certain. A sense of timelessness had descended upon us. There was no before, no after, only the gray morass of a present without end. A spiraling eternity with the Whatnot Shop at its center.

Perhaps it was Privett, perhaps the departure of the birds. Perhaps it was the bistro going into receivership. The day it closed its doors, turned off the big-screen TVs and the glass-fronted meat fridge, our community grew a little dimmer. Without its noise and light, without its menu of average but affordable pub food, without its modest assortment of micro-brewed beers and locally sourced wines, the heart of our suburb felt empty and black, the laneways grim. Under the unblinking eye of the Whatnot Shop's unwashed windows, the empty bistro stood, cowed, gathering darkness into itself.

With the loss of the bistro, a kind of malaise descended over our suburb. The hollow quiet of weekdays seemed to steal across the neighborhood, creeping out of the empty working hours into the evenings and beyond to the weekend. There was a new and altogether unwelcome grayness, as though the light of the world outside was filtered through a thickening layer of smog. There was a desolate, empty quality to the sounds—the whispers of trees, the distant hum of traffic, all were stifled, as though muffled by cushions. And, of course, there was the complete absence of bird song and the exodus of the neighborhood cats. The local oval, too, was now completely abandoned. No longer used for sport of any kind, nor even as a meeting place for the once-thriving community of dogs and their owners. The grass grew long, the cricket pitch obscured by drifts of unraked leaves.

People began to indulge themselves in petty failures, made poorly informed choices in pursuit of mad, unobtainable dreams. Professor Vickers left his wife for a student half his age and lost his job at the university. He haunted the neighborhood like a grimy specter, the newest resident of the halfway house. Ms. Wilkinson invested her life savings to establish a business making artisanal soaps. A mishap with a tub of lye left her blind in one eye and facially scarred. Mr. and Mrs. Nguyen dug out their garden to install a swimming pool, but triggered instead a sinkhole which devoured the back end of their home. One by one the members of our community pursued with abandon these ill-considered ambitions, and one by one fell victim to minor misfortunes of a mundane and entirely predictable sort.

No one doubted the role of the Whatnot Shop in these occurrences. It was clear to all that the black hole of our neighborhood affliction had its event horizon at the borders of the shopping precinct, and its singularity at a certain corner-most establishment. No one doubted— yet no one spoke of it either. When our favorite products no longer lined the supermarket shelves, only unrecognizable knockoffs and bland alternatives, we knew the underlying cause. When the banh mi from the Vietnamese bakery lost its flavor, when the local coffee became undrinkable rather than merely tolerable, we knew what lay at its root. And when the hairdresser closed its doors and the shutters of the bike shop were drawn down for the last time, there was no question in our minds. All had fallen victim to the pernicious influence of the Whatnot Shop.

We, ourselves, no longer visited the shop, no longer peered through its filth-smeared windows. There could have been anything on display in those last months—a dead shark, a murder scene, the remnants of a satanic ritual. We did not look, did not want to know. On trips to the supermarket—for our daily paper, our weekly Lotto ticket, or to stock our larders with the increasingly objectionable groceries—we none of us spared the Whatnot Shop a glance. We kept our heads down, our eyes set on the ground in front of us. We did not look to left or right, did not greet each other as we passed.

Perhaps that explains why not one of us noticed when the "open" sign disappeared from the window, and the barely literate splats of paint vanished from above the doorway. On the squalid concrete floor there is now nothing but dust. It is as though the "Wutnut Shope" never was, as though those weeks (months? years?) were nothing more than a feverish hallucination, a madness dreamt by all in our community.

The shop is still bare and will, we suspect, remain so. Perhaps the dead windows and grimy floors of the empty shopfront will spread further, slow and certain as cancer, until the center of our suburb is as hollow and empty as a tin can rattling down a deserted street. The shops abandoned, the square desolate, lifeless but for the dance of a single sheet of newspaper, pirouetting in the silent wind. We all of us feel we have lost something—something small, but vital.

But what exactly? None of us can say.

Our Last Meal

It used to be our favorite lookout. Our hangover lookout, Sallie called it.

We always got trashed the night we arrived and, the next day, would roll out of the cabin before dawn, woken by kookaburras and the first crystal shards of hangover. We'd slog our way through the rainforest, sweating poison, Sallie forever in the lead, boasting how she'd walked this track since she was a toddler and couldn't I keep up. At the top, we'd stretch out on the coarse rock and share the same, unchanging picnic: crackers, cheese and cucumber sliced with a knock-off Swiss Army penknife, all rinsed back with the warm dregs of last night's bottle of white. And there we would lose ourselves, gazing out across the canopy and the hazy blue exhalations that rose above it, into the deeper blue of the sky.

It could never be the same without her; I knew that. But something had drawn me back here, to spread out that same simple lunch and stare blankly at those same treetops. I'd invested in a bona fide Swiss Army knife since then, and was washing down the food with water instead of wine (I only ever drank because Sallie did), but whatever it was I'd hoped to recapture remained hidden, or had not been there to begin with.

There had been a storm in the night and the rainforest that morning steamed, lush with the smells of life giving birth to itself without cease. The foliage all about me resonated with the calls of whip birds and whistlers, the rustlings of scrub turkeys, and other sounds of creatures too innumerable to distinguish or identify; or too quiet and slight to acknowledge.

My feet were swollen from the walk, and aching. Trickling streams of ants converged on the cracker crumbs and flakes of cheese. I unlaced my boots and tugged them off, surprised to find my left sock was dark and soaking. As I peeled it off, my hand came away smeared with a watery redness. I rolled up my trouser cuff to uncover the wound and found instead a leech, bloated and quivering.

It was as round as my thumb and twice as long, shiny black with streaks of orange. Even as I watched, it seemed, with each of its hideous pulsations, to be getting larger.

I'm ashamed to admit it now, but I was so overcome with revulsion that I panicked. In an instant I was on my feet, kicking at the air; I wanted it off me, but I couldn't bring myself to touch it. I flicked at it spastically, trying to brush it away, but the leech held on, its engorged body flapping against my calf like a bloody balloon.

It would have drawn some odd looks, had there been anyone around to see it: a bearded young man hopping barefoot on the rocks, arms flailing against an outstretched leg, while his twisted mouth strangled noises of disgust. I can laugh about it now, but at the time I had no sense of how daft I must have looked. Only the hysterical thought voicing itself over and over: *It is drinking me!*

In the end the leech just let go. Engorged and rippling, it writhed among the remains of my ritual lunch.

Something welled up in me then, something I could not contain. I picked up my boot by the toe and slammed the heel down on the leech.

That first blow had no effect, so I struck again. And again, and again, and again. I felt the reverberation in my arm each time the sole struck rock. I was grunting. Jaw clenched. Teeth grinding.

When I finally stopped, I was panting, almost in tears. There was nothing left of the leech but a twist of black, like a burnt elastic band, and a burst of red the size of my palm pooling in the striations of the rock.

My blood.

—

All the way back to the cabin I was consumed with disgust.

The walk seemed longer than usual, and more perilous. I recoiled from every frond that brushed my calves, jumped at each drop of water that fell from the canopy above. The rainforest teemed with life-forms of every sort, both real and imagined. Every path was crisscrossed with the giant webs of orb-spiders. Every leaf was crawling with the black bodies of sucking, biting parasites. I swept and lashed at every sensation—on my arms, my neck, my shins. Every exposed patch of skin seemed to be alive with creeping crawling things.

Before I finally passed through the gates of the national park, I had removed three more leeches from my boots. It was an enormous relief to feel the concrete beneath me again: man-made, impervious, reassuringly lifeless.

But the disgust stayed with me.

It was a feeling I knew well, however indirectly. In the months before she left, I had seen it creep across Sallie's face like a shadow, seen it pull down the edges of her mouth, seen it in the way she turned from me, as though unable to bear the sight of me any longer.

"It's like living with a black hole," she had said.

And then: "I hate who I am with you."

And then: "You're draining the life from me."

It made no sense to me. I heard the words, but it seemed she was talking about some other person—someone I did not recognize and could not identify with.

In the time we'd been together, I'd done all I could to become the perfect partner. I was dedicated to her constant happiness, molding myself precisely to each contour of her personality. Every quality she disliked in a man—vanity, aggression, jealousy, protectiveness—I erased from myself as though they had never been. Her likes became mine. Her interests and opinions too. I cooked her favorite foods, met up with her friends in her favorite bars, massaged her feet to her favorite movies. I wanted everything to be perfect for her, for every one of our moments together to be a festival of worship, a religious devotion with her the central deity.

But as I came close to that idea of perfection on which I'd staked everything, Sallie began to change. That shadow fell across her eyes. That twist appeared at the corner of her mouth. Finally, there came the looks of unmistakable contempt.

"But I love you," I had said.

"You love something," she said. "But it isn't me."

"And you? Do you . . . ?" I couldn't bring myself to say it.

"Do I love you?" She said, and looked at me as though at a complete stranger. "What's there to love?"

Sallie and I continued to live together for some weeks after that, but we were just bodies drifting through a vacuum: all coldness and silence and the mounting fear of suffocation. I went through the motions, carrying on as though nothing had changed, perhaps believing that those words could be undone or overpowered by the simple repetition of established habits. But the change was written on her face. The twist grew into a sneer and, soon enough, I had to accept that it was over.

Within days of moving out, Sallie started seeing her ex—the one that I had worked so hard to be nothing like. Shortly after, she set off for Europe on some pseudo-existential jaunt; to 'find herself,' perhaps, or to put as much distance as she could between her and me.

I thought I had made myself exactly what she needed me to be. But in the end, it just wasn't enough. Or wasn't what she'd wanted in the first place.

—

The cabin was a basic affair, characterized by its size and lack of amenity; two small bedrooms, a smaller bathroom, and combined kitchen–living room, were compressed together beneath an old tin roof. It stood empty most of the year, so had become a home to every imaginable sort of vermin. I was kept awake each night by the rattle of possums across the roof and the skittering of rats in the walls, then deprived of sleep past dawn by the scratch of claws on tin and the cacophony of shrieks as cockatoos drove smaller parrots from the feeder. The back deck looked out upon the garden: a wild tangle of rainforest from which, at night, the faraway lights of the Gold Coast could be seen, shimmering through giant fronds of cycads and bursts of frangipani like a hallucination.

The cabin and surrounding block had been in Sallie's family for years. Her parents had bought it before she was born, in the carefree early days of their marriage. It was unique on this road of stately Queenslanders, of expansive and manicured gardens—a little island of wildness that her parents swore always to keep intact, never to develop. It had been their family retreat throughout Sallie's childhood and, later, when she and her brother were at uni, it had been their escape, a free space for their group's riotous weekends or an intimate one for their lovers. Her brother married and moved to Perth and her parents had followed to be closer to their grandchildren. For some time, Sallie and I had been the cabin's only visitors.

In the first flush of our romance we had come often, whiling away the days in blissful aimlessness. We would walk the local bush trails, loving the exhaustion and the closeness that came with it. Long, impassioned siestas in the heaviness of afternoon would drift into boozy dinners on the veranda, watching the night descend into the spatter of lights that marked the coastline. In those happier times, the cabin was our haven, a cocoon in which the best parts of ourselves felt safe to emerge, and love, with all its possibilities, could grow without restraint.

In the cold last days, however, the only retreats we made were into our own private worlds, and the cabin remained empty. We still walked, but only to work, and separately, immersed in the gloom that always followed our uneasy breakfasts. Work was a barely tolerable distraction that evaporated into afternoons of restless daydreams and morbid gazing. Sallie, at least, still had the boozy dinners—just no longer with me. She would come home drunk, caustic. Nights descended into bitterness and evasion: the unspoken conflicts that defined the boundaries of our relationship. And the wilderness that lay beyond it.

When the taxi dropped me off a week ago, the cabin was almost obscured by the encroaching garden, now as dense and unkempt as the beard I'd let grow since Sallie left. I had taken the key from its hiding place beneath the deck, peeling back the wispy vortices of abandoned funnel webs. Inside, the air was stale and damp and had a faint tang that I later came to associate with rat droppings. The draining board was still stacked with plates and glasses from our last meal here, now sticky with dust. A half-drunk bottle of wine had turned to vinegar by the sink.

When I arrived that day, I did not yet know what compelled me or why I had come. The cabin held me in a kind of relentless gravity, drawing me toward some notion of completion that, however vague, was left unsatisfied by Sallie's parting. Perhaps I felt that something had been left behind here—some ghost of the person I had once been, or, perhaps, some essence of those happier times, that I might reabsorb by simple proximity. It's possible there were other reasons, but, if so, they were obscure. On some days it felt as if I was here to say goodbye to Sallie, to finally let go of whatever it was we had shared and move on with my life. On others, I felt I was here to get closer to her, to connect with her once again through spaces she had once occupied and objects she had once handled, to rekindle an intimacy between us that existed now in only inanimate things, and in emptiness and silence.

Although I knew that I would not be disturbed as long as she was in Europe, I often fantasized about surprising Sallie here in some way. Returning home from her travels, seeking solitude in her old retreat. Or perhaps a romantic escape with some new man. These daydreams whiled away the long afternoons and left me with an unusual sense of calm and a feeling one might almost describe as joy.

How would she react to find me here, I wondered? What strange shape might that encounter take?

——

The wound left by the leech continued to bleed for many hours after I returned. The thin fluid streamed from my calf so profusely that I ran through the cabin's entire supply of Band-Aids to staunch it, replacing them each time the blood soaked to the edges of the dressing.

It also began to itch: a maddening tingling sensation that gnawed away at me, no matter how I tried to distract myself from it.

Between the itching and the incessant changes of dressing, that tiny puncture consumed my attention well into the afternoon. My mind came back again and again to the incident with the leech, the memory growing in vividness and intensity as I turned it over upon itself. And the more I dwelled on it, the more abstracted my deliberations became. Away from the rainforest, where every frond dripped with the threat of tangible parasites, my thoughts spiraled into a vortex of vague anxieties and phobic imagery. It was as though the heightened clarity of this memory was at the expense of a context that moored it in reality. Underlying everything, feeding and growing fat on my obsession, disgust coiled inside me like an unnameable black *thing*, writhing in my belly, gagging in my throat, and pulling back the corners of my mouth into a grimace. At first, this nameless revulsion was directed at the leech. But as the color drained from inside the cabin and the blue-gray dusk enveloped me, the feeling began to shift and I grew disgusted with myself.

On the one hand, my feelings toward the leech seemed completely justified, a primal horror that was only natural considering its grotesque otherness. It *was* repulsive. A hideous creeping parasite. An alien. A thief. Its very nature seemed an offense to warm-blooded creatures of every species. Its foul body: spineless and glistening. Its sickening gait: puppet-like and ludicrous. Its means of survival: stealthy, deceitful, insidious. Just picturing it made me boil with anger all over again.

And it was this anger that troubled me most of all, that kept me picking over the scene again and again, scratching at it and worrying it like the sore spot on my calf. How could I dare feel disgust at a creature simply for feeding on me, when my response had been to take its life? How much blood had the leech taken from me? And how much did I have to spare? Surely I could have shared that little bit of myself for the sake of a life?

The tension between these conflicting extremes bound me in an unresolvable, and quite intolerable, state of agitation well into the night. As I lay awake in the small bed that Sallie and I had once shared, I was overcome with pity for the leech and with remorse for what I had done to it. Like words of spite that erupted unbidden into one of my few arguments with Sallie, or the many times I let slip something about myself that did not hold with the image I had cultivated, I couldn't take this back—no matter how much I may have yearned to. I could not undo what I had done or return the leech to life. Knowing this, and finding no possible way to right it, was an agony that oppressed me like a storm that wouldn't break.

The rats that night were particularly bold. I had left a cupboard door open in the kitchen and I could hear their tiny feet skittering among the boxes of cereal and open packets of crackers. When I first arrived at the cabin, I had found a rat by the garden tap—the body of one at least—flat and completely desiccated. I knew the cabin was peppered with unsprung traps and boxes of poison, their lids peeled back to reveal the deadly green candy inside. My heart had gone out to this poor creature, who, believing it to be food, had filled her belly with the poison. It must have taken days to parch her from within, sucking all the moisture from her body. She had died beside the dripping tap, no doubt in a desperate, doomed attempt to slake her undying thirst. Before unpacking the meager supplies I'd brought with me, I had gone round to every corner of the cabin, every cupboard and cabinet, springing the traps and emptying the poison into the bin. As long as I was there, I wasn't going to be responsible for the death of an innocent creature. The rats had no less right to be in the cabin than I had.

The noise, along with my deliberations, kept me awake for many hours. Listening to the rats in the cupboard—gnawing on crackers, upending the open bags of rice—made me question still further my reaction to the leech. Why had my response been so extreme? What was the real root of my disgust? Where had the anger come from? And the violence? Why was I able to accept the rats, feeding themselves on the food that should have fed me, yet recoiled from the leech, following its instincts to precisely the same end?

These thoughts came from the shadowed border between sleep and wakefulness, folding over upon each other, collapsing together into a dream like soup of impressions and ideas that merged at last into a united vision—a vision at once transcendent and monstrous. It was as if a curtain had been pulled aside, revealing the inescapable perversity of nature: to be born hungry, a belly that lives only to feed itself, alive only at the expense of other lives. Purposeless and interminable, compelled to live, to feed, only to make meat to feed some other starving belly. The pointlessness and horror of it was overwhelming. The hunger never satisfied. The hunger unto death.

At the peak of the vision, I saw all life as nothing more than a grotesque sculpture of mouths devouring mouths devouring mouths. A multitude—an infinity—expressed as a single mouth devouring a single meal.

And that meal was itself.

———

I must have slept, for I dreamt: long vivid dreams that I had no memory of on waking. Still, I felt them weighing on me like an old overcoat, heavy with melancholy and a nebulous longing. It had been raining while I slept and the cabin was ripe with the perfume of the rainforest. This fragrance intermingled with the funk of my forgotten dreams, as though, for want of sleep, I had become porous and was both absorbing the moisture of the rainforest and, at the same time, spilling out into it.

There was little breakfast to speak of. I rummaged in the kitchen for whatever scraps the rats might have overlooked, but all they had left was a scene of devastation and abandon. Rice was everywhere. Spilled from the upended bag, it was pooled in dry rivers on the Laminex work surface and sprayed across the kitchen floor like the dead husks of fallen stars. The cupboards themselves were bare of everything but crumbs, shredded boxes, and the ubiquitous peppering of dry turds. In the fridge I found a small piece of cheese and the last apple. I tossed the cheese onto the deck for the possums and set out for my morning walk, eating the apple as I went.

The morning was oppressively humid, thick with moisture from the night's rain and already pregnant with the heat of the coming day. Even at this early hour, it was too hot for clothes—I walked in nothing but my hiking boots and a pair of cut-off shorts. Unlike previous mornings I had no plan, yet my feet seemed to know exactly where they were going.

I took the main track through the gates of the national park and down into the rainforest. Instead of turning up toward the lookouts, I continued to descend, leaving the path to follow the creek into the lushest nooks of the forest. I found a pool beneath a terrace of lazy waterfalls, where the canopy above was so thick that no sunlight could penetrate. I settled down in the cool gloom and pulled off my boots, sat on the moist edge with my feet in the water.

It wasn't long before they found me there.

Before I even reached the pool, several leeches had already attached themselves. I wasn't sure exactly how many. I could see one on my calf and another further up my thigh, both of them quivering as they drew blood into their expanding bodies. At least one had settled on my back, but there may have been others. Knowing they were on me, seeing them feed, the feelings of disgust arose again. But, unlike the day before, I did not react. The emotions where still there, just . . . detached somehow; only another tangled shape within that body, with its mouth and its belly, with its hunger and fear and other drives of a distinctly animal nature.

And more were converging, other leeches inching through the foliage toward the bare white flesh, heads twitching on the end of undulant black stalks. They swiveled this way and that as if sniffing the air, sensing the promise of warmth and of nourishment. I felt the feather-light touches of tail-suckers and mouths, the delicate end-over-end as the leeches made their ponderous climb, seeking out a space on which to attach. On which to feed.

I must have cut a strange sight as I returned from the park that lunchtime. The track was busier than usual and I encountered many other walkers before I reached the cabin: families, couples, lone hikers like myself. Every one of them recoiled when they saw me approach, flattening themselves against the edge of the path to clear the way. One man was so disturbed, he tripped over the snaking roots of a Watkins Fig and nearly toppled into the foliage. On his, and on every face, that same look: the flaring nose, the downward pull at the edge of the lips; the unmistakable grimace of disgust. They talked too, talked about me as I passed, as if I couldn't hear, as if I was in some way contrary to them. I heard one woman behind me retch.

I had to laugh. Hadn't my face been contorted by these same emotions only the day before? I felt for them. All they could see was the wild young man storming along the path, his eyes perhaps a little too wide, revealing a little too much white. They saw the expression—at once intense and serene—that encompassed a grin, uncomfortably twisted. They would have seen the body, bristling with the glistening black hairs that swelled and rippled and writhed as though with life of their own, pulsing shapes that dropped to the ground like rotten fruit, leaving thin ribbons of red to darken his shorts, streak his legs, and pool in the fluffy bands of his socks. I couldn't blame them for their feelings of horror and revulsion. They couldn't see beyond the mechanics. They lacked the vision.

Although it was all downhill, the final stretch to the cabin seemed endless. I must have given away a fair bit of blood by then, for I felt giddy and weak. Each step took considerable effort. When I finally reached the cabin, having left a breadcrumb trail of engorged leeches that led all the way back to the forest, I was so drained that I flopped straight into bed. I hadn't even the strength to pull off my boots.

—

I awoke later to the sound of rain drumming on tin. I had no idea what time it was; the light seemed to have leaked out of everything, creating an effect both shadowless and gray. It must have been evening, for I could hear the rats in the kitchen and feel the pinch of cold on my skin. The bed was soaked.

I made to sit up, to put my legs out over the side of the bed, to stand, change out of my bloody shorts and into something warmer, perhaps scratch around in the kitchen for a bite. But I could barely sit up. Even that small movement made my head swim and I lay there, feeling the world flip-flop around me.

Then the itching began.

Not the uncomfortable irritation that I had felt the day before, but a seething anger in my arms and legs and chest. Had I been suspended from a thousand burning hooks and slowly pulled apart, it could not have been worse than this. I longed to scratch, but even that movement was too much to contemplate. My arms lay lifeless beside me on the blood-soaked sheets, as flaccid and impotent as the swollen bodies still squirming there.

I think I began to cry then, for my body convulsed and my eyes were shut so tight that my head ached. It's hard to contemplate now exactly why I wept: despair perhaps, or regret. Perhaps it was the only means of escape from the pain, which swarmed beneath my skin like a colony of fire ants. Whatever the reason, those tears were cleansing. They didn't take the pain away, but they took me out of myself, out of my body. They allowed me to let go—of everything. And in that letting go I became weightless, unencumbered by the thoughts and feelings and memories that had bound me to myself. I felt as though I were floating upward, the itching and the weakness and the wetness now so dilute as to be almost imperceptible, completely overwhelmed by the greater flood of transcendence, of oneness, of interconnectedness with all things.

There must have been nothing left in the kitchen worth eating, for, sometime later, a rat came to visit me where I lay. Emboldened perhaps by my immobility, she hopped up onto the foot of the bed and perched on the toe of one of my walking boots. I watched her lift her head and sniff all around, teeth bared, nose twitching. The bed, I realized, must have smelled like a butcher's shop, of blood curdling as it dried, of meat that was just beginning to turn. She tiptoed down the ladder of laces and stopped at the bunched-up end of my sock, leaning out over my calf to take another sniff, not little sips this time but long questing inhalations.

I barely felt the first bite. Watching her little jaw at work, tugging—first tentatively and then with incredible focus—at the ligaments of my lower calf, I experienced . . . nothing. A distant pulling sensation, like someone unthreading a bootlace.

Soon other rats began to pop up over the sides of the bed. They didn't take long to tuck in. Before long, they covered my legs, tails curling, pulling off strips with those coarse yellow teeth. They were unstitching me, one red ribbon at a time. And by then I was too weak to even lift my head, let alone to sit up and sweep them away.

And, I wondered, would I even want to? I had shared my blood. Should I not share my flesh as well?

I had always felt I had so much to offer, so much to give, but Sallie never saw it that way, how good I could have been for her. She saw only a vacuum, an emptiness that emptied her. Her loss. She would never understand—I can see that now. Not like my new friends with their simple needs, so easy for me to satisfy.

What would Sallie think if she could see me now?

I picture her, weeks, maybe months from today, returning to the cabin. The doors—once the threshold between the small but civilized inner space and the boundless incivility of wild nature—are now open wide. The smell of damp and decay is everywhere. Frogs, birds, lizards, and the legion tiny marsupials, have made their homes here, in the water pooling from the holes in the roof, in the branches that pierce the flyscreens, among the rotting foam spilled from decrepit furniture, and in every one of the many boltholes and crawlspaces that now perforate the cabin. Fungi, molds and grasses bloom throughout. Like the veins of a great living organism, tree roots have burst through the mock-linoleum floor, vines have ripped through the ceiling. Twisting, coiling, interwoven, they lead Sallie to the living heart of the house, the bloody bedroom, and my parting gift. What will she think? How will she react to find, in that bed, which held us close so many nights, the hiking boots and the gleaming skeleton, so white against its flag of red, seething still, perhaps, with the life of a multitude. The center of a living ecosystem.

What will she think of me then?

Inside the cabin all is gray. It's as though all color has leached from the room, and whatever world still exists beyond. Even the crimson sheets are now just a deeper, darker shade of gray. It is neither night nor day, but a perpetual twilight, as though we are caught, my friends and I, hovering in a borderland between twinned worlds: light and dark, satiety and hunger, numbness and pain, life and the absence of life. It is as poignant as a dream. And I can't help but wonder if this grayness exists without—in the room, in the insatiable gnawing of the rats, in the droning of the flies, in the silent procession of the many ants—or whether this absence of color, of contrast or tone, is in fact mine, dimming, faltering, fading unerringly to white.

I can hardly believe I have anything left to offer. Yet here we still are, all of us together, sharing this last meal. My true friends and I.

The Black Massive

*Yet no matter how deeply I go down into myself
my God is dark, and like a webbing made
of a hundred roots, that drink in silence.*
—*Rilke*

1

It was a banging scene, back in the day. Before Cadman came out of the shadows, touting his weird black shit.

Back then it was all color and sound. Everyone off their bone, grinning like nutters, sweating and gurning and losing it to the lights and the tunes. Lasers slicing the dark. Bass beats kicking up from the floor. Fractal lead lines like living things, like creatures of light that danced the sound, that danced the rush that was all of us. It was like another world. A magic kingdom.

Fucking La La Land.

I'd tell Mum I was staying round Dog's, then we'd catch the bus out to Tescos carpark. The warehouse was always this big secret—the flyer in my pocket didn't say nothing more than a time and a place for all the ravers to meet. No one knew where they was going till the lead car pulled in and everyone drove in convoy to the night.

Me and Dog was too young to drive, so we had to be there in time to cadge a lift. We'd go early and slip into the bog before the supermarket closed. Sometimes we'd roll one. Other nights we'd sniff whizz off the bog seat, come out sipping Strawberry Ribena, breaking the seal on a brand-new pack of Benson & Hedges. Then we'd strut out between the cars, looking for mates or a friendly face, grinning and bobbing, blowing smoke rings into the cold, still night.

Dog did the talking. He told me once he could sell a man his own knob. I hung back, always tongue-tied in spite of the whizz. While he talked, I'd stand behind, looking out over the roofs of the cars, through clouds of whitish sweet smoke, past the touts dishing flyers and the dealers droning, *weed or 'ash, weed or 'ash*, out beyond the carpark to where the orange streetlights ringed the roundabout, uncoiling down the offramp to the A14 and the everywhere dark of the fens.

Would've been mid-March, the night we first met Cadman, still dark and biting cold. We was late for the bus and missed it, bombing our last wrap of whizz behind the bus station. By the time we got to Tescos, the convoy was already moving out. We panicked, me and Dog, ducking between the cars to catch eyes, make faces. But no one had space and car after car after car left without us. Thinking back on it's like a dream. I see them all pull out, become streams of red light snaking down onto the road and off. Then, as the car park clears like dirt brushed from some buried thing, there it is: the two-tone black Austin Allegro, headlights dipped, engine purring. Almost like it was waiting for us.

Even as the last car turned onto the roundabout, the Allegro didn't pull after. Whoever was inside was in no hurry to keep up with the convoy. I figured they weren't even there for the meet, but Dog went for it anyway and knocked on the passenger window. A pale hand gestured behind with a thumb. Dog popped the back door and leaned in, talked to someone I couldn't see. Then he give me a look—*This is a bit alright!*—slipped into the backseat and closed the door, left me to sit up front.

Inside, the Allegro was super-plush and looked brand new, though it must've been close-on twenty year old. The dashboard and doors was lined with dark wood trim. The seats, deep red leather. The driver wore a black hoodie with the hood all the way up and was so tall he had to stoop. All I could see of his face was a beaky white nose. He didn't turn to look at me or nothing and didn't answer when I said alright. He just dropped the handbrake and put the car in gear.

The bloke beside Dog was half sprawled, half slouched across the backseat, a leather trench-coat spread about him like a pool of oil. He was a sight: pasty white with a round, toady face and lips that was too wide, hair that hung in clumps like vines. His lashes was long and girlish, his eyes small and piggy, but there was a look in them that was hard as fuck. He didn't look like no raver. I thought he seemed a bit of a twat; not someone you'd want to get caned with, not someone who'd have a laugh. There was something wrong about his smile. He didn't introduce himself or nothing, but by the end of the night there was no one on the scene what didn't know his name. Cadman.

The convoy was almost gone, but neither Cadman nor the driver seemed bothered. We pulled out of the carpark casual, as if we'd been at Tescos for the weekly shop, turned onto the roundabout, drove straight past the exit and down onto the A14 toward town. I twisted in my seat, saw through the back window the vanishing stream of taillights.

"Where we going?" I said. "The convoy went that way."

I give Dog a look, but he didn't catch it. He was rolling one from a hefty bag of weed he'd not had before. He rolled it long and slim and ran his tongue along the gum. Cadman held out a Zippo and sparked it. Sweet smoke filled the car, edged with something else, something bitter and loamy. I give Dog the look again, but he just winked and grinned.

The driver pushed a tape into the stereo, turned the knob all the way up. The car must've been fucking wired, mate—bass bins in the back and whatnot—'cause what came out the speakers was *massive*. But them sounds was all wrong. No one had heard of Tendril back then, black-tracks neither, so my ears didn't know what to do with themselves. Awful, it sounded. There was the thumping beat, like you'd expect, but it was all mushy, buried, like a dying heart. There was no bass, no lead, just this sickly drone and a sound like some choir babbling mind-rubbish, all whispering at once.

It made me feel proper queer, the music and the whizz and the cloud of wrong-smelling smoke. Proper wrong. And not knowing where we was going. And not trusting Cadman as far as I could piss.

Outside, the lights of the A14 throbbed past, the tarmac glowing orange with streaks of yellow. Beyond the road was field after field of oilseed rape and out beyond that the fens, deepest black beneath the deep black sky. Like a bottomless black void, like infinite cold nothing, and the road and the lights the only thing real.

—

All the way to the warehouse, Cadman and Dog in the backseat was having a right old mothers' meeting. I couldn't catch what was said for the roar of the engine, the weird noise on the stereo. I didn't get word one from the driver, didn't find out his name or nothing. He hardly moved, except to change gear, to turn the wheel. The spliff made its way round the motor to me, Cadman bowing out with a polite wave. It was hot and harsh and didn't make me feel anywhere near as good as I wanted it to, made me tense, in fact, as I didn't know what to do with the ash and didn't dare ask; ended up tapping it into my cupped hand. I was paranoid as—couldn't figure why Dog was so chill. I didn't know where we was going and honest-to-god thought we was done, that we'd wake up next day in a ditch, bum-fucked and knifed.

We pulled up in an empty backstreet off the industrial area, dead and dark but for the security lights. When the driver killed the engine, you could hear bass pounding from the next street, somebody some-where tooting a whistle. He popped and held the door for Cadman. Dog was out and beaming like a knob-end, hopping from foot to foot and doing the moorhen to that faraway beat. He kept grinning at me and raising his eyebrows. I didn't know what he was on about.

Cadman led and Dog followed and I fell in behind the driver, cutting between the looming buildings. The pounding got louder. Then I smelled dry ice and hash smoke and saw the open door, a rectangle carved from the dark by purple, red and green lasers, and the silhouette of some big fuck-off geezer blocking the way. You could feel the bass all the way down in your guts.

Cadman walked right up and fuck knows what was said, but the bloke just stepped back and we all four walked past without paying penny one. Soon as we was in, Dog grabbed my arm and dragged me through the crowd of sweating, stomping, finger-pointing ravers, and out into what passed for a chill-out room—a derelict back office with fluorescent tubes on the ceiling, rotting carpet on the floor and nothing to breathe but second-hand smoke. He was so excited, he could hardly hold it together.

"Sonic, my son," he said. "We are *in*, mate. We are all the way in."

"What are you like," I said. "Just *what* is it you reckon we're in?"

"In business, son," he said and opened his hand. "Magic beans."

I looked down at the black shapes in his palm and I looked back at Dog and his grinning mug and I near enough pissed myself laughing. Ten gleaming rabbit turds.

"Dog," I said. "You are a twat. We've been proper skanked."

"Nah, mate. Nah," said Dog. "This Cadman geez is on the level. Proper bigtime. He's got his connections, got his crew. Got his own night coming up and all. He says they're the bollocks, mate. Black Suns. They'll shift quicker'n a cat can lick its snatch."

I snorted and shook my head, took one of the pills for a closer look. It was an almost perfect sphere. Pure black, so black it almost shone. Where it caught the light, rainbows shimmered on the surface. On one side, there was a detail embossed: a circle with squirly lines all round it, like rays of the sun. At least, that's what I figured.

"And there's more where they come from," Dog was banging on. "We keep two in every ten, so if we shift four each that's our night made. That, or we go back and back and make ourselves some proper wonga. Either way," he dropped another four in my palm, "you come and find me when you're clear and we'll hatch a plan for the rest of the night."

Dog plunged his hands in the pockets of his fleece and stepped out with a practiced strut, a side-to-side glance, an over-the-head peer; moves he'd lifted from the grownup dealers.

I looked down at the pills in my hand, rolled the other round and round between my thumb and finger. Dog loved this bit, doing the shuffle, flogging his wares, acting like Mr. Bigtime. But I could not stand it. For me, I served up only to indulge *my* special skill, *my* unique talent: getting so far off my bone I'd need a map to get back. And this, mate, was uncharted territory. These was untested waters. I couldn't in good conscience sell some muggins one of those little black balls if I'd never tried one myself.

I slid the four into the pocket of my jeans, popped the one in my mouth and swallowed it dry. The *taste*. Fuck, mate—it was like necking the crypt. I gagged getting it down, sparked a Benson straight off to get that death-taste off my tongue. But when I took a drag, my belly did the flip-flop. The Black hit my stomach like poisoned meat. I legged it for the bog.

The queue was long as the corridor, but when I burst through with hands cupped to my mouth I was pushed along fast enough, shoved in as soon as the door opened. Next I knew I was squatting over the bog, the bowl all black like someone'd tipped out a bottle of ink. Fists banged on the toilet door. My eyes was shaky. Standing up, I thought I was falling. I hung onto the edge of the sink, splashed water on my face, tried to focus on the cracked mirror. My pupils was so wide there was no color round them. I grinned, then grimaced. All my teeth was black.

I fell out into the corridor, hand fumbling with the four Black Suns in my pocket; only I was so off it, I'd forgotten what they was. My fingers made no sense of the shapes, but the feel of them woke some gnashing dread, something I was supposed to do. Faces swam like the moon in a puddle. Everywhere the lights cut into me and I staggered, tripped through the crowd, fell into deep shadow at the edge of the warehouse.

And there I dropped, back to the wall, legs spread, head hung like a puppet with its strings cut.

The ground was cold and I felt it in my hands, in the backs of my legs, felt it creep into me, like roots bursting from the grubby tiles, snaking round my ankles, tangling my wrists. The dancers seemed miles off, some mad revel at the farthest end of a graveyard and all between wreathed in coils of mist, the smell of long-dead fires and rotting leaves. The music was far away too, the highs receding like stars in endless night, into that pit of deep tone, of bottomless bass. And at the center of everywhere, that formless persistent beat that was both my heart and the heart of all things, pumping black blood through the veins of the world, through the roots that curled from my blackened fingertips, down into the winter earth.

Fuck, but I was off it.

A face congealed. A voice from beyond the grave. "I see you've had one, then," said Dog.

I tried to answer, but I couldn't move my lips, couldn't nod even. Dog laughed and shook his head.

"Sonic, mate—you are the original lost boy." He was crouched before me, looking back over his shoulder at the forest of legs. "They're alright then, are they? You got any left? I can't clear 'em fast enough."

I pushed myself back up the wall, feeling the pull of the earth, the drag of the roots that Dog didn't seem to notice. I rubbed my pocket and nodded, fumbled inside till I found the four shapes, buried in fluff. When I pulled them out, my fingers was gnarled like a claw. Dog shook his head again.

"Lost boy," he said. "Let me shift these, then I'll neck up and join you." He looked right in my eyes then, as if through that window he might see inside to the wonders in my skull. "Wherever it is you are."

He patted me down until he found the Bensons in the pocket of my fleece, shook out two and lit them both, handed one to me. The flare of the match burned in my eyes long after he was swallowed by the crowd.

—

That was the first night the Black hit the scene.

You could tell the deadheads from the ravers at a glance. The ravers was bouncing, stomping, shaking fists and pointing fingers, grinning like Cheshire cunts, toot-toot-tooting on their daft fucking whistles. Me and Dog and the rest danced to a different tune. We rocked like loonies, nodded like puppets, trembled like bone-people strung up by wire, getting down to the throb that was the heartbeat at the center of everything. Our hands was gnarled as though draped with vines. The Black poured off us like breath from the tomb.

It was just before dawn when the coppers shut it down. This was back in the day, before the fuzz came down hard on the illegal nights, when both sides still played by Queensberry Rules. If they made it to the warehouse before the convoy, that was it, the party was off. But if the ravers made it in, the rozzas wouldn't do nothing till morning.

The music stopped dead with the grind of a needle. But everyone, raver and deadhead alike, kept moving to the sound of their own footfalls. Gray light, thin as skimmed milk, dripped through windows in the ceiling. Over by the decks stood two constables in full uniform.

It took a while for everyone to shuffle out. Dog swayed beside me, slit-eyed, lids fluttering. All around us ravers was still bopping: shirtless blokes chewing their cheeks, scrawny as plucked chicken; girls in sweat-soaked catsuits and body-tops, skin blotchy and sick; everyone's eyes bulging like the dead. There was no more coppers on the street, just the empty panda car of the two inside, so the crowd milled, aimless and vacant.

Out on the pavement, some kid was handing out flyers. He wore a black hoody just like Cadman's driver, with the hood pulled up and over so all you could see was his chin. As we passed, he pressed something into my hand. The flyer was matt black, with a shiny black design—the same symbol as on the pills. *The Black Massive*, the flyer said, *Presents: ABYSM*. Cadman's night.

The man himself was nowhere to be seen and Dog was in no state to talk us into another lift. We walked back to town and over to Dog's, with the dawn coming up all around and us coming down as it rose. In the dead half-light before morning, the only trace of the Black was the shadows that crept between paving stones, the darkness that snaked from the cracks in the walls.

The comedown was brutal—the 'nameless horrors,' we called it. Like being hollowed out from inside, like your soul was bleeding black through your pores. It hurt, but it weren't all bad. Spliff took the edge off, until all that was left was the emptiness.

And there was something about that bottomless nothing that was alright; it was just a void. You didn't care about nothing.

And that was alright.

2

Me and Dog hadn't always been mates. When we was younger, he'd been a bit of a bruiser, a bully. They was hard times, I learned later. Rough times. In those days, his dad was hard on the piss, before Dog's mum told the old boozer to get the fuck out and never come back.

Dog never beat me up or nothing, but him and the boys he hung with used to make things hard. They'd nick my bag, or chuck my books or my pencil case between them so I'd have to run round after while they all laughed. I didn't have any proper mates, so all this seemed like a bigger thing than perhaps it really was. Each morning, when I stepped through the school gate, my heart would start to thump, and break times I wouldn't go outside. But things changed between me and Dog just before I turned thirteen. That was the year my dad died.

It weren't a shock or nothing. We'd known it was coming—at least, it was something Mum and Dad had sat me down about. I don't know if I ever really took it serious, or thought about what it meant beyond the words. I watched him get sicker, thinner, paler. Then he weren't there no more, and it was just me and Mum.

The ragging from Dog's mates didn't die down or nothing, though Dog seemed less a part of it. If anything, it got worse. They started to push me, took the piss. It was a prick called Miller who crossed the line, made some crack about my dad. Next I know, Dog was pounding shit out of him, broke Miller's nose, his cheekbone, dropped him in a groaning, bloody heap on the rockery. I never saw him go mental like that on anyone, before or since. Dog was expelled, but the pricks never touched me again, and that weekend I took a bus out to the village where Dog and his mum lived.

After that, we was inseparable. Tight as, mate. I smoked my first cig with Dog, rolled my first spliff. We dabbed whizz in the bus shelter, dropped acid down by the Tubes, sat up nights in Dog's bedroom playing games on his Megadrive with the sound down. That's when I got my name.

Soon as Dog turned sixteen, he moved into town, signed up for the Benefit and got himself a bedsit round the corner. From then on, we got fucked up pretty regular.

—

The first black label came out the week after we rode with Cadman. It was by an outfit called Tendril and carried the Black Massive symbol. The next weekend, it was all anyone was talking about. By then, the whole scene was dark, with everyone out necking the Black. Going crepuscular.

That first black-track was called *The Beating Black Heart in the Bottomless Void,* with a twisted remix on the flip side. Dog bought it the day it dropped and looped it ever after. I didn't like it, not at first. It give me that same queer feeling as the tunes in Cadman's motor, the same unlistenable drone and the freakish whispered mumbling. Hear it straight and that track sounded like the record player was broke, like the needle was bunged with dust. Have a smoke and listen to that shit and it give you straight-up nightmares.

But on the Black . . . On the Black you was fucking suspended. Tendril held you hanging in infinite black space and the beat was the beat of your own black heart bleeding out into blackness blacker than black. It was the void within void veined with wisps of black smoke from the snuffed black sun. It was a well without end where the black vines tangled and groped, and where the heart at the bottom of everything beat.

It was something else.

Dog was serving up for Cadman full time then, earning his place in the Massive. There was a steady stream of punters through the bedsit, fives and tens changed hands, the ashtray overflowed. Tendril looped and looped. Every few days, Cadman's driver would appear in Dog's room. He never stuck around, just stood silent by the door. Beneath the shadow of his hood, in the flicker of the TV, his eyes was black as dead stars. Dog would hand over a ragged stack of cash. The driver would slip him a brown paper bag. It was always paper—the jiffy bags dealers used for pills and weed and ounces of whizz was no good for the Black. In plastic, a handful of Black Suns would be dud in hours, and by morning they'd be nothing but stinking black sludge. I learned that one the hard way.

I was hitting it hard. At the weekends, out, or back at Dog's place. But in the week too. It got so I only went in to school when I had Black to clear, flogging just enough to make personal. Then I was gone, leaving excuses and half-cooked explanations, miracle sick notes in Mum's forged handwriting. My absence from school was like a debt I couldn't pay—I'd been gone so many days it seemed easier to just never go back. And why would I've wanted to? Life outside the abyss had lost its color, had become brittle and empty, a hollow gray husk. Only the Black made sense. Only the Black hooked you in to that deep living, with its roots in the bottomless dark.

School was one thing, but home was another. I knew Mum worried, knew that she fretted over all the time I was gone. But she never said nothing, just made me dinners I couldn't bring myself to eat, cups of tea I left to go cold. She'd look at me with her face all sad, trying to read something in me that weren't there. I had to hide my eyes, not wanting her to see their fading blue, or how the whites was darkening by degrees. I couldn't smile for fear she'd see the color of my teeth. I'd lower my gaze, purse my lips, mumble this or that as I staggered past her and up to my room.

I could hear her in the kitchen as I lay awake at night. The chink of plates, the clatter of pans. In every corner of my room, snakes of shadow writhed.

—

It was a month or more before things really went bad. A Friday it was, the last day of term before Easter. Far as Mum knew, I was off to school then over to Dog's place for the night. Instead, I monged on Dog's couch till evening, caught the bus to drop in on his mum and get dark with his old village mates.

We rode on the back seat, sharing the earphones from his new Walkman, bobbing to a proper eldritch Tendril mix. Dog was putting a spliff together in the creases of his jeans, tearing roach from a flyer for ABYSM. Cadman's night was still a ways off—the solstice, midsummer night—but it was all the deadheads was talking about. It was going to be *massive*. Word was even Tendril was going to be there. Dog's laundry lay across the seat between us, stuffed in an old kit bag.

The bus dropped us by the village pub and Dog left me the spliff for company, while he rolled home to see his mum, have dinner, drop off his dirty undies. I went down to the edge of the village, out past the derelict playground, with its Seventies swing-set like a scaffolding gallows, out to the abandoned construction site and the heap of concrete pipes that Dog and his mates called the Tubes. Beyond the collapsing fence of barbed wire lay the gray-green expanse of the fens, a horizon of blurred plane trees melting into the darkening blue-gray of the sky. I smoked the bifta, perched on the rusted tracks of the old bulldozer, killed time pitching rocks at the last flecks of glass in its windscreen. It was twilight and still warm. A faint breeze rattled the cow parsley.

Dog's mates showed up before he did. I shared around cigs and Gav, the eldest, licked his along the seam and peeled it open to crumble into a spliff. With him was a Polish kid with a name no one could say right that they all called Chewy, and Ellis, a gangly raver with bug-eyes and a ringlety bob. Ellis had brought his sister, Mandy. Gav passed the spliff around and we toked, blowing smoke rings into the dimming sky, waiting for Dog to show. Mandy was watching me. I didn't know where to put my eyes.

"What's it like, then?" she asked.

I was figuring what to tell her, when Gav cut in. "It's the darkest. Like crawling with spiders in a shallow grave. You're going to love it, Mand."

But something on his face told me he was bluffing, that he'd never had the Black. They all seemed a bit tense, was puffing on the spliff a bit too earnest. Ellis was restless. Mandy, almost afraid, kept looking from me to Gav. I remember feeling a swell of something—importance I guess. It was me what had the secret knowledge.

"I reckon you've been done, mate," I said. "It's not a bit like that."

Gav scowled and narrowed his eyes, but Mandy laughed and something in her look, and in the way Ellis leaned forward to listen, urged me on. I told them everything about the Black, about the snaking vines and the bottomless void, about the black heart that beat forever in deep time. I was the grand wizard, boasting how often me and Dog had gone crepuscular, telling all about the nameless horrors, leading them step by step into the darkness.

I didn't tell about the dead, empty feeling that stayed with me even into the daylight, the feeling that the world I'd known was crumbling, like a stage set of rotten cardboard. I didn't tell them that only the Black was real. I didn't talk about that 'cause I had no words for it. And 'cause it frightened me.

"Is it true you've met Cadman?" Ellis's eyes was wide, filled with awe.

"Met him?" said Dog, coming round the side of the Tubes. "We're like fucking brothers, mate."

Dog looked washed and well-fed. His hair was still wet from the shower. He'd changed his clothes: clean jeans and a brand new Black Massive hoodie. When he sat down beside me, Ellis leaned over and touched the glossy black symbol on Dog's back. The black sun, or whatever it was supposed to be.

"Come on then," said Dog, pulling out the brown paper bag from his hoodie pocket. "Hand over the dollar and we'll all get stygian."

They all must've given their cash to Gav, as he pulled out a fair wad and peeled it note by note into the dirt between us. Dog counted ten of the shiny black pills into Gav's palm. Gav handed one to Ellis, one to Mandy, took one for himself and pocketed the rest. Dog took one from his paper bag and I rooted in my johnny pocket for my own: six Blacks to last me the weekend, and into the week if I could squeeze them out that far.

We all necked up. Me and Dog dry-swallowed and I had a laugh at the others, all of them gagging on that foul taste. I hardly even noticed it anymore. Even before the Black hit my stomach, warm excitement was tugging at my belly, shriveling my nuts. Mandy kept looking my way, her glances nervous and eager, and every time our eyes met I felt a thrill of—I don't know what—a kind of electricity that tightened my thighs, crackled up my spine. Then the darkness closed in and we all went crepuscular.

I don't know what made me keep going. Some buried urge drove me to reach back into my pocket, to lay out the scrap of brown paper with its five black pills. As the darkness opened inside me, the Black Suns breathed, giving off gusts of shadow like smoke. What made me pick up another, make such a show of knocking it back? The others was going dark hard, already swallowed by the pit that yawned for all deadheads. But maybe that was it, that as soon as the others was off it, there weren't nothing to set me apart. The only way to claw back that scrap of power was excess.

Maybe that was it. But maybe, too, I was nervous, edgy 'round people I didn't know so well. And maybe—just maybe—I wanted Mandy to think something of me.

I'd built up a fair tolerance over the months we'd been going dark, necking Black for breakfast, lunch and dinner. I figured I could pop a few and not sink too far down; not so far that I couldn't pull myself up again. Thing is, I weren't the only mug playing the double-up game.

Though Gav'd never done the Black before that night, he had his own reasons to stay ahead and matched me neck for neck. Before the moon was out he'd sunk four to my five. By then, I was just putting them down to stay ahead. The sickened awe of Mandy and Ellis was its own reward, only I weren't around long enough to claim it.

Curled in the Tubes, the world beyond was a disc of sodium and debris, swirling wind and distant, dopplered traffic. Within, the blurred murmur of voices, the cave-fire flare of a sparking Bic. My heart sank deep, beneath the curve of concrete I couldn't feel no more, a distant pulse disconnected from my body, from the flow of my own blood. No air went in or out of my lungs. My fingers curled and twitched, not fingers anymore but coils of fetid black roots that snaked and rippled and writhed. From the farthest reach of the fens, darkness encroached—the night itself not as black as this blackness that tore at the real and stole toward me like the end of all light. It crept from the seam of the horizon, engulfing everything. The living world fell away into a mouth of nothingness that came closer and closer, devouring the last of all things, until existence itself was extinguished and all that remained was the void.

But this was not the bad thing. It was not what I saw as the world collapsed and plunged me, limbless and adrift, into bottomless nothing. Not what *I* saw—but what saw *me*.

Out of the infinite night came a wordless murmured chant and the beating of a soul drum, the heart of that living darkness. Two vast eyes peeled open, as red as glowing coals. They fixed me and I shriveled, and a fist of knotted roots closed around me to crush all that was left.

And there was no escape. And I would not wake. And the terror yawned and swallowed me forever.

——

The chant faded to whispers, hushed voices at swim within the deeper drone, the rising and falling vibrations as the car accelerated, slowed to take a corner. Ahead, the two red lights of the truck in front blurred, leaving trails smeared across my vision. My hands was in my lap, fingers twisted and gnarled. The nails was black.

Dog helped me out and guided me to his front door, propped me against the wall as he fumbled with the key. The streetlights pressed against the living night. Threads of shadow like smoke crept from between the bricks, from behind closed curtains. The darkness throbbed and swelled, its eyes everywhere. It followed me up the stairs to Dog's room. It lurked in the corners where the glow of the TV couldn't reach. It wafted from beneath the bed, cold and rank. Even as the madness of the night drew back and the familiar shapes and smells of Dog's room pressed in, even then the fear didn't go away. It stayed with me, a rippling chill that prickled from inside.

Dog stayed crepuscular all that day, dropping half after half to keep the dark steady. I couldn't bear it—even the crinkle of brown paper was enough to make me shiver. We kept the curtains closed and looped the new Tendril mix, flipping the tape every time it clunked at the end of a side. I smoked spliff after spliff just to get real, to forget that the darkness was everywhere, that it was alive, and that whatever was inside it was trying to get out.

I must have nodded, as next I knew it was night again. I was crashed on a mattress on the floor, looking up at Dog propped forward in bed, lit flickering blue by some shit on the TV. Whatever I'd been dreaming must've followed me out, 'cause Dog looked all wrong—his eyes was crazy, half-lidded and wobbling, his body swaying like a flagpole in the wind. But it weren't that what made me freak. It was the roots that snaked about him, that tangled round his neck, bulging like black veins. They pulsed and wriggled and writhed like tongues coiling into and out of his mouth, flickering round the edges of his eyes like maggots, like filthy black maggots eating out the hollows of his blacker-than-black eyes.

I grabbed for the light.

Dog was rocking forward and back, his gormless gob pouting and puckered, his eyes fluttering, half awake. He was rolling a spliff best he could muster with his fingers all twisted by the Black.

He turned to me, licked the back of the skin and rolled it closed. "Whassat, my son?"

My heart hammered at my ribcage like it wanted out. I'd finally lost it, gone full fucking mental.

"I gotta go, Dog," I said. "I gotta go home is all."

"Awright," he said, without looking up. "Catchya."

Last I heard as I staggered out the door, half falling down the stairs to the street, was the *scrit scrit scrit* of Dog sparking his Bic.

———

I slipped in through the front door, released the latch as slow and silent as a burglar. Shadows writhed in the entryway, but the smell of the house was old and familiar and a comfort. I'd never been so grateful to be home. The reading lamp was on when I snuck past the living room, stepping careful over the boards I knew would creak.

"Stephen?"

Mum had never waited up for me before. If she'd have yelled at me I might've told her to get fucked, stalked up to my room, packed up and gone back round to Dog's. I'd be there now, or on the street, with hollow eyes and missing teeth, selling some shit or other. I'd have followed Dog into the darkness. But she never raised her voice or nothing.

When I stepped inside, leaned on the doorframe too fucked and beaten to hide my eyes, my teeth, my blackened nails, she didn't say nothing, just give me this look. And that look was all love and sadness and disappointment, with nothing in it for me to push against. She patted the couch, and though something held me back—maybe shame, maybe something else I weren't ready then to see—I shuffled in and slumped down beside her.

It hurt, to be this close, to be looked at so kind and forgiven. There weren't nowhere for me to hide. From all the wrong I'd done her; from the way she loved me anyhow. There'd been nothing in my heart for so long that to feel it wake, like some small frail thing, so helpless, so vulnerable, it hurt like I can't tell you what.

Mum picked up my hand, squeezed it. That was all it took. Whatever I'd been holding onto, out it came. I cried like a fucking baby, eyes burning, gut heaving, face smeared with snot and tears. And through all of it she never said a word, just held my hand and sat with me.

I don't know how long I lay that way, staring out of focus at the weave of her skirt, smelling ancient dust in the sofa cushion, hearing the old house creak. We'd been quiet a long time when Mum stirred, patted my hand.

"I'll run you a bath," she said, "bring you up a cup of tea."

That's all she said. I nodded, let her pull me up, help me to the stairs. It weren't till I was tucked in bed with dawn tugging at the blind that I figured what she really meant, the thing what all this time she'd been wanting me to understand.

"I can't lose you too."

———

I saw Dog two more times after that. Just two more times.

I didn't go back round his place or nothing, and I never heard word one from him. I suppose he could've come round looking for me, but if he did Mum told him I was out or something 'cause I never heard about it. Or maybe he never did come round. He was in pretty deep with the Massive by then.

Me, I went back to school to face the music. Mum drove me in each day and waited in the car till she saw me in the front door. Before, I would've just waited her out and split, gone straight round to Dog's to get trashed, but things had changed. Something had opened up between Mum and me, like I saw her for the first time just as she was, saw how much she needed me to be there for her. I'd been too caught up in my own shit to see how lonely she was, how much losing Dad had taken from her. I hadn't noticed how old she'd got, the streaks of white in her hair, the lines around her eyes and the corners of her mouth, the slight tremble of her hands whenever they weren't doing nothing. It hurt to be close again, to see just how much wrong I'd done her; and to admit, at last, that Dad weren't there, that he weren't never coming back.

Facing up to all that and the mess I'd made of things at school weren't easy. But I owed it to Mum. And to Dad.

And I was afraid.

Ever since that night in the Tubes, I'd had this lingering terror, an anxious kind of dread that wouldn't leave me alone. Though I'd not touched the Black, it was still in me. Things still moved in the shadows. The darkness still clung, still had eyes. School was a necessary distraction. Exams was just around the corner and I had half a year to catch up on, spent every break in the library and every evening taking notes under a mountain of textbooks. Each night, I read until I couldn't hold my eyes open and slept with the light on. I was building a wall, surrounding myself with all the color and solidity and occasional sunshine of this material world, pulling it toward and around me, pushing back the darkness that pressed in from everywhere.

After I'd been back at school four or five weeks, Mum let off picking me up. I'd catch the bus home and sometimes see kids in Black Massive hoodies, handing out flyers for ABYSM by the record shop, or flogging Black out back of the supermarket. Maybe one of them was Dog. I couldn't tell: they all looked the same with their hoods up. I never went to see, never sought him out. It pained me deep to cut our old tie, but the thought of seeing him again pained deeper. So it threw me to run into him unexpected.

I was late leaving school that day and missed the first bus. By the time I got into town, I'd missed my connection. The bus station was packed with school kids and the afternoon wave of workers heading home. Over by the bogs I saw Cadman's driver and another Black Massive crony dishing flyers. I ducked my head, doubled round to find a sheltered spot to skulk, crashed straight into Dog coming the other way.

He didn't know me at first. His hoodie was pulled down over his eyes and his jaw was tight. He looked pale as fuck.

"Dog?"

As soon as I said it I wished I hadn't, wished I'd just let him grunt and walk on. But then he looked up, took me in. His eyes was vacant, filled with darkness.

"Sonic?" he said. "Fuck . . . Where've you been, mate. It's been *time*!"

"Stephen," I said. "It's Stephen. And . . . alright. I'm alright." I felt I had to explain, or something, that Dog deserved to know why I'd cut him dead. I never got to tell him why I ran, what I'd seen, how it weren't him but . . . *survival.* I'd run for my life. But then all I said was, "I couldn't come over."

"Y'alright, son," Dog said. "Y'alright. I been kind of busy myself, see." He patted the front of his hoodie and I heard the rustle of a paper bag. "Yeh, boss man keeps me busy, right enough. You're coming, intcha?"

I must've looked confused 'cause Dog pulled a card from his back pocket. It was all black, with the Black Massive symbol catching the dull light and that one word, ABYSM. "To the night, mate. The night. Trust me, Sonic, there won't be another like it. A night so dark it'll last forever."

I cringed. That kind of rubbish had always rung so deep on the Black, but now it just sounded like bollocks. I took the flyer, looked down at it like for the first time.

"I can't do it, David." I said.

Dog snorted. "What are you, my fucking Mum?"

"I can't do it, Dog. I'm out of the scene. I've stopped the lot: going out, getting fucked. It's not for me. I'm back at school—"

Dog grabbed my hand. His grip was tight and hard like bone. His fingers was gnarled.

"Listen to me, Sonic." Dog's voice was urgent, a hiss. "Trust me, mate. *You won't want to miss this.*"

He closed my hand around the flyer, pushed it back toward me.

"Catch ya," he said, and pushed past me into the crowd.

—

As the summer term wore on and end-of-school exams loomed, so too did ABYSM.

Maybe it was the pressure, everyone losing their shit over the GCSEs, but I was getting edgy, afraid that all I'd done to turn things around would be for nothing. I couldn't concentrate, found it harder and harder to focus on revision, couldn't see nothing ahead of me but failure. Even if I made it through the exams, or by some miracle actually *passed*, there was still the endless blank page of the summer holidays. Until now, I'd kept the urge to get trashed at bay through fear and tireless work, but the urge was still there. I didn't dare think what'd become of me if I give in to it. The stress got so bad I had to roll myself a spliff each night just to get to sleep;

and even then it didn't help, just monged my body while my head churned and churned, imagining everything that could go wrong and probably would.

I was still haunted by what I'd seen, by what'd gripped me down there in the dark. I never remembered my dreams, but woke cold and soaked, heart pounding, the echo of a cry in my silent room.

I thought a lot about Dog. I'd be staring at a textbook, some page on the War of the Roses, or how ox-bow lakes was formed, and find I'd been reading and re-reading the same words over and over, thinking about me and Dog back in the day. We'd had good times, right enough. Some proper laughs. And Dog'd always looked out for me, kept me steady, kept me safe, all the way back to that time pounding Miller. I thought of that day in the bus station, of Dog's clawed hands and black eyes, of his skin blue-white as a corpse. I thought about how I'd left him that last night, run and left him and not turned back.

I started looking out for him in town, walking closer than I dared to the Black Massive wherever they was huddled. They must've seen the old trails of shadow round me 'cause they'd holler, as I passed, in the deadhead lingo: "eldritch," "stygian," "crepuscular." And the darkness in me'd respond so strong I'd have to about-face to break it, walking away quick like running in a nightmare, moving but getting nowhere. Dog was never among them.

I went round his house after school one time, hoping to catch him, to say to him—I don't know what—something, anything to get him out of the Massive and back into the daylight. I wanted things back how they was before, back when we was still mates and there weren't no Tendril, no Black, no Cadman. The bloke downstairs remembered me, let me in, and I climbed to Dog's bedsit for the first time in months; the first time ever straight. My hands was shaking and I felt sick to my stomach, like I had to shit. The bloke stood below me at the foot of the stairs, watching every step.

Dog's room was unlocked and the door swung open when I pushed. His stuff was all over the place, but the smell was stale, like nobody'd been there in weeks. In the corner of the room, the TV flickered. On the bed, a mess of flyers, the half-light from the screen reflecting off a hundred shiny Black Massive symbols. And that one word, repeated over and over. ABYSM.

If I wanted to find Dog and make things right, there was only one time and place I'd be sure to catch him.

<h1 style="text-align:center">3</h1>

Mum give me a lift out to Tescos. I didn't want her to see the convoy or nothing, so I got her to drop me off a half-hour before the meet. I bought builder's tea in a Styrofoam cup, sat in the supermarket caff and sipped it, watching the cars roll in.

I figured she'd never let me go, which may be why I came straight out and asked her. I thought she'd crack one and say no, maybe get all teary and hysterical, maybe lock me in my room to keep me safe. I'd be off the hook then. No one could blame me for walking out on Dog; no one could say I abandoned him. But she thought it was a good idea. She said I'd been working so hard it would help to let off a bit of steam. Only—

"I know," I said. "I won't. That's behind me now, Mum."

But even as I said it, I wondered.

When all that was left of the tea was dregs, I slipped into the bog for a couple dabs of whizz, a half-wrap untouched from the night we met Cadman. Just to keep me awake, you understand—I didn't want to get fucked or nothing. I had a couple of spliffs pre-rolled to take the edge off, but otherwise I was going straight. I stepped through the sliding doors and into the car park.

It was a bleak scene. The vehicles gathering in twilight, engines throbbing, headlights off. Black-tracks bleeding from half-cracked windows. Smoke curling into the almost-night. The sweet smell of hash mixed with something rank, like breath from the grave.

I walked between cars, looking in windows for someone I'd know. There was faces alright, but no response. Everyone looked tragic. Fingers snarled and palsied like a seizure, nails inky-stained. The eyes was all smoky, vacant. I saw the pit in every one of them.

I heard my name and turned and there was Ellis, lolling in the passenger seat of Chewy's Peugeot 205. Gav slouched in back, with his arm round Mandy's shoulder. All of them looked empty, like they'd been hollowed out. Mandy scooched over and I slid in beside, give her an awkward smile. She looked at me blank. I pulled out the wrap of whizz and took a dab, offered it round, but no one was into it. I asked if they'd seen Dog, but Gav just laughed, said he had his own connection now. The car was heavy with shadow and I felt it tug at my own darkness. They was all packing the Black.

Outside, purple light crept from bonnet to bonnet. The car park sounds—hushed chatter, black-tracks and distant traffic—was overwhelmed by a deepening drone, filled with whispers and growls of bass. Ellis whooped as Cadman's black-on-black Allegro rolled past, slow as a hearse, an eerie glow in the windows.

The cars moved out in silence, sliding into the slow-moving stream of the convoy, out to the roundabout and down onto the A14. It was late, but sickly warm and still almost light. The fens slipped by in parallax, the blur of nearby hedges and the distant slow procession of silhouetted trees was shadow-black against the blue-gray dusk. Some coppers drove past on the other side of the road, but no one said nothing or even seemed to notice. Chewy closed the window, shut out the bitter smell of oilseed rape. Brown paper rustled and someone said "crepuscular," then they was all dry-swallowing Black Suns. The convoy turned off the dual carriageway onto an unlit B-road.

We snaked through backwater villages, through suburbs raised from fen fields and flood plains, past the mock-Tudor facades of identical cul-de-sacs, past the darkened windows of a business park and into some industrial zone. I had no idea where we was, couldn't tell if we was still in the same county even. Ahead of us brake lights rippled, indicators flashed, cars pulled in.

Chewy killed the engine, lit a cig. I could see from the curl of his fingers that the Black was already working on him. The others was slack-jawed, eyes dark and bleary.

It was a weird vibe, following the trail of deadheads down through the scrubby wasteland, along walls of collapsing breeze-block, past overfilled skips and rubbish heaped on rotting palettes. The long shadows and stark bright security lights made the night seem darker, closer. No one spoke. Not even whispers. It was like going to church.

A creeping unease rose from deep in my gut. Everyone around me was shuffling forward, going dark, or dark already. To be among them all yet not *with* them . . . well, it did not feel good. I couldn't see Dog anywhere.

Out of the debris of upturned shopping trolleys and charred oil drums, a black building loomed. Like a hole cut from the scene, the warehouse was a void, a door into some space darker than the deep blue night. The entrance flickered shades of purple. Black-tracks rumbled and thumped. The deadhead procession staggered out of the night and into ABYSM.

—

I lost the others as soon as we got inside. Cadman's driver was on the door, flanked by a shaved-head, thickset goon who stared down everyone as they stepped in. The deadheads handed over their cash and slipped into the dark and the noise. But I fumbled my note, had to drop to my knees to pat the grimy concrete round the goon's feet while he glared and glared. By the time I'd found it and handed it over, the others had been swallowed by the crowd.

Inside, the warehouse was like a cathedral, vast and unadorned. Purple light glowed in the corners, the ceiling a vault of impenetrable black. Deadheads bobbed and shuffled to the booming heartbeat, to shifting swirls of feedback and TV-static hiss. The black noise was so loud it filled the space like something you could touch.

Eyes peeled, I began the search for Dog. The eerie purple glow—which didn't seem to *come* from anywhere—was barely enough to see by and I had to step careful not to trip. The deadheads had no bother, moving easy through the near dark. On the dance-floor, they swayed like an underwater forest, lost to the music and the downward drag of the Black. And I felt it too. That buried shadow twisted inside me, daring me to let go and merge with the crowd. I pulled against it, kept straining to make out Dog in all those shadowed faces, but the closer I moved toward the sound system, toward the squalls of feedback and that bottomless beat, the worse the feeling became. I had to clench my fists to keep the fingers from curling.

Dog was nowhere round the outside, so I pushed in among the hung heads and the shifting bodies, trying to clock him. Before I reached the middle, I was stopped short by a band of plastic construction tape. There was an enormous space in the center of the room, marked out by traffic fencing. In the weak purple glow, I could just make out the floor tiles, warped and cracked, folding downward, falling away into . . . nothing. A vast black space, darker even than the unseeable roof above. The deadheads shuffled and bumped against the tape like they didn't even notice. Gusts of cold, rank air wafted up from the hole.

I staggered backward, away from the fence. My head spun like vertigo, like I didn't know up from down. The ground weren't solid no more, felt thin as paper with nothing beneath. I pushed back through the crowd, trying to find the wall, but the weird light threw me. The smell coming off the deadheads was so thick and feral, like the Black itself, I felt the blackness inside me respond. I couldn't get my bearings, couldn't find the wall. And then there was Cadman.

His rubbery face was smeared with purple and shadow. In the unlight his eyes was all black, with not even a glimmer. He took in the crowd, lips pulled back in a smile that was wide and oily and unkind. Something glinted in his hand. A chain looped round his fingers caught bursts of the purple light, the reflections trailing away from his fist and down to the studded collar of the creature skulking at his heel. It was hideous—a huge, half-naked thing that turned on me with bulging black eyes, bared rows of jagged black teeth. My stomach lurched.

It was Dog.

Some noise escaped my throat, a word maybe, or a cry. I backed away, shaking my head, but tripped on some deadhead's foot, fell backward into the crowd. I flailed, in a right state—without the Black, the music was driving me half mad, and what I saw tipped me over. I crawled among the feet, pushed up and between the mass of bodies, back to where the door should have been. But I couldn't find the door.

Then someone cut the sound. And all the lights went out.

———

A drone, like flies, like a thousand flies both distant and everywhere, rose from every corner of that boundless dark. Then a voice. Deep. Present. All gravel. All bass. Words I didn't understand in a language that never existed. The voice was rhythmic, hypnotic.

Out of the darkness, some shape emerged, a glowing form that hovered in the cavernous vault of the warehouse roof. A circle ringed with squiggles, like the rays of the sun—only they was writhing; and I understood they weren't rays at all, that the symbol had never been the sun.

I'd backed into a wall. The rough feel of breezeblock against my palms was the only thing what made sense. I pressed against it and started to edge, fumbling, feeling my way with trembling, terrified fingers, sliding one foot then the other, tensed against what my feet, my fingers, might find in the dark. The door had to be somewhere along the wall. It had to be *somewhere.*

The drone swelled, filling the darkness like a living thing. A kind of whisper-filled hum that came from everywhere. From the dead-heads. My hand found the door frame. I fumbled, turned, groped wildly for the handles. When I yanked at the doors they rattled but wouldn't open. My hands slipped down to thick coils of chain, to a padlock the size of a fist.

When the beat began, I felt as much as heard it, a pounding that made the floor tremble. Distant at first, buried deep—the beat of a distant, buried heart. I wrenched at the door, slamming the handles against the chain again and again. Then sheets of blue-white light-ning tore at the dark, a strobe that pulsed in time with the thunder from below.

What happened next come in flashes, freeze-frame bursts in black-and-white. Flickers of movement from around the hole—gnarled roots, whipping, tangling, grasping—deadheads bent and crooked, root-meshed, bodies merging—Cadman intoning, arms raised, head to the pitch-black heavens—Dog, buckled, howling, twisting against the chain.

The beat was louder, the floor shaking. From the center of the room, a roar, like wind, like a tornado erupting from the depths of the earth. Black smoke poured from the darkness-eaters, coiled and spun above the hole, sucked down like a vortex, like a whirlwind in reverse.

Strangled with the black roots, clothed in the black smoke, some-thing rose from the hole. Each burst from the strobe was a colorless still that tracked its movement. It was a hand. A *massive* hand, each finger as big as the biggest deadhead; bigger, even. The fingers scratched at the edge of the hole, like it was grabbing for something.

And then . . .

And then . . . oh god . . .

The ground buckled, lifted, began to split, to break apart. Dead-heads tumbled left and right. Someone screamed. The great hand—the *hands*—was tearing at the edges of the pit, shaking the warehouse as they scrabbled for grip. Out of the widening hole, a black dome rose, veined with thrashing vines. Everywhere, the sounds of collapse, of the warehouse tearing apart. The rising dome became a hill, then a mountain, and in the darkness of that great mass two lines of red fire grew wide. Two blind red eyes.

Pressed back against the exit, frozen, I saw Cadman, head back and eyes rolled, arms out and open. His hands lifted, lifted, like this motion alone would bring up that mad horror from below. Dog thrashed, gnawing at his wrists, trying to chew off his own hands.

Deadheads was lashed, tangled, strapped in a mass by the whipping tendrils. Bodies was flung this way and that, dragged to the very edge of the pit as the head emerged. It rolled as if in pain. The mouth yawned and billows of stinking blackness gusted from the hole. It groaned, a birthing roar that rose above the chant and the whispers and the screams like the din of slaughtered cows.

Something smashed against the exit doors and I was chucked forward. Another smash and the door hammered against the chain, the handles buckled. Through the crack, a flash of blue, the flicker of lights. I scrambled to the side as, with one last smash, the door burst open and in poured the fuzz.

Torch beams scoured the crowd, caught flashes of madness, scenes that only might have been. Deadheads festooned with decomposing roots. Gnarled bodies in half-human shapes. A giant mound of rotting veg. The chant had died, the roar just an echo; only the warp of sirens on half-pulse, the chatter of police radios, the officers' shouts as they drove the crowd away from the hole.

As the coppers took control, I saw, in the streaking torchlight, Cadman disappear into shadow at the back of the warehouse. I followed, but was caught in the tide of deadheads driven toward the exit.

It was a proper commotion. Cops yelling, deadheads stumbling, the strobe mutely blinking. As I was pushed back and out into the throbbing blue of emergency lights, the high beams of police vans and ambulances, I caught a glimpse through the ruined doorway of the thing. But what had been there, what I'd seen, weren't there no more; at least, not as I'd seen it. Only heaps of filthy black debris, like tangles of cable, slumped around the edge of the hole.

—

From the comfort of the living room, warmed by the morning sun, I lay on the couch with a glass of juice, reading the paper over and over. *Lives lost in illegal rave disaster.* The article was short, low on fact, but squished up beside an opinion piece, all snotty and self-righteous. It talked about "irresponsible organizers," railed against "the corrupters of our youth."

A lot of bollocks if you ask me. There was no mention of what may or may not have been found in the condemned warehouse. No mention of the pit.

There was no mention of Cadman, either. From the moment I saw him slip into shadow, it was like he'd never been. The Black Massive disappeared from the streets, and with them the Black. With no one going crepuscular, there was no market for the black-tracks. There was no more reverent whispers of Tendril, who'd vanished along with Cadman. The only evidence that any of it had ever happened at all was the stacks of ABYSM flyers on every stoner's coffee table, still torn and rolled and roached into spliffs the town over.

Even without the Black, the scene weren't never the same—not that I went out no more, but that's what I heard. Over the summer, there was a few more cracks of the whip, ravers trying to claw back that old colorful vibe. But the efforts was limp, half-arsed, shut down by the rozzas before the convoy even made it to the warehouse. After the health and safety nightmare of ABYSM, the police was under pressure to clamp down on the illegal scene. Within a year, it was dead.

I weren't that bothered. By then I was back at Sixth Form, head down, working on my A-Levels. I'd got a Saturday job washing dishes in town. I'd met a girl.

I never did see Dog again. I like to pretend he made it out of that warehouse alright, that whatever Cadman had on him was snuffed as soon as he and the Black was out of Dog's life. I like to pretend that what I saw I didn't see. A couple weeks after ABYSM, I went round to his place to check on him, but all his stuff was gone and there was someone else in the room. Took me forever to pluck up the courage to call his Mum, but when she answered I froze and couldn't say nothing. Her voice on the other end of the line was distant, teary. She just said, over and over, "David? Is that you, David?"

I don't know. I don't think back often to that night. I suppose I've tried to put it out of my mind. But sometimes it comes back, sometimes I'll wake with the sweats and a pounding heart and I'll remember those red eyes peeling open in the blackness. As the dream falls away, I'll feel tendrils of shadow snaking back from the edge of the bed, pooling in the corners of the room with that other, living dark.

No matter what I believe in the daytime, with its light and noise and warmth, in the deepest reaches of night, my body knows different.

At those times, the beat beneath my ribs seems deeper, older, marking time not in seconds but in centuries. And that beat is everything, all there is and ever has been. Just the emptiness and the fall and the heart that beats forever in the everlasting night.

The Face God Gave

They were somewhere between LAX and Sydney, way out over the Pacific Ocean, when the plane hit rough air. The boys were both asleep, finally, and Karen lay in a waking doze, drained of all energy yet too wired to submit to sleep.

It was a relief to see them unconscious. They'd been awake so long, passed through so many time zones, that both boys had lost it completely. They had become so feral that even the endless loop of movies and TV no longer subdued them. But now Dylan was curled beside her with his head in her lap, snuggled under the airline blanket, one small, sock-less foot poking out from beneath. Torin lay rigid as a plank, mouth wide, with his head against the window blind. The arm of Karen's seat was up and dug painfully into her shoulder with the sudden dip and shudder of the plane.

Karen had never before confessed this to herself, but she was terrified of flying. For the sake of the boys, she had pressed down her true feelings, wore a brave expression she hoped concealed how tightly she gripped the armrest as the plane peeled from the runway, how her belly churned each time, as now, they hit a bad patch of turbulence.

Her TV screen showed a pixelated map of their location. The plane icon was hemmed in by rippled shades of blue. There was nothing beneath them but air; and, beneath that, only water. Karen forced herself to breathe slow and deep, suppressing the panic that tugged at her insides, that forced her to picture each of the ten-or-more-thousand meters between the plane and the ocean. The limitless void of black waves. The chill, fathomless depths.

The plane shook again and Karen felt her stomach drop, the

sickening feeling of weightlessness. She clenched her fists, counted backward from ten. The cabin was dimmed for nighttime and, apart from the few insomniacs with their glimmering screens, most of the passengers were slumped beneath cheap blankets and eyeshades in restless sleep. No one but Karen seemed concerned by the lurching, rolling motions of the plane.

Something changed in the movements then. Something sudden and sick making.

The plane banked hard to the right and the cabin tilted sharply down. Bags slid out from under seats. Untethered headphones skittered down the aisle. Torin's head bumped the window-blind and he woke with a jerk, yanked off his eyeshade, searching for Karen. She reached out to comfort him, but even that small movement almost pulled her from the seat. She gripped the outside armrest, clutched at the stirring Dylan with her free hand, looked to Torin with eyes she hoped betrayed none of her panic.

They were dropping, the plane in a mad spin. Karen couldn't see it, but she could feel it, in her guts, in her madly popping ears. People were waking now, yelling, trying to stand but pulled back into their seats by the plane's relentless drag. A voice squelched over the Tannoy, words lost in the din from whining engines, from frightened passengers. A businessman across from Karen forced himself from his seat to open an overhead locker. Cases tumbled into the cabin, banged off seats, clattered down the aisle. One struck the man and knocked him to the floor. People were screaming. The captain had switched on the fasten seatbelts sign.

There was a gasping sound then, a deep hissing sigh, and masks dropped from the ceiling.

Karen struggled to remember the brace position, the location of the emergency exits, how to find and deploy her lifejacket. But her mind was a blank. Throughout the safety demonstration she had been racked with shame and anxiety as Dylan kicked the seat in front and Torin badgered her without cease about some game he wanted her to buy. She had felt the eyes of the other passengers, of the cabin crew, burning into her: the bad mother. Now she wished she had ignored the children, ignored her self-reproach, paid attention instead to the formalized ritual of the cabin crew's safety display, to the comforting infographics of the flight safety card.

She reached for the dropped masks and Dylan gripped her arm, buried his face into her belly. Torin clutched at the seat, his face stretched and pale with terror. But when her fingers found the edge of the mask, Karen recoiled.

What she had pulled toward herself was not made of plastic, but of fur. Stiff and leathery, the feel was of something long dead, desiccated with age. It was the face of a fox.

There was a hissing sound and the cabin filled with thick white mist. The lights failed and the total darkness was broken only by a strobing exit sign. The plane was still falling, falling. Karen's breath came in stifled gasps. Beside her, Dylan wheezed and Torin scratched at his throat. Karen gripped the fox mask and pressed it onto her face.

The mask smelled of dried meat and ancient taxidermy, with a faint but unmistakable tang of musk. Yet it did not repel her, as she had expected. It was, in fact, oddly comforting. She could breathe without effort. Her night vision had improved.

She reached for another, saw Torin doing the same. The mask she pulled over Dylan's face was dark brown, with round ears and a snub nose. A bear. Torin, when she turned to him, looked back at her through the eyes of a young stag, the twin forks of antlers jutting from the back of his head. All around them, passengers were donning their own masks. Faces of geese, of badgers, of echidnas, bilbys and goannas. There were starlings, salamanders, pigs and toads and tigers. There were lemurs and lions, all manner of creatures, many Karen had no names for.

But there was no impact.

One moment, the plane was plummeting, in a desperate, twisting, terminal dive. And the next . . .

Stillness. Silence. The dark.

All along the aisle, tiny lights fired one after another, illuminating a path to the exit doors. Looking closer, Karen saw they were glow-worms.

Passengers slipped from their seats and followed the lights. Not in the chaos of panic, but in a respectful, orderly procession. Some padded on paws, others trotted on hooves, others still scratched at the carpet with claws. Some even fluttered and flit from seat-back to seat-back. As Karen guided the boys into the aisle, she too felt the change, the acuteness of her sense of smell, the way she turned to lick

Dylan as he rolled out of his seat. By the time Torin clopped past, she no longer thought of him by his name, but by the complex grammar of odors that poured from his tautly muscular body.

Daylight poured in from a hole in the side of the plane. The emergency exit door had been fired and a gazelle, still wearing the hat and scarf of the cabin crew, was guiding the procession out and down. Torin nuzzled her as he passed, reared and snorted, before stumbling down the rubbery yellow slide.

Karen nudged Dylan with her snout, persuading him with gentle motions toward the lip of the inflatable slide. As he spilled, slipping and rolling toward the jungle floor, he looked back toward Karen with round eyes full of desperation and loss. But by the time he reached the bottom, the look had faded and he turned from the slide without pause to carve his own path, following the slowly dispersing crowd of animal passengers. Torin had already vanished into the living green.

The smells that came to Karen were rich and alive, danced in her nostrils like scent poems. From deep within the boundless jungle, sounds came to her, unfamiliar calls, the cries of unseen birds. The weight in her breast was already lightening and lifted entirely as she stepped forward onto the slide. When her paws connected with the moist ground, tangled as it was with vines and the roots of vast fig trees, there was nothing left of Karen but the lightness.

She followed her sons into the understory of that first and final garden.

The Boon

"Oh, Eric. You simply have to see it. It's quite, quite magical."

Beth gestured toward the latticed window, the waving fields of wheat, still green, and the dark line of forest beyond.

Eric looked from Beth to Jon to Dani. What they had just told him was absurd, the secret Beth had invited him round to share. It was . . . ludicrous. Impossible. Yet their faces betrayed nothing but gravity and veiled excitement, gave no hint that this might be some kind of elaborate practical joke.

"You're messing with me," he said. "If I say I believe you, you'll all just fall about laughing or something. I'm not that gullible."

"Ooh, big word," said Jon with a sneer. "You learn that from the dictionary?"

Eric flushed. Jon was two years his senior and the older of the three siblings. There was something about him that frightened Eric, something hard and strong. Jon was about a head taller than Eric, with taut, scrawny muscles. He looked as though he never slept, his eyes like hard shining lumps of coal.

Eric tried to hold the older boy's gaze, but the humiliation overwhelmed him. He looked away, cheeks burning. Knowing that Beth had witnessed this easy defeat made him flush hotter still.

The girls' bedroom was tight and cold and unadorned, the two single beds draped with patterned quilts that Eric could tell were homemade. Outside, a silent breeze rippled in waves across the field. The wood that marked its farthest edge might have been a cut in the world, an opening between earth and sky within which lay hidden movements and shadow.

"We're not joking," said Beth. Her eyes were open and blue and impossible to ignore. Her hair, the gold of ripened wheat, her cheeks dotted with bronze freckles. "The forest really *is* enchanted. The trees really *do* whisper secrets. There *are* magical creatures in there, ancient forest folk who grant boons to those who believe in them, who show them kindness."

"I *want* to believe you," said Eric. "It's just . . ."

"You don't have to believe us," said Dani from the floor, where she knelt. "We'll show you."

———

Eric had not been in the village long. He'd moved there with his mother only a month or two before. So short a time, but already it felt an eternity. He missed their flat in the city, missed the library, the museums. He missed his friends.

That was the hardest part of the transition for Eric—the loneliness. Slow to connect, at school he felt like a ghost, already a pariah because he'd come from the city. In a way it wasn't so different from before: he just noticed it more here. There was so little to *do* in the country. So little to distract him from that desolate, empty feeling.

They'd moved here in the holidays, just before the start of the summer term, and everyone already knew each other. They all knew each other anyway, of course, having grown up in one or other of the villages hereabouts. Some of the families, Eric knew, had been here for generations. The looks they gave Eric and his mother made it clear that they, as newcomers, would always be on the outside, would never be truly welcomed.

Though the Wintons were a well-established family in the area, there was a misfit quality to them as well. The siblings were not so much shunned as ignored, a tight-knit clique which others were unable to penetrate. Though at eight and ten and twelve, Dani, Beth and Jon were all in different years at school, when the bell rang for break time, they sought not the company of their peers but their own family circle. They would walk the outskirts of the cricket pitch or disappear together into the shallow copse at the edge of the school grounds. When the bell rang for home time, no parent came to collect them. The three children walked together by lane and bridle path back to their little whitewashed cottage on the farthest edge of the village.

The father did not work, but kept a small plot out back for vegetables. The mother did odd jobs for small change, scrubbing floors, folding laundry. The children, too, were often seen running errands, carrying produce or clean, pressed clothes to the handful of village customers. The family seemed barely to subsist. And yet, though gaunt and lean, the siblings brimmed with confidence and energy.

Beth in particular was full of life. She and Eric were in the same class at school, and he'd been captivated by her since his first day in class. He'd never had such strong feelings for a girl before: hot, confusing feelings that tangled his gut and muddled his head. He wanted above all things to be close to her, and yet whenever he'd tried to speak around her, his tongue turned to chewing gum in his mouth, his hands shook and his face went so red it felt like sunburn. In the quiet privacy of his bedroom, with its large bed, its new furniture, its walls bedecked with posters, he lay for many hours, staring at the ceiling, fantasizing scenarios in which Beth came to him. He imagined her knocking on his window at night. "Come out, Eric. Come with me. I have a secret to show you." It was like the answer to his prayers when she strode up to him at lunch break yesterday, inviting him round to her house.

Of course, he hadn't expected to be spending the day with Beth *and* her siblings. But Eric felt he was already living in a land of make-believe—one where Beth approached him at all—and he would take whatever he could from it. Even Jon and Dani. Even stories of pixies and elves in a magical forest at the bottom of the garden. If it came with Beth, he'd take it all.

—

"Come on, slowcoach. Keep up!" Beth ran, laughing, ahead of him, green ears of wheat dancing in her wake.

Jon strode in front, carving a path through the field that all of them followed. Dani skipped behind him through the young grain, her head appearing and disappearing with each bound. Beth had almost caught up with them now, holding aloft the battered leather satchel that their mother had filled with sandwiches, apples and a tartan thermos of tea.

Eric turned and looked back the way they had come. The cottage was just a blob of white in the distance, no bigger than a match box. Beyond it he could almost make out the red smear of the village telephone box. Ahead of him, drawing closer with each step, the dark wall of the forest loomed.

The siblings were almost at the foot of it now, Jon and Dani disappearing into the hawthorn bushes at its edge. Beth turned again and waved him onward with a pantomime gesture. Eric pressed toward her through the hissing wheat.

There was no path into the wood. Eric had to force his way through the hawthorn behind Beth, the twigs bending back, scratching as he passed. Once through, he stumbled beneath towering conifers onto a drift of pine needles, spongy, soft and fragrant. As the bushes closed behind him, Eric became aware of the hush, the deadening of all sound. And the dark. After the heat of the afternoon sun, the chill of the forest was like a cellar, or a tomb. He shivered and goose pimples ran up his arms.

"Is he coming, or what?" Jon said gruffly to Beth. Apart from the occasional jibe or veiled threat, Jon had not spoken directly to Eric all afternoon. He seemed to resent his sister's insistence on bringing along this stranger.

It was this obvious hostility, the plain fact that Jon made no effort to hide his dislike of the younger boy, that reassured Eric of Beth's earnestness. If this *was* a trick, surely Jon would play along more convincingly? And Beth, all of them, seemed to believe so completely in the "secret" they had shared with him, there had to be *some* truth in it, didn't there? Eric felt himself teetering between fear of falling victim to a practical joke, one that all were in on but him, and that longing which swelled in him with each step closer to the dark boundary of the wood: the hunger for magic to be real.

A breeze he could not feel fussed at the upper reaches of the pines. The whispering sound of thousands of needles caressing each other was like a lullaby's shush, rising and falling, almost singsong. Almost like . . . Wouldn't it be wonderful if this forest really *were* enchanted, if even half the things Beth and Jon and Dani had told him were true. He ran to catch up with them, his feet sinking in the heaps of fallen needles.

"I can hear them," he said, falling into step beside Beth. "They really *do* sound like they're whispering to one another."

He glanced ahead to where Jon and Dani strode. Had Jon cocked his ear to listen? Eric's cheeks flushed.

"Isn't it wonderful?" Beth responded. "If you're lucky, the forest folk will teach you to understand the whispers. It's one of the boons they grant."

"Boons?"

"Gifts. Sort of presents, I suppose. When we first encountered the forest people, we weren't afraid. We shared our lunch—sandwiches and some toffee Mum had made. We gave it freely and they granted us a boon. That day, it was to understand the whispers of the pine trees. But we've learned other things from them too, been granted other boons."

Eric didn't know what to say. The sense that this was all some incomprehensible prank still nagged at him. If he spoke, he felt, if he were to engage with Beth's unusual, impossible tale, it would embroil him more deeply in the deception, make a greater fool of him when they finally whipped away the rug. And yet it pained him to stay silent. Beth was opening a door for him, granting him a boon of her own: to spend time with her, to share her secret. In a way it didn't matter if it was true or not. The idea that he might be about to encounter uncanny, boon-granting beings both amazed and frightened him. He was afraid that the magic of this moment—Beth's attention, the imminent possibility of an actual miracle—would vanish if he imposed himself upon it in any way; that, like a dream drawn back from the sounds of the waking world, it would slip through his fingers, never to have been.

"You'll have to introduce yourself, of course," Beth went on, unbothered by Eric's silence. "In a moment, we'll come to the clearing and you'll see the Great Mother Tree. You'll need to approach her fearlessly—she'll know if you're afraid, or if there is malice in your heart. You'll approach alone and make your offering."

Ahead of them, the pines were thinning. Jon and Dani waited for them at the edge of a wide amphitheater of trees.

"My . . . offering?" Eric's voice sounded weak, deadened by the stillness of the wood.

"A sandwich ought to do it," said Beth, patting her satchel. "Perhaps an apple. This is your first meeting, after all. You don't want to look too showy."

They reached the clearing, stopped beside Jon and Dani. Eric stared. The meadow was almost perfectly round, the width of a cricket pitch, ringed by wavering pines. The whispering of the many thousands of needles was louder now, and everywhere, rising and falling as it swirled around the edges of the wood. Clouds had rolled in since they first entered the forest, like a lid over the clearing behind which the sun was obscured. Across from the children, beyond the circular expanse of overgrown grasses and the profusion of wildflowers, loomed the most enormous—the most *monstrous*—tree that Eric had ever seen. It was easily the width of a house, the trunk deformed by hideous shapes. Though, from this distance, the vast thickness of the tree gave the impression that it was squat, the halo of leaves, effulgently green, reached higher than even the tallest of the pines. The top disappeared into swirls of gray cloud. Great dark boughs snaked from that hulking mass, reached out as though grasping, as though enclosing the outer edges of the forest glade in a suffocating maternal grip. There was no sound but the shushing of the trees. Not a bird, not a voice, not even the distant hum of the motorway. Eric tried to swallow, but his mouth was dry.

"Did you tell him?" Jon asked Beth, as though Eric wasn't there.

"He knows what he has to do."

"But what about the open heart?" asked Dani. "What about not being afraid?"

Jon caught his sister's eye, scoffed and turned to face the clearing.

"He knows," said Beth. "He'll be fine."

She rummaged in her bag, pressed something into Eric's hand. He looked down, dumbly. He was holding a sandwich, wrapped in clingfilm.

"Go on then," said Dani. She gave him a little push from behind.

Eric stumbled forward, turned to look at them: Dani, wide-eyed, grinning; Jon, eyes narrowed, daring him to fail; Beth, stroking hair from her eyes with one finger, a faint smile muddling the freckles on her cheeks.

"That's the way," she said. "Just stride right across the middle of the clearing, straight toward Mother Tree. If you pause, if you hesitate for even a moment . . ."

"She'll know," croaked Eric. "She'll know I'm afraid."

"That's right," said Beth. And this time her smile was warm and wide. "You don't want that."

Eric took one step, two, then turned back to face them again. "And what do I do with—" He gestured toward the sandwich in his other hand, limp by his side.

"Don't worry," said Beth. "You'll know what to do when the time comes."

Eric nodded stupidly. He turned, strode falteringly toward the enormous tree, willing his steps to appear strong and purposeful. His feet shush-shushed through the long grasses, through wildflowers, purple, white and yellow. As he approached, the great tree seemed to grow, towering before him. The shapes that girdled the trunk appeared to shift with each step he took, warping its surface, writhing almost, like bodies contorted in pain. By the time he reached the center of the meadow, his nerves were jangling, fear pounding at his heart. Then the clouds above him parted and sun flooded the clearing.

The warm brilliance of midafternoon lit the glade, gilding the tips of the waving conifers. The grass all around him came alive, joyous and radiant. The wildflowers fluoresced, their colors now vivid and intense. In the glorious sunshine, even the Great Mother Tree seemed kinder—vast still, but somehow less ominous. A kind of simple joy bloomed in Eric and he turned, grinning, to where the siblings stood at the treeline.

As he turned, still walking, he felt a sickening lurch in his stomach, heard the snap of splintering twigs. His foot sunk through a thin layer of torn grass and wildflowers, crunched through the lattice of branches underneath.

Eric tumbled forward into the pit.

———

Eric's earliest encounter with the siblings had been with Jon on the first day of school.

Eric and his mother were running late that morning and the bell was already jangling when he climbed out of the car. He raced to follow the last of the stragglers into the school building's musty corridors. As he bumbled awkwardly with his bag in the cloakroom, he was bumped from behind and spilled his books.

"Watch it!"

Not a warning, but a sneer. Jon looked down on him with those coal black eyes, a hard look that made Eric shrivel.

His heart was still pounding when he lowered himself behind the one empty desk in his classroom, face flushed from running and the teacher's snide remarks. Everyone in the class was staring at him. The new boy.

Not everyone. The girl ahead of him to the right didn't look up when he entered and did not turn around when he stammered his apology. When it came to his name on the register, she didn't titter at his accent like the other children. He might not have noticed her but for the quiet, almost singsong way she said "here" when the teacher called out "Winton." The strangely antiquated frock she wore. Her hair, the locks that fell softly around her shoulders like summer wheat. Once he saw her, Eric was transfixed.

When the bell rang for break-time and he followed the golden-haired girl from his classroom, he was horrified to see her skip across the playground to join his antagonist from that morning. The look Jon gave him almost stopped his heart. But then another, younger girl joined them and the siblings turned and made for the playing fields. Eric continued on to the library, as if that had been his plan all along.

In class, Eric stole glances at Beth whenever he could. He was powerless to prevent himself. When, at one point in the tedious second hour of double maths, she turned slightly, slid back her hair with one finger to reveal the pale perfect shell of her ear, something in Eric's gut fell awkwardly and he felt heat rise to his face. He longed for her to turn around fully and notice him.

She did glance back, once, perhaps aware of his gaze burning on her. But there was nothing in the look. Her eyes took him in—the boy behind her and to the left, with his red cheeks, his eyes that flicked from her to the blackboard, feigning a sudden interest in two-step functions. Her face registered nothing. She smiled faintly: the barest acknowledgment of the presence of another. He might as well not have been there at all.

When Beth finally *did* approach him, it came completely out of the blue. Eric had grown so used to her blank looks, her total lack of recognition, that he assumed she was smiling at someone else, walking toward some other child on the playground. Yet at the same time, wasn't this exactly as he'd imagined it? Lying awake in the lonely quiet of his bedroom, didn't he picture precisely this? Beth singling him out—him alone.

Eric was so flustered by the sight of her approaching—her eyes fixed on his, her smile incandescent—that he was hardly aware of

Jon and Dani behind her in the background. He failed to notice that, before she caught his eye, Jon had seen him first.

And he had leaned down and whispered in his sister's waiting ear.

—

The pain in Eric's leg was so sheer that, for a moment, the world disappeared. Had he passed out? Woken again? It took him some moments to adjust to the darkness, to recognize where he was and what had happened.

Far above him, a luminous disc hung like a full moon in the night sky. Only it wasn't night, and the edges of the disc were tufted with branches and tussocks of grass, with sprays of snapped twigs. A dribble of sunlight bled from the mouth of the hole, illuminating the upper reaches of what looked like a well. Eric reached out a hand and felt rough-hewn timber, thick wooden beams holding back the great weight of earth that towered on all sides above him. He panicked, struggling to gulp air into his lungs. The pit stank of dampness and rot, like the compost heap at the bottom of his garden. He fought to slow his breathing and take stock of the situation. The sound of his convulsive sobs reverberated dully off the walls.

Eric strained to make out his surroundings in the gloom. The vague shape of his legs was just visible, but all else was shadow. Beneath him he could feel tight-packed dirt. From the darkness at the other side of the pit, a scratching, skittering sound.

Eric shifted to get a better view of his leg, but the movement thrust spears of agony up from his shin. His yell bounced back at him from every side.

With a gurgling cry, his teeth clenched so tight his jaw locked, Eric pulled himself upright. Brilliant whiteness, like the burst of a flashbulb, popped behind his eyes. He looked down, warily, not wanting to see. Seeing, sobbing, he retched dryly into the mud. His thighs lay parallel, with his knees almost touching. But below the knee, his right shin bent back upon itself. His right foot pointed wrongly up toward him.

"No," he moaned. "No no no no no."

He stared at the ruined leg—as though staring alone was enough to will himself awake, back to his bed at home, warm and safe and unharmed.

"Help!" he yelled. "Beth! Dani! Jon! Help me, I'm . . . I'm—" But the shouts sent fresh pain shooting from his leg. He collapsed into snorts of tears.

Sounds from overhead. The siblings? Eric sucked in his breath, tried to quell his sniveling. Yes, voices. Definitely the Wintons. Dani's singsong, Jon's gruffer tone. He could hear them talking above, but the acoustics in the pit were strange, disorienting. He couldn't make out the words.

"Beth! Help me! I'm down here!"

Three heads peered over the side of the pit, three featureless silhouettes. They muttered to one another, too soft and fast for Eric to distinguish. Then one of them laughed—Jon, unmistakably—and two heads vanished. Only one remained.

"Eric," said Beth. "Eric, I'm sorry."

Then she too was gone and there was nothing but the dirt and the pain and the disc of sky above, impossibly distant.

—

Eric drifted in and out of consciousness, each spell of numb black a mercy. He felt drained and weak. The broken shin bone must have pierced the skin, for his trousers were sticky and wet and he felt empty, barely able to open his eyes.

He was too weak to move. The pain of his last attempt had been so shrill and all-consuming, it had erased his will entirely. He was starving, but the sandwich he dropped when he fell into the pit lay just out of reach. The skittering sound turned out to be a rat. He had shrieked when it scuttled over his good leg. It gnawed now at the sandwich, the sound of its teeth terrible in the dark.

When had night fallen? Sometime in between his bouts of unconsciousness, the shadows in the pit had clotted into an impenetrable black mass. The ring above was distinguished now only by its peppering of stars. Strange noises bled from the wood, eerie cries and sounds of movement. Just animals, Eric told himself. Squirrels and birds and foxes. His mind was dulled by the fall, the loss of blood, but his body still thrilled with a kind of mute tension, poised, despite its injury, to fight or flee.

After the siblings left, Eric had shouted himself hoarse. He shouted their names, shouted every swear word he knew, his shouts collapsing into sobs that shook his body and made his wound scream. When no help came in response to his cries, he lay there weeping, back propped uncomfortably against the splintered boards, legs splayed in the dirt.

His mind tumbled over the events of that day, of the preceding weeks, rifling through memories in search of a reason, the thing he must have done or said to anger one or other of the siblings. But though he looped through the moments of his encounter with Beth yesterday, through the procession of hostile looks from Jon, he could find no incident, however small, that might justify . . . *this*. As his thinking slowed, his mind hazing over from loss of blood and the grogginess of sleep, a far worse thought emerged, one so terrible that he could not look at it directly: that there might be *no* reason. What that said about Beth, about Dani and Jon, he could not fathom. It was too alien to comprehend in its entirety. What sort of a person would *do* this? And *why*?

At first, he thought that it was just a practical joke gone wrong, that the siblings would return with a doctor, with help from the village. But this mad sliver of hope had long since dissolved into pain and tears and self-pity. He thought instead of his mother, imagined her waiting for him to push open the back door, knees covered in dirt and smelling of the fields. How he wanted above all to be home, to be in his own bed, to be held by her. Perhaps she was out there now, searching for him. But how would she, or anybody, ever find him here? Where even was he? Would they look for him? Send out a search party? Surely not in the dark. They would do nothing before morning.

Eric began to shiver. The warm light of morning was an eternity away. And would it even reach him down here?

There was a cry from above, near the mouth of the hole, a hoot, something like the call of an owl. Unlike an owl's cry it was a pure, flute-like sound, and its unusualness, its proximity, brought Eric quickly to attention.

There was a rustling above and then the call again, mournful and unnatural, but further away this time and coming from the other side of the hole. Eric's teeth began to chatter and fear stole from the pit of his belly. The rustling became a white noise that hissed from every side at once, distorted by strange acoustics. Waves of movement rolled through the tall grass, from the outer edges of the clearing, toward the mouth of the pit.

Then silence.

The quiet was so still and deep that Eric could hear his blood thumping in his veins. He strained to listen, scanned the dark for any sound, anything. But even the nattering of the rat on his sandwich had stilled. For a terrifying moment Eric thought he had gone deaf, but he heard his fingers grabbing at his ears clear enough. The silence was *out there*. In the total dark.

A disc of light cracked over the edge of the pit and Eric glanced up at the rising moon. A full moon, perfectly round and silver and brilliant, casting a limpid phosphorescence that reached almost to the bottom of the pit. He could see all of it now, the huge glowing disc, and only his relief, only the flood of hope prevented him from noticing what was wrong. The moon was rising too fast. It was too huge in the sky.

Then two eyes popped open and the moon grinned.

Its voice, when it spoke, was scratchy and thick, distant, like the sound of his mother's old records.

"Yes, children. Yes!" said the Moon. "This will do *nicely*."

And Eric heard muffled voices whispering in reply. Jon and Dani. And Beth. Somewhere.

Looking up into the terrible glow of the moon-faced creature, Eric saw, poised around the rim, shapes and silhouettes, the writhing of many small and sinuous bodies.

The moon grinned again and said, "Yes, this is a *fine* offering. Name it, children. Name your boon!"

Eric heard talking, unmistakably the siblings. And their voices rose with excitement and surprise and then he *saw* them—Beth and Dani and Jon—holding hands as in ring-a-ring-a-rosie, only high above the mouth of the pit. Lit dimly by the luminous head of the moon man, they floated upward, giggling and shrieking with delight as they flew.

And the shadow shapes descended at once into the pit. A landslide of shriveled skin and teeth and horrible, horrible warmth.

Eric was spared the sight, for the moon-faced man, still grinning, withdrew his luminous head. But before he was plunged into darkness and the tide of unknowable horrors seethed around him, Eric caught a last glimpse of the siblings, flying high above the clearing. Whooping for joy. Delighting in their boon.

—For EB, with apologies.

The Measure of Sorrow

1

The sun was low, like a distant fire on the horizon, as they closed the last few miles to the farm. The amber light withdrew from desolate pastureland, strobed gently through black tangles of eucalyptus. They hadn't seen another car since the last town, an hour or more behind.

The road twisted, narrow and unforgiving, all tight corners and no turning places. Chris kept one eye on the cracked and dusty tarmac, the other on the odometer, anxious not to miss the entrance.

He tilted the rearview mirror to see if Callum was asleep. The boy had been silent ever since the iPad died, and Chris half-hoped he'd dropped off. But, though he lay still, his head against the window, Callum's eyes were open, gazing out across the farmland to some place beyond, where only he could look.

Chris almost drove past the sign. He braked sharply, hooked a tight left through a gap in the crumbling stone wall and bumped over a cattle grid. The lights were on up at the farm but he didn't pull in, followed the gravel drive past the shadowed mass of an old barn, down toward the solitary light of the shearers' cottage. A dog barked as they passed and shadowed them behind the darkening hedgerow.

Callum was out of his seatbelt and spilling from the car before Chris even pulled the handbrake. "Can I ride my bike now, Dad?"

Chris started to say no but checked himself. "Sure," he managed. "You must need to stretch your legs. Just don't go too far. And don't be *long*; it's getting dark."

He wrestled the bike out from a tangle of occy straps in the boot, set it down beside the boy, turned back to rummage for a helmet. But

Callum was already gone, the crunch of wheels on gravel receding behind the cottage. The urge to yell after him welled up in Chris, but he pushed it down. The least he could do was not trample this last moment of freedom. Soon they would be home, back to the relentless cycle of days and weeks, of work and school, and the grief that had no end.

There was a lamp above the front door of the cottage that lit the poky veranda, reflected starkly off the one window, summoned moths and mosquitoes from the encroaching dark. Inside, it was tiny and smelled of soot and old cloth. At one time it would have slept ten or more farmhands; now the cottage felt it would be cozy for just the two of them. There were only three rooms: an outside toilet, walled in to create an entryway; a combined kitchen/living room, with a huge fireplace that took up most of one wall; and a small, neat bedroom, with windows along one side and modern sliding doors along the other. Chris dropped their bags on the bed, slid open the glass doors and stepped out onto the back deck.

It seemed darker now, with the light from the cottage behind him, and very still. The sky had turned slate-blue, smeared with sickly yellow clouds; the trees and the farmhouse were just silhouettes enveloped by the descent of night. A dog barked over at the farm and, somewhere in the darkness, cockatoos bickered. He walked down to the fence line, peered along the snaking drive. The gray gravel phosphoresced. He hoped to see Callum returning, hoped he wasn't going to have to go and find him, bring the boy back himself.

Going back to lock the car, Chris saw again the barn they had passed driving down. Even from across the yard, the old building loomed—over the farmyard, the desolate wool shed, the derelict pens. It towered over Chris where he stood, a black monolith with a distorted center of gravity, sucking what light remained into its infinite silhouette.

Something compelled him toward it, some dark attraction he mistook for curiosity.

Tires crunched on gravel. Headlight beams and shadow dragged over tufts of grass. A whitish ute pulled up beside him.

"Looking for your boy?"

The driver half-leaned from the window, dim lights from the dashboard outlining her broad, angular physique, the square jut of her chin. Her face was obscured by darkness and the brim of a beaten Akubra, but Chris made out the glint of incongruously fashionable, rimless glasses.

There was a skittering sound in the tray of the ute. The restless shape of a dog pacing out the enclosure.

"He was just down with the alpacas, watched me bring them in. He'll be on his way back now, I expect."

"Thanks," said Chris. "I was just admiring your setup here. It's a lovely spot."

She grunted, gave the faintest of nods.

"Brekkie's up at the farmhouse from eight. There's a bottle in the fridge. And I brought you some feed, in case the boy wants to get up close to the animals." She reached across to the passenger seat and passed over a bucket, loaded with pellets.

Chris stepped forward to take it, but she did not let go. The ute growled. The dog scratched in back. Blue-white fluorescence pooled on the ashen gravel. Chris and the driver, half leaning from the window, both gripped the bucket of feed as though frozen in time. He couldn't see her eyes, but could tell she was looking over his shoulder, up toward the roof of the old barn.

"Um . . ." he began.

She turned back to him as from some distance greater than their outstretched arms could measure, released her grip on the bucket.

"And you best keep that gate closed behind you." She gestured at the fence surrounding the cottage. "Unless you don't mind company."

She popped the ute into gear and moved off up the driveway, the dog still prowling in back. As she pulled away, she gave a little half-wave, touched the brim of her hat with two fingers. Chris stood for a moment, watching the taillights, still clutching the bucket of feed.

Callum broke the spell, skidding in beside his father to drop his bike at the gate. As Chris gathered up the last of their things, carried them into the cottage, Callum walked backward in front of him, just slow enough to be maddening. He wittered on about the big lady and the long-necked creatures and all that he had seen and done on his grand adventure. Chris ground his teeth, biting down the irritation that had been brewing all week.

The boy was still jabbering as Chris stood in the small kitchen, tore open a packet of sausages, poured himself a glass from the complimentary bottle of wine. Chris carried the wine, the meat and a handful of implements out, through the sliding doors of the bedroom, to the veranda. He let the hiss and spit of the griddle drown out the chatter from the bedroom. He watched oversized moths beat themselves against the doors, drank two glasses of the wine.

By the time the sausages were finally done, Callum was laid out on the bed, legs and arms outstretched. Fully clothed. Fast asleep.

—

That night Chris dreamt of Miriam for the first time since they saw her buried. She was paler than he remembered, and her hair was black and straight as a ribbon. But it was her just the same. He knew her by the ache in his chest, the sensation of falling, of descent without end.

She ran ahead of him through the darkness, her nightdress billowing. Through fields of tall grass wet from the rain, through a maze of black chambers inside the old barn. Then he lost her, and was lost himself, wading through black waters in an underground tunnel, through the smell of mold and stone and decay, calling her name into the dripping echoes. And all around, from within the walls, and behind and above, the grinding of colossal but invisible gears.

Chris woke in wetness, his hand cold on soaked bedsheets.

His first panicked thought was that Callum had a fever and had sweated the sheets through. Then he remembered the boy had fallen asleep fully clothed and hadn't put on his training pants.

He and Miriam had been so proud when Callum decided, quite by himself, to give up nappies at bedtime. The boy had been three at the time and they—younger, happier, oblivious of what lay ahead—saw in this decision more evidence of his inherent genius, another ray of glory from the wonder they'd created. The night of the funeral, Callum wet the bed for the first time in two years. He'd been unable to get to sleep on his own and had cried until Chris let him into bed. That morning, Chris had stripped the sheets, taken the mattress out onto the balcony to dry, performing the new tasks mechanically. Callum had been embarrassed, and his shame at this thing, so small in the light of everything else, was a weight that Chris carried still, that plummeted every time Chris saw in him all that was left in this world of *her*. Callum had slept in bed with him every night since the funeral; afraid, perhaps, that without this physical constant, he would wake one morning to find his father gone as well.

Chris rolled out of the bed, leaving Callum spread across the wet mattress like a starfish. The curtains were thin, barely holding back the cold morning light. Chris squinted as he pulled them apart, then yelled, swore, heart tumbling at the sight of two large eyes, just inches from his own.

"What is it, Dad?" Callum sat up, rubbing his face.

"Come and look," said Chris.

Outside the window, calmly ruminating, holding his gaze with indifference, was a huge caramel alpaca. Two more, dark brown, stooped behind it, bending to munch the grass around the cottage. He had forgotten to close the gate.

It was an ordeal, getting the alpacas out onto the driveway. They seemed quite content where they were, not a bit bothered by the man and boy at the window, entirely resistant to their claps, threats and cajolements. Father and son dressed quickly, stripped the bed, spilled into the cottage's small garden to oust the stubborn invaders. At last, after much fruitless pushing, Chris remembered the food they'd been given the night before. He sent Callum out beyond the gate, shaking the bucket and calling to them, while he drove from behind.

At last they got them through and closed the gate. Callum stood, laughing, completely surrounded, the alpacas peering down at him as he scooped handfuls of pellets from the bucket.

Chris's attention was drawn again to the looming barn. In the daylight it seemed even larger, even more out of place. It stood completely apart from the other farm buildings, twice or more the height of the wool shed, built of raw boards blackened with age. The barn seemed ancient, as though hewn from the landscape's earliest trees, a shelter for its first European settlers. But it was unlike anything Chris recognized from that era; in their long drives through rural towns and old farm country, they had passed nothing to match it, nothing with even the vaguest resemblance. The whole structure was surrounded by a fence of orange and white construction tape, giving it the appearance of a creature penned.

Echoes of the dream came back to him then—the distant whir of machinery and the grinding of hidden gears. And Miriam, at once close and impossibly far away. The darkness blooming and billowing and—

"Dad?"

Chris stopped, dazed. He had been walking away from Callum, toward the barn.

"Dad, I'm hungry."

"Right, let's . . ." It took Chris a moment to get his bearings. Callum had emptied the bucket of feed onto the ground and the alpacas were stooped around the pile. The boy stood beside them, holding the empty bucket. Chris rubbed his eyes, ran a hand down his face. "Let's get cleaned up and go for brekkie."

Callum gave him a strange look, one he found impossible to read. It gnawed at him as they closed the gate behind them and went back into the cottage to get ready. He gathered the bundled sheets, rinsed and wrung them, draped them, still dripping, over the fence. He pulled out the mattress and stood it on the deck—the familiar rhythms and routines, transposed to this unfamiliar setting. Once they were washed and dressed, he and Callum followed the driveway up to the farm.

As they passed the barn, Chris felt his head turning to keep it in sight. It really was exquisitely unusual. He longed to ignore the construction tape, push wide the rotting doors and cloak himself in the darkness and decrepitude that lay beyond. Callum pulled at his hand, urging him forward. The boy kicked at the gravel as they walked, head down.

"I hate this place," he said. "When are we going home?"

2

I do not remember my mother. Nor do I know the year in which I was born.

The passport I earned when I fled to this country tells me I came into this world on 14 March 1937. That was the day that Lotty and, later, Stephen would celebrate my birthday. Not that I ever cared much for it, the presents and the cake, the foolish song. The day meant more to them than it ever did to me. Perhaps because I knew it had no meaning: the date was plucked from the air, a fabrication necessary only to make concrete the identity I adopted when I became an Australian, the day Johannes Wolfgang Helmholtz became John William Hemming.

My stepfather told me I was born in Germany, though I have good reason to believe that my mother was from Poland. He told me many lies about my past, perhaps because he was afraid of how I would react were I to learn the truth, more likely because he was shaping me in the image of his belief, his idealistic longing for a new 'pure' Germany. And I, and all the other blond-haired, blue-eyed German children like me, were to be the vanguard of that new utopia. No matter where we were originally from.

I do not remember my mother, nor do I have any memory of my first two years of life. I say it is likely that she was from Poland, that I was born Polish, because my first memories are of the Kindererzie-hungslager, *the children's education camp where I and my fellow* Lebensborn *were taken for selection. I remember a tall, windowless building, made entirely of brick. I remember how the bricks weathered from red to ocher, to sooty black. I remember our 'mother,' the sour-faced matron who oversaw every detail of our lives at the camp. I remember the pride I felt when I was selected for the* erwünschter Bevölkerungszuwachs; *of course, I had no idea what the words meant, only that these children and I were the special ones, brothers and sisters smiled upon by Mother, the doctors, the SS officers. I remember my disdain—Imagine! The disdain of one so young!—for the* unerwünschter *children, those with the round heads, the degenerate skulls, the Gypsy characteristics.*

There is, somewhere, a photograph of us, the 'desired.' A grainy black-and-white image of fifteen or twenty little Aryans, stood erect before a mottled brick building. Mother stands in the open doorway with her hands behind her back, in the fashion of the SS officers who visited the camp. I am the youngest child, a plump-faced toddler in the arms of a tall girl with a tight plait curled round her shoulder. The faces in this picture are indistinct, white blobs with dots for eyes, dots for mouths. It is a picture not of children, but of an idea; an idea only half-formed.

I do not remember where I have seen this photograph. Perhaps it is a figment, a fantasy I saw once in a dream. Or perhaps I saw it here. In the old barn.

3

The trip had seemed such a good idea at the time. Summer holidays along the beaches of the South Coast had been their getaway since before Callum was born, but in the past six years it had become their *family* holiday. Crammed into a three-man tent in the narrow strip of grass between road and beach; the sticky dryness of salt-crusted hair; the tingling tautness of skin too long in too-hot sun; the inescapable presence of sand everywhere, in everything. Chris had wanted them to return to the simplicity of those times, to escape into them. He had imagined that, in going back to all those familiar places, repeating those patterns of experience that, in the past, had brought them so much happiness, they would again be happy. They would be able to forget, to move on.

But all they found were ghosts. *Her.* Everywhere. In everything.

Chris could see it in Callum's eyes, see Miriam reflected in them. In the tent, at the beach, staring into a box of hot chips. It was always with them—her absence. A silence so loud it enveloped everything. He wished the boy would open up about it, the feelings that had hollowed him out since Miriam died. But he seemed only to withdraw further into himself, into his private grief.

Chris brooded as he swung back the gate, and he and Callum entered the gardens of the farmhouse.

The old building was newly painted, a blue and white prefederation weatherboard, ringed by a low fence of scaffold piping and chain-link. A border collie lay on the deck with a forlorn expression, its head on its paws. There was a scratching at their approach and a chocolate-and-tan kelpie came into view, trotting up and down the deck and barking at the invaders.

They followed the fence round to a grassy clearing shaded by a grand, gnarled fig. There was a tire swing and some tables and chairs, white-painted wrought iron flecked with rust. Adjoining the farmhouse was a dilapidated tin shack oppressed by wisteria that clung to the roof and entirely dominated one side. A hand-painted sign, like the one out on the road, said simply "café."

Callum ran to the tree and clambered into the tire, begging Chris to be pushed. Chris ignored him, wanting to order breakfast, order coffee, before having to face another moment of the morning.

Inside, the café was clean and spacious, with sunlight streaming through glass panes in the ceiling. Light glanced off the chrome of a vintage espresso machine, behind which hung a shop sign painted in the old vaudeville style—*Madam & Eve: books & antiquities*, and a Newtown address. The room smelled faintly of good coffee and new-cut wood, of fresh paint and old books. The inside walls were decked with custom-made shelves, stacked to the ceiling with second-hand paperbacks.

Callum, having abandoned the swing and followed Chris inside, spotted something in the corner of the room and raced over to investigate. From the raking rattle that followed, Chris could tell he'd found a huge box of Lego. Chris paced aimlessly around the room, running a finger down the spines of thumb-worn murder mysteries and poetry collections, idly scrutinizing the canvasses of local artists.

"Chris, isn't it?"

He turned to see a compact, muscular woman in a farmhouse frock and apron. She had dark hair, plucked eyebrows, and a wide, easy smile that creased her cheeks and sparkled at the edges of her eyes. Something in that smile and the way she carried herself suggested that the frock, the apron, and her pinned-back hair were all props in a role she was playing. Or perhaps it was the tattoos that adorned both her arms, disappearing beneath her frock to emerge again on either side of her neck. Her gait and the prominent bulge at her front suggested that she was seven, maybe eight-months pregnant.

"Eve said she saw you last night. How's the cottage?"

"It's all been great, thanks. Perfect," Chris said and gestured at the sign. "And I suppose that makes you *Madam*?"

She laughed. "Paula will do. Why don't I get you started with some coffee while you work out what you're after."

"Thank you. Was it yours then? The shop I mean. I think I remember going there once or twice. What made you pack it in?"

Chris was cut short by the roar and hiss of grinding beans. The doser clicked, steam hissed and the air filled with the smell of fresh coffee.

"I'm a city girl," Paula said with a smile. "Born and bred. But Eve grew up out west. And, well, you can take the girl out of the country, but you can't . . . you get the picture. We started looking for homestead fixer-uppers around the same time we started talking about this little one." She patted her bump, poured milk into a metal jug.

"Well, your shop is missed. My wife always used to drag me in there after her, whenever we went out in Newtown. I remember how gutted she was to find out you'd closed down."

"Your wife is clearly a woman of good taste and discernment." Paula grinned, frothed the milk.

Chris's face darkened. "Was," he said. "She—"

Paula's smile collapsed into an expression of concern. "I'm sorry. How tactless of me. I should never have—"

"It's alright," said Chris. He turned to look at a triptych of black-and-white photographs on the wall beside the counter. "You couldn't have known."

He leaned in toward the photos, pretending to examine them minutely.

"So what's the plan with the old barn?" He asked over his shoulder, turning back as Paula coaxed milk froth from the jug.

"That old thing?" Her face crinkled like she'd smelled something bad. "It should be condemned. Hot chocolate for the boy?" She nodded toward Callum, still ensconced in the corner.

"Sure. He'd love that." Chris sipped at his coffee. "I thought you might be looking to renovate it. The tape . . ."

Paula squeezed chocolate syrup into a cup. "I've wanted it pulled down ever since we set up here, but Eve has a sort of obsession with it. Has some plan, apparently. Maybe one day she'll let me in on the secret."

She gestured with a raised eyebrow toward a glass jar half filled with pink and white marshmallows. Chris nodded.

"It seems so out of place," he said. "Something you might see in Eastern Europe or Germany. The Black Forest, maybe. But here . . . ?"

"You tell me," said Paula. "I haven't looked at it that closely—try to steer clear of it, myself. Only Eve's been inside, says it's gutted, structurally unsound. That's why we put up the tape."

Chris sagged, faint but distinct. Paula's expression changed.

"You were hoping to look around? Sorry to disappoint, Chris, but the whole thing could collapse any moment. And I'm going to crack a bottle of bubbly when it does. Did you want breakfast?"

She slid a menu over the counter and Chris ran his eyes over it. He was hungry, ready to order, but couldn't hold his attention on the words. He was thinking about the barn—knowing he couldn't explore it only stoked his curiosity. And aroused something else too, some deeper thing he did not yet understand.

"If you're up for a big feed, I can recommend the cooked brekkie. The bacon's from pigs up the road, the eggs are fresh this morning. And I make a mean sourdough."

Chris blinked, looked up at Paula, for a moment uncertain where he was. "That sounds great. Two of those."

Paula smiled. "Coming up," she said, and started toward the back of the room, the door to the farmhouse.

"Before you go," said Chris, an idea, half-formed, compelling him to speak. "Do you have any bookings in the cottage tonight?"

"No, we're all clear for tonight if you wanted to stay on. Some nice walks start just beyond the fence, and the pub in town is good for a feed. Want me to put you down for it?"

Chris thought for a moment of Callum, of the dislike the boy felt for this place, what he had said as they walked up to the café.

"Yes," he said. "Please. That would be perfect."

—

Callum was not happy they were staying. He whined all along the path back from the café, yelled and stamped when they got inside the cottage, threw Chris's wallet and keys round the bedroom. Now he was curled on the couch with the iPad, rubbing his arm where Chris had held it too tightly. His eyes were ringed with red, his cheeks and forehead blotchy from the tantrum.

Chris made tea and took it out onto the back deck, carrying the bound booklet of farm-stay information and local business leaflets he'd found on the mantelpiece. He pretended to look over them, but could not really concentrate. He stared at glossy brochures, at photocopied menus, quietly seething.

The sun had fully risen, melting away the chill of morning. It looked like it might turn into a scorcher. But as Chris sat on the shapeless outdoor couch, sipping tea, flicking without interest through the pages of the booklet, scudding clouds merged and blanketed the sky.

The farm was set on a sloping ridge that curved down toward unseen gullies. All around, hilltops arched like the backs of sleeping beasts, furred with pale green and sandy-brown. Far away, the sleepy drone of a tractor, the distant excitement of a work dog. From where he sat, Chris could not see the barn, but was aware of it behind him, like a shadow falling across the cottage.

He drained the tea, stepped back inside. "Come on," he said. "We're going for a walk."

Callum did not respond, just tapped and fingered the iPad screen, absorbed in some game.

"I'm talking to you, Callum."

"I don't want to go for a walk," he said without looking up.

"Well, we're not going to lie around here all day. You need some exercise."

Callum poked at the screen, lips tight. Chris grabbed the iPad, ripped it out of his hands.

"Get dressed," he said. "We're going for a walk."

Callum glared at his father, eyes ablaze, jaw locked with a rage too great to express. Chris threw clothes onto the couch beside him.

—

They crossed the paddock to the fenceline, wading through the uncut grass, past the pond, the ducks, the geese, down toward the skeleton of a gargantuan eucalypt around which the alpacas were stooped.

Callum dragged behind his father, head sunk, hands in pockets. The alpacas had lost their magic apparently, for he shambled right past them without raising his head. His excitement reappeared at once on discovering the mountain of deadwood beneath the ancient tree's graying husk, inviting him to climb up and about it.

Chris made him get down, told him it was a breeding ground for snakes and spiders. Which it was, but really he just wanted to start the walk, had no patience for Callum's dawdling.

They clambered over a stile, followed a sheep trail down into the gully. The half-path led to a dry creek, then up to another stile and a barbed-wire fence tangled with blackberries. Chris picked a handful, offered them to Callum, but he shook his head, climbed over the stile without looking up.

Following the creek round and down into the next field, they startled a mob of kangaroos that lounged in the shade. The roos gazed warily in their direction before rising, one by one, and loping off into the trees.

"See," said Chris, gesturing after them. "This is fun. Look what we just saw."

"I hate the bush," said Callum.

They stopped for a break at a sharp bend in the creek, ate an apple and some cheese. Chris tried to stay cheerful, to lighten the mood that had clung to them all morning like a shadow. But Callum was a black hole, still doggedly refusing to connect. He sat at the edge of the path, dropped crumbs of cheese for the streaming ants. He pretended to give this all of his attention, pretended that Chris was not there at all.

"We'd better get going," said Chris.

"I'm tired," said Callum. "I don't want to walk."

"So, what? You're just going to sit there?"

"I told you I didn't want to come."

"Come on," Chris stood. "Get up. Once you start moving you won't even—"

"You're not listening to me," said Callum, and he turned and locked eyes with his father. "You're not *listening*."

Later, Chris would see that look for what it was, a hurt young boy talking about something other, something bigger than a stupid bushwalk. But, in that moment, his vision was clouded. All he saw was the confrontation, a disobedient little brat yet again opposing his will. All he heard was the sound in his head, like the grinding of vast but distant gears.

"Get up," he snapped. "Get on your feet and stop whining. It's pathetic. I'm sick of it, Callum."

Callum didn't say anything. Just stared down at the dirt, the ants. His jaw was set, askew. He was grinding his teeth.

Chris stepped forward and grabbed his arm, but the boy wrenched himself back and away, eyes bright with an emotion Chris mistook for defiance.

They stood as though frozen, eyes locked. Callum, poised like he was ready to run. Chris, stooped, towering over him. Each held the other's stare, neither willing to back down.

Chris laughed—a gesture intended to break the tension. It came out as a snort, his face twisted with contempt.

"Fine," he said. "Fine. Fuck you. Just stay here by yourself and rot."

Chris turned and stormed ahead, leaving Callum crouched at the path's edge, alone.

Chris heard his tears even before he rounded the bend in the creek.

—

The anger faded quickly, but he did not turn back. Chris must have walked at least a mile before it registered what he was doing, what he had done.

Through a graveyard of gray eucalyptus boughs, across the creek again and up into an orchard of knotted apple trees. Ahead of him was a paddock, marked out by barbed wire and bushwood fenceposts, where sheep were grazing. Their complaints hung in the air and Chris heard, too, the bark of a dog and whistles, gruff instructions. Though he could not see her, Eve must be somewhere in the field.

Embarrassment stopped him there, in the orchard, among the white nets and the distant groans of livestock. He couldn't bear to walk across that paddock, past the sheep and the dog. Past Eve. He couldn't bear for her to say, "Where's your boy?" or worse, "I've seen your boy."

Chris's throat tightened, stomach knotted. He felt he might be sick. What was he *doing*?

Chris began to run, back through the orchard, down toward the creek. Callum's face haunted him—that look. Callum had needed him, and Chris . . . What had he done? He couldn't even remember what had made him so angry. Only that look on Callum's face, that expression of distrust and betrayal and—

And fear.

Chris's heart writhed and wrung in his chest—an anguish that even the burn of his sprint couldn't reach. What had been done could not be undone.

Above, the clouds were roiling. He could smell rain, felt the chill on his skin, even as he ran, burning. Back through the deadwood graveyard, round the bend in the creek, back to where—

But Callum was not where Chris had left him.

Chris tried to think, but his thoughts were scattered, tripping over one another. He tried to calm himself, but his heart was pounding from the run, breath coming in gasps.

Maybe he'd gone back to the cottage. That would be the sensible thing. Chris should go and check and . . . But the rain was coming. If he got back to the cottage and Callum *wasn't* there, then . . .

Chris was too panicked to think clearly, too afraid to be decisive. Callum could be anywhere.

Chris shouted his son's name, hands on either side of his mouth like a bullhorn. His voice echoed flatly around the gully, the low, heavy clouds muffling the sound. The trees across the creek began to rustle and bend, the dry leaves chattering like voices. The wind was picking up.

Something pulled at his heart, some heavy black thing that crushed and squeezed. "Callum," he yelled. "Callum! Callum!"

The wind paused and the rustling died for just a moment, just long enough for smaller sounds to reach him. A sob. He strained to listen but the wind picked right back up again and all he could hear was the white noise from the trees, from the long grasses alongside the path.

Chris turned round and around, scanning the path, the creek-bed, the scattered trees on this side of the gully, some of them blackened with fire damage. One of these had been hollowed out by the flames, a twisting husk of charcoal and dead wood. Huddled against the back of this gnarled shelter, his head against the black wall, arms hugging his knees, Callum shivered, his face splotched and eyes ringed with red.

He startled when he saw his father, but did not move. Just looked at him with raw eyes, as if waiting to see what Chris would do. Waiting to see who he would *be*.

"Callum," said Chris, crouching down to meet eyes. "Callum, I'm so sorry."

Chris held out a hand and Callum sprang forward, wrapped his arms and legs about his father so tight Chris was almost winded. Callum's breath was hot on his neck. Tears and snot mingled on his collar.

Chris held him like that, the boy's small body shuddering against him, even as the first rain began to drum against the creek bed and the path.

"Don't leave me, Daddy," Callum said into his father's neck again and again. "Don't *ever* leave."

4

Paula was woken by a distant crack that reverberated across the valley. The crack was followed by the sharp ping of raindrops on the tin roof of the farmhouse; first one, then a second, then a brief tattoo. Then the deluge as the skies above the farm opened and water striking the roof drowned all other sound.

She had fallen asleep on the couch with Gypsy Rose curled beside her, sprawled across her legs. The black-and-white border collie sat up and sniffed the air, whined, rested her head back down on Paula's calf.

Paula gasped as the baby shifted, pushing some sharp and knobbly part of itself hard against her pelvis. Gypsy Rose tilted her head, looked at Paula with a concerned expression.

"I'm alright, girl," said Paula, scratching the dog behind the ear. "It's just his nibs here, throwing his weight around."

She pushed herself upright, brought her feet down to the floor, rested that way a moment to let her body settle. The old house creaked and complained at the drop in temperature. It had been sunny and bright when she lay down on the couch, but now the lounge was heavy with shadow. Paula hated falling asleep in the day. It left her feeling dull and groggy and hungover, worse even than the feeling of constant exhaustion. Now the baby was so big, she couldn't get comfortable at nights. Just lay there, hot and fussing, with restless legs and everything aching. If she slept at all it never felt like it. Then every day up and straight to work, feeding chooks, collecting eggs, cooking, cleaning, pottering in the kitchen. With the pregnancy moving into its final stages, the romance of life on the farm was losing its sheen.

She stood and arched her back, waddled, hands cradling her belly, up to the window. Gypsy Rose hopped down from the couch and padded over beside her. The downpour and the grisly lid of clouds had sucked all color from the landscape—from the rolling hills, the hidden valleys, the line of poplars that marked the boundary of their property where it met the road. The farmyard itself looked bleak. Eve was out somewhere with the sheep and the pens had an abandoned look. The dark lump of the barn was like some hideous charred *thing*, a disfigurement that drew the eye, drew the light and energy from all around into itself. Beside it, the shearers' cottage looked cowed, a defenseless animal cowering beneath its predator.

From the edge of her vision, Paula caught a movement, two figures sprinting across the open field from the gully and the stile. A man and a boy, arms over their heads to protect them from the pelting rain. *Chris*, she thought. *His name was Chris*. And the boy? The cottage looked dark and cold. An uninviting place to return to for someone soaked to the bone. She wondered if she should grab the umbrella, head down there to see if they needed anything. Perhaps she could light the fire for them, make them some tea. No. That would be too much. They'd be alright, would work it out for themselves. Besides, there was work to be done here—always. And she wanted to be around when Eve returned.

In the kitchen, the cups and plates from their guests' breakfast were still heaped by the sink from the morning. Paula ran the water till it steamed, put in the plug and a squirt of washing-up liquid, pulled on a pair of pink rubber gloves. She would have laughed, as she had in the past, imagining what she must look like. Only now it was too depressing. Somehow she had become a housewife, utterly conventional—those rubber gloves were the final nail in the coffin.

Paula had always believed that the life she'd been born into, the lifestyle she had chosen, somehow transcended gender roles. She loathed the constraint of definition, refused to identify as this or that, would be and be with whoever she wanted. She loved her own parents, of course, but abhorred all they represented: the relentless homogenous everyday of the nuclear family. The path through her twenties had been a zigzag away from that bland constant, always in search of the edge, those experiences, people and sub-sub-cultures that would mark her forever—gleefully—an outsider. And perhaps it was this willful mutability—as well as a certain nagging biological imperative—that compelled her toward motherhood in her late thirties. She could never have guessed that, from the moment the fertilized egg began to grow inside her, she and Eve would become more and more—*normal*. She, the stay-at-home mum. Eve, the breadwinner, out at work from morn to midnight. Instead of bringing them closer, it had driven a wedge between them.

And there was something else, too. Some pressure building inside Eve that she refused to release, refused even to acknowledge.

Paula had thought they were past all that, that they had left the long shadow of Eve's 'episodes' behind them when they moved from the city. Hadn't that been the rationale for the move in the first place? After that night, closing down the shop, climbing the stairs to their apartment to find steam illuminating a shaft of light from the bathroom. The roar of the hot tap, the flooded tile floor, the dark wetness spreading across the carpet in the lounge. Paula found the dogs whimpering and pawing at the closed bedroom door, and Eve, naked and blank on the other side, just—staring. Staring. Responding to nothing. Neither words, nor touch, nor Paula's desperate embrace. Hadn't they chosen, with Eve in recovery from that latest and most terrible of her depressions, to leave the darkness in the past and scratch both of their midlife itches—to return to the country and bring a baby into the world?

And the move to the farm had transformed Eve. Paula had never seen her so . . . *herself.* She was liberated by toil, by dirt and animals, by the endless project of restoring the homestead. And if Paula caught her now and then staring out into the farmyard, eyes held by the lumpen sore of the old barn, there was no need for alarm. She was . . . planning. Daydreaming the transformation of the property that was her sole preoccupation.

But something changed when they at last became pregnant. The tiny, unborn boy had literally come between them, keeping them apart in the old iron bedstead they'd painstakingly restored. Paula couldn't tell if it was a hunger to do right by her family, or a desire to flee it, that kept Eve away from the farmhouse for so many hours in the day—and often, too, at night. Eve seemed almost afraid of the baby, as though she saw in Paula's belly something beyond the bump, some old film that played and replayed, twisting the reality of the present, sending her spiraling. Paula knew that Eve had lost a baby brother when she was a child, that she'd blamed herself for his death. Could it be that? The old ghost resurfacing as the pregnancy came to term. Or perhaps there was grief, jealousy, even resentment, that it was Paula and not *her* carrying the child? Perhaps it was the simple fact that they would soon be introducing into their home a human male. Eve had always nurtured a fear that Paula would leave her for another woman, or worse, a man. Perhaps . . . ?

Perhaps if Eve ever opened up. Ever told her *anything*—

Heavy footsteps thumped up onto the deck, stamped on the mat outside. Paula peeled off the rubber gloves and opened the door to the hall, where Gypsy Rose was already waiting, poised to greet her other master. Eve towered in the doorway, her broad shoulders almost as wide as the lintel. Her Akubra hat was a shapeless sodden mass. Water poured from her Drizabone and pooled on the floor. Her expression was blank, eyes distant. In her right hand she clutched a dull metal tube.

Paula approached as though everything was normal, as though her skin weren't prickling in alarm. She reached up and laid a hand on Eve's chest, on the cold oilskin. Eve looked ahead, as though Paula were not there.

"Where's Zorita?" Paula asked, noting the kelpie's absence.

Eve turned her eyes down to Paula, as though drawing back from the horizon. "With the sheep."

"Is she—"

"She's fine. Busy. She'll be down soon, I'm sure."

Paula reached for Eve's hand, flinched at the cold touch of metal.

"Eve, why—what's with the bolt gun?"

Eve's eyes scanned Paula's face. Something flickered in the look, something that made Paula flinch. Was it suspicion? Contempt?

"Sick sheep," said Eve, and pushed past her into the hall.

5

Like many of my "desired" brothers and sisters, I was adopted by the family of an SS officer, took his name, became his son.

I learned later that the other Lebensborn fared poorly in their new families; those who went back to Germany were never allowed to forget their Polish origins, or that they might be "SS bastards." But I was lucky. My adopted father was an ambitious young officer, stationed with SS-Sturmbannführer Wirth at the new processing camp at Belzec. It was outside the camp, in a pristine, whitewashed villa surrounded by the Polish countryside, that I spent the first years of my memory.

Those years at Belzec were like a dream, a fairy tale, filled in equal measure with wonder and with horror. My stepsister and I were cared for by a huge, bustling Polish woman, who we called Teddy Bear, Miś; although only when our parents were not in earshot. Miś had thick, dark hair and kindly eyes, and always snuck us treats from the kitchen, or sang to us when we were hurt or woke crying in the night from some bad dream. Those songs still haunt me, Polish lullabies with lugubrious melodies and words that, while I was too young to understand them, seemed always to drip with melancholy. And her voice, so rich and deep and filled with a sadness beyond the reach of healing.

My stepmother was a vain woman, with a mean mouth and a reek of perfume and cigarette smoke. She had little love for my stepsister, and even less for me, resenting me perhaps for the biology we did not share, or the regard in which my stepfather held me. She spent her days sulking in her bedroom, or smoking cigarette after cigarette on the balcony, sneering at the golden fields. Like a vampire, she lived for night, for the extravagant dinner parties she held for the officers from the camp and visiting SS dignitaries. My sister and I were never present at these events, of course, but we heard them; the ribald shouts, the music and coarse laughter often kept us awake long into the night. We knew also to avoid our mother in the day-time—particularly the days after—when her usual irritation toward us inflated into a kind of hostile disgust.

My stepfather was a sadist, a man of such ruthlessness and cruelty I can hardly give credence to my own memory. But, unlike my step-mother, he was also a passionate man, a man driven by the vision of a new Germany. While my stepmother's racism was innate, an outward expression of the hatred she felt toward all 'lower' forms of humanity, for my stepfather it was a science, and his work for Wirth at Belzec was the cutting edge of a new technology that would see Germany back in its rightful position as leader of the modern world. I have said before that he was an idealist, and perhaps it was this that shaped his relationship with us, his children. Certainly, he was always kind to us, and to me in particular, perhaps seeing in us the potential of his dream future. No matter the scorn heaped on me by my stepmother, SS-Hauptsturmführer Helmholtz never once treated me as anything less than his son, and for that I will be forever grateful, in spite of all that was to follow.

Perhaps it was his longing for an heir to his bold utopian dream that encouraged him to bring me into the camp, to bear witness to the fine work in which he was engaged. My memories of that day are conflicted. The man who writes these words cannot hide from view the sorry passengers that disembarked the train; a train built not for humans, but for cattle. The weeping and the wailing of the naked creatures driven from the makeshift platform toward the shower block, a dirty brick building snaking with pipes, their purpose and destination unclear. The Ukrainians sent into the train, to 'bring out the trash' as Unterscharführer Hackenholt jokingly referred to the heaped bodies of those who had not survived the journey.

These are sights that, once seen, cannot be unseen. Yet, my clearest memory of that day is not of these things. It is of the excitement I felt at being invited into my father's inner sanctum, the pride in his voice as he introduced me to Herr Wirth and the other officers at the *camp, the feel of his great hand around my small hand. It is to know that I had a father, and, on that day at least, my father loved me.*

I have not thought about those days for many years. When, from the deck of that bustling ocean liner, I caught my first glimpse of Sydney harbor; before I stepped down from the gangplank, touched my young feet on that new land; before I became John Hemming, leaving Johannes Helmholtz forever behind; I vowed that the days of my youth should never have been.

Yet no memory is ever completely lost. The storehouse of our minds is a living thing, bottomless and blind. Though we may hope to forget forever our most shameful secrets, though we may veil with mists and drape with cobwebs the unpleasant truths of our childhood, though we hide the horrors of our past in our deepest, darkest corners, nothing is ever truly lost.

And the vastness of that gulf between our private shame and the face we show the world is the measure of our sorrow.

6

"Dad? Dad? What're we doing for dinner?"

Chris was staring out the window, the glass streaked and spotted with droplets. The rain had calmed, but the wind had picked up and the orange and white tape around the barn flapped wildly. The sky was a curdled gray of post-storm clouds and impending dusk beneath which the old building seemed to throb, sucking the last light of the day into its blackened walls. Chris's tea had gone cold.

The fire, too, was dead in the grate. When, earlier, they had burst into the cottage, drenched and dripping, shedding their sodden clothes in the bathroom and drawing a steaming bath, Callum had asked if they could light the fire. The *no* had risen instinctively to Chris's throat, but he swallowed it, eager for any sop to appease the boy. He had been, and he remained, horrified by what he had said and done—the harshness of his words, the wound he had inflicted by abandoning Callum on the path. He was not . . . *himself.* As he showed his son how to scrunch up the newspaper, how to stack the kindling, he was relieved to see on the child's face not the grief and terror of the afternoon, but curiosity and excitement. Chris let Callum strike the match, let him rest it against the edge of the newspaper until the flame began to flicker and rise. And there they had both knelt, watching the wood catch, and heat and light bloom in the firebox.

After the bath, Chris had wrapped Callum in a blanket, set him up on the couch with a movie. Now credits music blared from the iPad, wedged into the corner of the couch where Callum had tossed it. He was half out of his cocoon, poised for action, for some decisive move from his father toward their evening meal.

"We're going out, that's what," said Chris. "And no restrictions. Tonight you can have whatever you want."

"Ice cream?"

"You can have ice cream."

"*Only* ice cream?"

"You can't have only ice cream."

The "pub in town" that Paula recommended turned out to be a forty-minute drive away. Even though it was against the law, Chris let Callum ride in the front passenger seat; they didn't see another car the whole way there, let alone the police, and Chris wanted to treat Callum in every way he could. He didn't know how else to show how sorry he was for his part in their fight that afternoon.

Callum seemed to have forgotten it already. He was so excited to be up in front, kept twisting round in his seat until his legs were under him and he could press his face to the passenger window and see the darkening world pass by. He jibbered and jabbered all the way to the pub, a cut-up monologue part comprised of things he saw as they drove, part made up of bits of the film he'd watched that afternoon, the incomprehensible actions of nameless characters, snips of dialogue free of context.

But Chris had not forgotten.

Whenever he thought back on the afternoon, his stomach churned and his heart throbbed like it was infected. He just couldn't imagine himself *saying* anything like that. Though he replayed the scene over and over in his mind, he could not understand what had made him so angry. What had come over him?

When at last they pulled up outside the country hotel, Chris was just about ready to give Callum anything he asked for. Three courses of ice cream. Anything. If it would only heal the fresh scars Chris imagined on that already troubled soul.

It was bright inside the hotel, in the way of country pubs, but there was a fire in the family room and it was still too early for whatever might pass for a Saturday night crowd. Chris and Callum sat by the fire playing snakes and ladders until the food came. Callum ordered the kid's chicken nuggets with chips and no salad. Chris had the porterhouse, done medium, and two bottles of the closest thing they had to craft beer. The kid's meal came with an ice cream sundae—two huge scoops of supermarket vanilla, lathered in a choice of bright red or shiny brown goop. Callum had squirts of both; and, because he'd flirted with the young woman that brought out their meals, she covered the sundae with mini marshmallows. Chris rolled his eyes but buttoned his lip. *Anything*, he'd told him.

"You staying down at Eve's place?" the barman asked when Chris got up to pay. He looked about Chris's age, but twice the size. A burly man squeezed into a clean check shirt, tucked into worn blue jeans.

"That's right," said Chris. "Paula told me to come out here. The food was everything she said it would be."

The barman's pleasure showed with the slight nod, the vague curl of his lip.

"Been a long time since I've been down on that old farm," he said.

"You knew the previous owner?" Chris asked.

He took Chris's card, punched numbers into the card reader. It was a wireless unit and he held it up toward the ceiling, waved it from side to side as though to catch some faint waft of signal.

"That's some sad shit right there," he said. "I didn't know the old man, Hemming, but I knew his boy. Me and my little brother used to go dirt-biking with Stevie . . ."

He squinted at the machine, held it out beside him. At last the connection was made and the receipt began to print.

"Don't see him so much these days. He moved to Sydney for uni and never came back, except to visit his old man. And to fix up the estate. You want a copy?"

Chris shook his head, took back the card.

"What's your interest?"

"Just curious. Staying at the farm . . ."

"Those lezzers have really turned the place around. From what I heard, the farm went pretty much to shit after Stevie's mum passed. Stevie didn't like coming back. The old man went kind of loopy out there on his own. Livestock died. Sad shit."

Chris didn't know what to say, so just nodded, standing there still holding his card, afraid to move a muscle in case he broke the moment.

"The old man had been dead a good year when Stevie found him." At this, the barman leaned in toward Chris, glanced over his shoulder at Callum down by the fire, petting the dog. "Hanged himself in the barn. He was dry as a strip of biltong when Stevie cut him down."

The barman shook his head. "Sad shit."

———

The drive back was longer and more perilous than Chris remembered. In the dark, without borders, without painted lines, the road seemed hardly there, a dream to which he madly clung, revealed only in the sweep of the high beams.

Callum was asleep long before the car bumped over the cattle grid and onto the farm. But the drive had woken Chris, made him tense. He was glad of the bottle of red he'd picked up before leaving the hotel.

He carried the sleeping boy into the cottage, wrestled him out of his pants and into a night nappy, tucked him up in the newly made bed. Then he went through to the living room and stoked the fire, cracked the bottle of wine. He sat by the window, poured himself a glass. He couldn't see the barn, but it was there, a patch of darkness deeper than the blue-black surrounding it.

Chris must have fallen asleep where he sat, for he dreamed again of the barn. He heard Miriam calling, but could not see her, just her shadow stretched across the gravel outside in the full moonlight.

In the dream, he crossed the drive in bare feet, chasing the shadow and the voice that called him. He peeled back strips of construction tape, scrambled over heaps of rubble and brick to reach the looming void of the barn's double doors. Silver light caught in the boards above and he saw the inscription: *NIECH SIĘ SKOŃCZY TO ROJENIE.* The words resonated, though they made no sense as he read them.

Miriam's voice echoed from somewhere inside. Chris lifted the rotten beam that held fast the doors, let it drop against the heaped debris. He pulled and the doors swung back soundlessly, making a space just wide enough to squeeze through.

Inside, all was dark. A deep, boundless dark that felt like falling.

Only his hand on the splintered wood of the door kept Chris from losing his footing and slipping into unfathomable depths.

From somewhere within, Miriam laughed. A sound like water, like the tinkling of sweet bells.

"Miriam," he called into the shadows. "Miriam, where are you?"

His voice sounded flat and hollow, instantly absorbed within the unseen architecture of the barn.

As his eyes grew accustomed to the gloom, he saw ahead the outline of a doorway and, beyond, a faint, pulsating glow, a pinkish luminescence that throbbed like the beating of a heart. There was a sound as of huge machines, a wheezing exhalation like industrial bellows, distant clangs of metal against metal, and the click and grind of enormous gears.

Chris stepped toward the faint light with arms outstretched, sliding his feet forward in an awkward shuffle, afraid he might trip or whack a shin.

"Miriam," he called again. "Miriam, wait for me. I'm coming. I'm coming as fast as I can."

Chris's foot caught on something and he fell headlong into the darkness. He expected the dark floor to be littered with rubble, rotten beams, bits of debris from the collapsing roof. But whatever his foot had caught on had been . . . soft, squishy almost, had collapsed repulsively as he tripped.

He yelped and scrambled away, heart pounding.

Somehow, in among the distant industrial clangor he heard the patter of footsteps, somewhere around and ahead. Soft steps like bare feet. Someone calling his name, singing almost. Was it Miriam? Or the voice of a child?

He pulled himself to his feet and stumbled toward the sound, toward the ghastly light that pulsed beyond the doorway.

On the other side of the door was a vast room, illuminated faintly by that amorphous pink glow. The space was like an abandoned school shower room, though tileless and long, its ends consumed by shadow. The entire room was skinned in rough concrete, crisscrossed with pipes that snaked just below the ceiling. The cement had crumbled in places to reveal bare brick, and in the cracks and hollows bloomed some hideous colorless mold, black in the florid half-light. The walls were streaked with what looked like phosphorescent paint, huge pink characters like words in an alien language, or gibberish. They pulsed softly, throbbing in time to a rhythmic drone, fleshy and dull. The light they gave off was eerie, like a gas seeping out from the walls and into that huge dark space. Chris felt grit and brick shards bite into the soles of his feet.

As he called again and again for Miriam, his voice echoed off the concrete. He felt very small, very alone in that dim expanse. He heard his name again, but this time from behind.

He turned, peered toward the far end of the room, where the flaking mottled walls dissolved into shadow, where unidentifiable black sludge pooled on the grimy floor. The voice diminished, reverberating, as though Miriam were vanishing down an unseen drainpipe in the chamber's darkest corner.

He shuffled toward it, straining to make out the receding voice from the throb of pink noise that devoured all other sound.

Gravel crunched to his right, impossibly loud and present. It was right there and yet . . . Chris turned, tripped, fell past the floor and into fathomless dark.

He awoke with a lurch. But he was not at the table, not in the bed. He was standing, awake in the dark, with the feel of cold dust and splinters beneath his bare feet.

He was inside the old barn.

7

I had nothing when I first stepped down onto the shores of my new homeland. All I have now I earned from the sweat of my brow and a survivor's instinct for opportunity, never shirking from labor. I worked to eat, to make something of myself—a new life unencumbered by the shame of my past. I worked to forget.

Love, too, worked its magic on me. Forged, on the surface at least, a new man from the pig iron of my youth. Life with Lotty was like a dream, radiant with simple happiness. We bought the rundown old farmstead when we learned that we were to have a baby, that we were becoming a family. Those first years on the farm together were a paradise of toil and simple pleasure, building a life out of nothing, building a whole world.

In all those years, the barn was to me just another of the many tasks I must one day perform in the unceasing maintenance of the farm. It was an eyesore, its beams rotted, its boards weathered and unkempt. It served no purpose, too unstable to store anything of value. Lotty detested it, pestered me to get rid of it. I would tear it down, I swore—one day, soon. But I put it off and off, always with more pressing demands on my time. And that day never came.

It was not until many years—decades—later that I grew to understand. By then, Stephen had left to start a life of his own, Lotty had passed from her second stroke. I was alone.

Then the singing began. And I grew afraid of that dark structure.

I shunned it by day, giving it the same wide berth as the animals. At night I turned my back on it, pulled down the blinds, stoked the fire, played music, read, anything to distract me from that heavy blankness, that blot of black upon the land I otherwise knew so well. Each day I vowed that the next day I would, at last, have it removed. But each new day brought distractions, more reasons to skirt around the monstrous old building, rather than confront its purpose. And what it contained.

One night I woke inside it. Woke in the arms of Miś. I was rocked, lulled by the melodies of her sorrowful voice.

Had I been dreaming? I know only that I ran screaming from that barn as though from the devil herself.

But I could not escape her thrall. Each night I dreamt of that old barn, each night of Miś. And her song became a labyrinth in which I was lost, a subterranean maze from which exit was impossible, whose solution was eternity. Each night I awoke in the dark of the old barn. Each night Miś cradled me in her arms.

How long had she been there? I cannot say. Perhaps Miś had always dwelled there, in the shadows of the old barn, wreathed in cobweb, spangled with dust. Perhaps she had always sung to me, from deep inside that old wooden hulk, her voice reaching me in the depths of my dreams. But as long as Lotty was alive, as long as Stephen kept me company, those songs were drowned in the noise of the living. Perhaps it was only in the quiet of my solitude, the silence of old age and neglect, that those sorrowful songs made themselves known to me, plucked at my heart with their dolorous melodies.

It is her song, I know, that urged me to write these lines, to commit to paper these words. My confession. My shame.

At first, I hoped that this would be enough. That the simple act of writing would be a release from those events of so long ago that have haunted me my whole life; no matter how hard I tried to push them down, no matter how deeply I tried to bury them.

But it was only the beginning. Miś told me herself.

I was afraid, and yet . . . And yet I was—I am searching, here, for the word—compelled. In the days, I ached for her, longed to be near to her. Something was emerging from within, some Miś that was no longer the woman I had known, nor the woman I had, in the short-sighted selfishness of my childhood, betrayed. But some eternal Miś, some goddess from beyond who was growing inside of me, inside the barn. I was weakening, I knew this. I was not eating, barely slept, spent every moment inside the labyrinths of that ancient and inestimable construction—or dwelling on them, seated on the deck staring out across the farmyard, down toward the intolerable architecture of that barn that was no barn, that was no building at all.

It sickens me to behold it. And yet, I am compelled. I cannot keep away. For, inside, Miś holds me in her arms and sustains me with her black milk, nurtures my unbounded guilt. Within the storehouse I am eternally unforgiven, suckled at her devil breast, consumed by my own shame. And, while I am thus devoured, she lulls me with her voice.

The song she sings is the music of the spheres. But the spheres are malformed, chaotic centers of foulness and deformity that hurtle through space toward nothing, away from nothing. And the music is not music at all, but a cacophony of need, a hunger that can never be sated, a thirst that can never be quenched. It is a song of sadness, for her universe is infinite and without purpose or mercy and cares not for the purposelessness of one life or another. Cares not that my guilt will not ever be assuaged.

I cannot even long for death, for, having seen the cold blackness of the beyond, I know that will be no escape. Instead I long only that the dreams may end, that all vision, all feeling, be stifled in that eternal vacuum.

This, my most earnest desire, repeats itself without cease in a tongue I never knew to call my own.

Niech się skończy to rojenie. Niech się skończy to rojenie.

Let this dream end.

8

Eve did not come to bed.

Paula lay for many hours in the dark of their bedroom, hot and uncomfortable, a pillow wedged between her legs. The farmhouse settled and resettled itself as a light wind agitated the tin roof and the windows in their frames. The old floorboards ruminated sullenly. Straining to listen, Paula reached out into the old house with her attention, searching for Eve, willing her to come, to lay down, to hold her. For all to be forgiven.

But Eve was still brooding in some far corner of the house and did not make a sound.

This silence was worst of all. That Eve should be physically present, somewhere in their home, and yet absent, so far away that Paula could not reach her, was unbearable. Ominous. A sick sense of dread battled with the ache in Paula's lower back. She longed for sleep, but her physical discomfort, the movements of the baby and her churning thoughts left her wired. She longed to simply get up and go to Eve, to wrap her arms around her, to heal everything with the oblivion of physical contact. But she did not dare. Their fight from that afternoon still resounded between them, like the hum of a bell long after it is struck.

Was it her fault? Certainly she blamed herself. She had been fussing, disturbed by the sight of Eve dripping in the hallway, by her coldness and distance. She had drawn a bath for Eve, mopped up the water by the front door. She tried to help Eve undress, but Eve shrugged her off, pushed her away. The look she gave Paula still burned. Paula had only been trying to help, masking her awkwardness and anxiety with action, the need to do *something*. But Eve seemed to interpret her every move as a sign of—what? Of guilt? She oozed paranoia. The things she said to Paula made no sense.

Paula remembered none of the words. Only the tone. Venomous and cold, filled with hate. Paula had wept in confusion. Eve had sneeringly accused her of manipulation, of *control*. It was madness.

Who knew how much further it might have gone if not for Zorita. The kelpie had returned, pawed, whining, at the glass of the front door. She was soaked to the bone and had gotten into something. There was blood all round her mouth. Eve's sick sheep, no doubt.

Paula had pushed down her grief and distress, fetched a worn old beach towel, rubbed the dog down. Eve locked herself in the bathroom and remained there so long that Paula began to fear the worst. All the while Zorita paced, peering out into the dark beyond the front door, then through the house again to peer out the back, watching for intruders, unable to shake herself and relax. From her bed beside the fireplace, Gypsy Rose observed the restless movements of her companion, her head turning this way and that as she tracked the kelpie with her eyes. When, at last, the lock on the bathroom door clicked and Eve emerged, Zorita followed at her heel. Eve shut herself in the spare room they used as a walk-in wardrobe, leaving the dog on the outside.

Lying awake, Paula played and replayed the scenes from that afternoon, struggling to make sense of it. Eve was not herself. It was as though she had become poisoned against Paula, as though someone had been whispering lies, filling Eve's mind with doubts and deceit. Paula found herself caught between her longing for Eve to be alright, to be here, with her now, with everything forgiven, and her very real fear both for and *of* the Eve that now brooded somewhere in the midnight house.

A chair creaked in the living room. Floorboards protested in sync with socked footfalls. A heavy clunk, as Eve put on first one boot, then another. The front door opened and closed and the deck shook as Eve tramped down the steps and away.

With a groan, Paula pressed herself upright. The baby chose that moment to stretch inside her, pushing hard against her already compressed organs. She sat on the edge of the bed for what seemed a long time, trying to control her breathing, willing the intense discomfort to subside. When at last the movements eased, she rolled forward and stood. Her lower back was stiff as a board and protested this new and unwelcome activity. She unhooked her dressing gown from the door and tugged it on over her nighty. Moonlight pooled in the hallway. Paula slipped her bare feet into gumboots by the front door and tramped out into the night.

Behind her, claws scraped at the glass. She turned to see the outline of Gypsy Rose in the doorway.

"Come on then." Paula went back to let out the dog and, together, they followed the path down to the gate, the crunch of gravel loud in the stillness.

There was no sign anywhere of Eve, no hint as to where she might have gone. A light was still on at the cottage, though its faint orange glow barely reached the drive, let alone the foot of the old barn. Silvery highlights edged the cottage roof and outlined the pens, but seemed to shy from the black mass of the barn, which dominated the nighttime farmyard with its supercondensed concentration of shadow.

Where to now? Eve could have gone *anywhere*. Paula's only certainty was that she did not want to venture near the barn in the middle of the night. The building disgusted her, made her feel almost physically ill. The idea of approaching it in the darkness gripped her insides like an icy fist. She veered from the path, repulsed rather than led by a clear sense of direction. The soft shushing of her boots through the long grass, still sodden from the afternoon's rain, was a relief after the loudness of the gravel. Somewhere across the paddock, a mopoke let go its mournful *boo-book*.

Gypsy Rose trotted ahead of her, pausing now and then to track night sounds inaudible to Paula. She sniffed the air and veered sharply to the right.

"Where you off to, girl?" Paula hissed. But sighed and followed the dog, almost tripping over an unseen tussock of grass.

The tussock turned out to be a leg, cloven hoofed and thick with fine wool. The leg was attached to an alpaca, cold and wet and rigid. Paula stumbled back, away from the body, toward where Gypsy Rose was snuffling, nose to the ground. There, Paula found another dead alpaca, and another—solemn lumps of shadow edged with moonlight. She swallowed, throat dry, stepped forward to where the dog crouched, and stooped to her haunches. She touched the neck of the nearest body. The muscles were stiff and yet the wool was soft, warm almost, and smelled as it always did, not like death at all. Silvery light glinted from the black globes of the alpaca's eyes. Above and in between, like a third blind eye, was a ragged hole the size of a five-cent piece. On either side of the hole were dark patches, like burns or smears. Paula reached out a finger toward the marks, but drew back with a shudder, not wanting to know.

She stood slowly, achingly, stretching her back. Gypsy Rose continued to sniff at the corpse. Paula toed her away.

"Stop it, you minger."

She scanned the dark around them. Faint outlines of trees against the blue-black sky. The distant dark of the hills. And behind her, back toward the farmhouse, the light from the cottage and looming hulk of the barn.

"Where are you, Eve?"

The baby turned. And with the movement a sick, ecstatic feeling rose from Paula's belly—a realization she wanted never to dawn. She took off at a loping trot toward the far pasture, where the sheep had been feeding that morning.

At first, she thought they were bushes. Humps of silvery gray that dotted the field. The scrubby hummocks stood out against the near-black grass as though lit from within, phosphorescing dimly. When Gypsy Rose stalked over to the nearest bush and began to sniff, Paula put a hand to her mouth to stifle a moan.

Sick sheep.

She did not need to look to know that every one of them would have the same glassy eyes, the same ragged hole.

Paula bent over and retched, came up weeping. "Oh Eve. Eve, where are you? What have you done?"

A single report echoed around the farmyard. A muffled crack from inside the old barn.

9

When Stephen was a boy, he had an imaginary friend. A woman he played with in the shadow of the old barn. She had no name, this woman, but she was kind. So Stephen said.

One day, Lotty heard screams from the barn. She ran to find Stephen surrounded by dust and shards of wood, by splintered beams. He had broken his leg falling from the barn's rickety loft. The woman, he said—his friend—had told him to climb up there. After, Lotty would not let him near the place. And Stephen never spoke of it again.

I had forgotten all about Stephen and his mysterious 'friend,' all these years. Only now, writing out these words, striving to compre-hend my own experience, only now does it come back to me. And I wonder: Was Miś, even then, reaching out to me through my boy? Or was Stephen's woman some other apparition? A figment of his own imagination? Or yet another avatar of the barn?

I have in my possession three photographs. The first shows the farmhouse porch and, standing before it, a weathered looking man in faded overalls, with a wild, tangled beard. The man leans on an upturned axe, has a sunken, faraway look. A date was scratched onto the negative and shows white in the corner. 1881.

The second is from 1923. It shows a man and woman in the foreground in front of a penned herd of sheep. The man leans against the pen, a cigarette drooping from his lip. The woman wrings her hands within her apron. In the background is the barn.

The third shows the cottage and a raggle-taggle group of shearers. The date, 1937. The men look tired and affect nonchalant poses, eyes shaded by dusty hats. All look to the camera. All but one. He looks across the others, beyond the frame, to where the barn stands now.

I see in these photographs a window on the past. They tell the history of this farmstead, of the barn. And yet that history is opaque. I look to these pictures for answers and find only questions. When I think of the old barn, it seems to me that it has always been there, that there was never a time when the looming mass of blackening hardwood was not a feature of this landscape. And yet I know it is a construct, that one of the men in these pictures built it with the toil of his own back.

Did he know what it was he built? Was there in its design some cruel intent? Or was there instead some aberration of material, of alignment, of chance?

What did they find in there, these men and women of the past? What private shame was disinterred for them, resurrected within the infinite rooms of that storehouse?

There is a room inside for every one of us. To each who treasures in his heart some black and corrosive lament, there is a room all his own.

I have found my room. And in it the secret I had hoped to take to my grave.

10

It was so dark that Chris could not tell forward from back, up from down. He was utterly disoriented, could hardly tell if he was standing or falling. Something, though, felt different about the room. It was close, dry, musty. There was no pink glow, no concrete echo to suggest he was still in the shower room. There was only the blackness and the silence.

The grinding had stopped. As had the wheezing respirations of ancient bellows, the faraway clanking of machinery. The air was dead and still and stale.

He was afraid to move. Without knowing exactly where he was or the path he'd taken to get there, he didn't dare step blindly through this darkness. The wet filth in the shower room was still fresh in his memory, as was the disgusting soft *thing* he had tripped over. He had no desire to tread down on some unknown horror, or to step out into nothingness and break his neck.

Cautiously, he reached out, tensed against the hideous and the unexpected. But there was nothing. Only empty space. He swung his arms slowly to either side, then circled, pivoting on one foot, hoping to find a wall or some other landmark. Straining his eyes, Chris could just make out a faint shape: an inverted *L*, only slightly less dark than the blackness all around. His first thought was of the strange symbols that cast their throbbing light around the concrete room. But as he focused, the shape cohered into a half-open doorway, only just illuminated by moonlight in the farmyard. He was not lost in the depths of an illimitable maze. Just a few broad strides and he would be outside.

Ahead of him the L widened and what little light streamed in was blocked by a figure, as tall and broad as the doorway. Chris froze, recognizing immediately the shape of the farmer, Eve. The moment to alert her to his presence came and went and he stood there without moving. As she stepped into the barn, her shadow stretched toward him, then receded as the double doors closed behind her and they were plunged back into darkness.

Chris barely breathed, listening for any movement from Eve, any sound at all. But there was nothing. Just the absolute blackness, the stale dry air. He closed his eyes, tried to picture in his mind the position of the door. Instead, there came a sound from the far corner, way over to his right. Sobbing. And a small voice saying over and over, "I'm sorry I'm sorry I'm sorry I'm sorry I'm—"

Heedless of the dark, of the obstacles that might lurk between him and the unseen door, Chris ran. He burst forward with arms outstretched, slowing only after a few strides, afraid of crashing into the wall of the barn. He fumbled forward, taking step after step until his fingers made contact with splintery wood. The sobbing seemed louder now and came from his left, closer it seemed. Chris panicked, grasping at the surface in front of him in desperation, hunting blindly for the door. His fingers found a rough-edged lip and he pulled, stumbled out into the night.

Only there was no outside. No moonlight. No farmyard. There was no deep and cleansing breath of night air. Beyond the door was only darkness and the suffocating closeness of a walled in space no wider than a cupboard.

Chris turned, groped for the door. And, like the *pop pop pop* of a fluorescent bulb, a neon-pink glow flickered into life around him.

11

Callum awoke with a start, disoriented and confused. The bed felt weird. The room was the wrong way round. The curtains had not been pulled across the sliding doors and, in the moonlight, Callum could see the edge of the deck, the fence beyond. Of course. They weren't at home, but at that stupid farm.

He reached out beside him, searching by touch. The mattress was cold and empty. His father had not yet come to bed.

Callum desperately needed a wee, but felt snug under the covers and was afraid to get up. Some ghost of his dream still clung and decked the shadows with unspeakable horrors.

"Daddy?" he said into the empty room. "Daddy?"

No reply. All was silent but for the hiss of wind through long grass outside the cottage. His bladder throbbed.

"Daddy?"

Callum crawled to the edge of the bed and peered down. The faint seam of light around the edge of the door reached only a hand's-length into the room. The space beneath the bed was darker than ink. Afraid to leave his back exposed to any part of the room for too long, he turned, checking the corners. Faint silver moonlight illuminated the edges of things, outlined shapes corresponding to nothing Callum remembered from the daytime. That looming mass in the corner must be the cupboard. But the lump over by the door . . . what *was* that?

Callum stared and stared at the thing, struggling to identify it by its shape alone. When it moved, he exploded from the bed, rattled at the cold brass knob and yanked the door open.

"Daddy!"

The main room of the cottage was empty. The fire in the grate, dark and dead.

A shadow moved in the window at the far end of the cottage and Callum froze, almost emptied his bladder in fright. But it was just his own reflection, silhouetted by the orange light of a standing lamp.

His cry hung in the empty room. The silence closed in. He wanted to call out for his father, but was too afraid to make a sound. Chris was not here, and behind him there was—

Callum forced himself to turn around, to confront the dark portal of the bedroom. Not daring to go back inside, he fumbled through the door for the light switch and gasped when his fingers made contact with the cool Bakelite. He flicked the switch and watery yellowish light flooded the bedroom.

The lump in the corner by the window was their suitcase. The open flap rested against the wall. Their clothes were heaped inside, spilling over the edge. Nothing was moving.

There was the cupboard, the bed, the one bedside table. Callum got down on his knees and peered. Under the bed there was nothing but dust. He could see all the way out to the wall on the other side.

With no immediate danger, Callum's fear began to subside. The more urgent needs of his bladder pressed at him. The toilet was just inside the cottage entrance, through the gritty concrete boot room. It would be cold and dark. He didn't know where the light switch was and did not want to brave more shadow. Crossing and uncrossing his legs, he rummaged in his school backpack, pushing aside reading books and loose Lego to find the flashlight his dad had bought him for camping. It was a small black Maglite, with a bright and power- ful beam. He clicked it on, lifted the old-style catch on the door and stepped out into the entryway.

Though it was cold and dark, and though the raw concrete chilled his bare feet, armed with the flashlight, Callum was no longer afraid. He found the light in the toilet easily and stood relieving himself for what seemed like forever. Though he felt braver now, he knew better than to flush, knew that the roar of water could hide the movements of any of the host of monsters beyond the light's protection.

Where was his father?

He left the bathroom light on, switched on the fluorescent in the entryway for good measure, slipped back into the living room, tugging the door shut behind him.

As he settled the latch, Callum heard, unmistakable and clear, a gunshot, reverberating around the farmyard.

12

It was the night of Obergruppenführer Heydrich's visit. My father had been anxious all week, knowing that the 'Blond Beast' himself was coming to review progress on his pet operation. But from my father's high spirits, when he arrived at our villa that evening with Wirth and The Beast in tow, I could only assume it had been a success.

Mother was over the moon, of course. She had been planning the party since she first heard Heydrich was coming; nothing fulfilled her quite like showing off in front of visiting SS dignitaries. From the noises that echoed up the stairwell, the party was raucous and bawdy. Above the guttural laughter of the men, her shrill voice resonated like a discordant flute, as she sought every opportunity to draw the attention back to herself. They were all in their cups and the noise was keeping me awake.

I crept to the top of the stairs and looked down but didn't want to be seen, didn't want to see them in this state, drunk and fawning over some notorious superior. Instead, I slipped along the landing to my father's room and sat there on the edge of his bed, admiring the play of moonlight on his hanging uniform, the silvery glint of the collar piping, the dull gleam of the Iron Cross. I was caressing the material, fingering the medal when I heard the door downstairs close. I must have jumped for the medal came away in my hand and there was no time to fix it. I slipped out of the room and back into bed with it clutched in my hand.

I lay awake with the medal under my pillow, my childish mind a turmoil of wonder and terror. To touch the symbol of my father's bravery was an honor that made my heart pound, yet I was terrified of what would happen in the morning when he saw it was gone.

My parents did not rouse until late that Sunday; a grave measure of the festivities the night before, for my father was a scrupulous early riser. I thought of sneaking back into the bedroom, but the prospect was too much like creeping into the lair of a dragon. And returning it might not be enough. I was afraid the cloth had torn when the medal came away in my hand.

Miś made breakfast for me and my sister, but I could not eat a bite I was so anxious, my ears so keenly pricked to the sound of footsteps descending the stairs. When she sent us out into the yard to play, I tore away from the table, the Iron Cross heavy and hot in the pocket of my shorts.

What made me hide it where I did, I cannot say. I am sure it was not any spirit of youthful malice—I can't even be sure I knew what I was doing. Had I known what would be the result of my action, perhaps I would not have hidden it at all. Or so I like to imagine.

I was terrified when at last my father sought us out, myself and my sister, ordered us into the courtyard. When he stood before us that morning, it was not as the proud and loving father but as SS-Hauptsturmführer Helmholtz, and I felt I knew, if only for a moment, the terror that the human cattle must have felt as they spilled from the train into his presence.

My sister was sobbing beside me, too young to understand what was happening.

He did not shout, did not raise his voice. He did not betray the merest hint of passion. And that was what frightened me the most. My father had gone and in his place there was this . . . machine. Absolutely without feeling. I dared not imagine what punishment might be in store for a criminal such as I, dared not speculate whether brick buildings laced with pipes were built for little boys who displeased their fathers. I could not meet his eyes, stared instead at the black gleam of his immaculate jack boots, at the breeches bursting from their top.

No, I told him, it was not me. But . . . I might know something about it.

Without looking up, I raised my hand, pointed past my father, across the courtyard. Toward the kitchen.

Miś was sent for. She stepped into the courtyard, drying her hands on her apron. Something about her presence made me brazen. The story had run so many times round my mind that I had begun to believe it myself. And the lie made me bold. My father did not look at her as he spoke, did not once take his eyes from me.

"Johannes has an interesting story to tell, Urszula," my father said, his voice betraying nothing. "Tell us, Johannes. Tell again the story you just told to me."

"Last night," I began, and wavered as I saw her eyes upon me. "Last night, I was awake and . . . and I saw the lady creeping out of your room, Father."

"Yes," he said. "Yes. Yes, Johannes. And tell us, what happened then?"

"I . . . I was suspicious, Father. So I followed her down the stairs, past the room in which you and Mother and Captain Wirth and Herr Senior Group Leader Heydrich were . . . dining." My body straightened as the lies fell from my lips. My feet together, my back erect. Every bit the model of Aryan youth my father saw in me. "Mi—the woman—stole back to her room and . . . and . . ."

There was the faintest hint of a smile at the edge of my father's lips, as though pulled taut by invisible threads.

"Yes, Johannes. Yes, go on."

"And she . . . And . . . And . . ."

Miś went pale. Her hands ground at the edges of her apron. Her eyes did not leave me.

"And I saw her hide something beneath her pillow."

"Very good, Johannes," said my father. Then he turned to Miś with raised eyebrows and that same mirthless half-smile. "Well, Urszula? What do you have to say for yourself?"

Miś did not look at my father. When she spoke, her eyes were fixed on mine. Her deep, sad eyes. And in that look? Pity? Love? More than sixty years have passed and I still do not know how to read her expression. Yet one thing I know. In her look there was forgiveness. And, in her forgiveness, the seeds of my damnation.

"For myself," Miś repeated. "It is just as the young master says."

The shot echoed round the courtyard. Smoke curled from the Luger at the end of my father's outstretched arm. Miś crumpled.

With slow precision, my father bent his arm, lifting the gun above his head, then lowered it once more to his thigh, sliding it into the leather holster at his belt. A red lake bloomed around the heap of rags that was, only moments before, Miś.

My father smiled thinly, his eyes boring into me.

He had known from the beginning.

I hear her songs every night since Lotty passed. I hear them as I lie awake in the dark, hear them in the wind that blows through the valley, through the trees.

In that mournful voice, a depth of sorrow that reminds me like nothing else of the homeland I never knew. The voice, the sorrow, they are inside me, inside my head. And yet, they are outside also, wafting to me from the silhouette in the doorway of the old wooden barn.

13

Ahead of Chris stretched a long corridor, lined with doors. It twisted imperceptibly, the perspective somehow wrong. There was a fizzing sound, the crackle of electricity. Was it a trick of the weird pink light, flickering from scrawls of illegible graffiti on the walls? Or was the corridor—moving?

Chris's sense of balance failed and he almost fell. The distant movements of the corridor made his stomach tumble. He reached for the wall to steady himself and recoiled at the feel of it, warm and malleable, with a pulse that throbbed in time to the sound of distant machinery.

A door opened and closed up ahead and Chris lurched toward the movement. He heard the tinkle of laughter, saw shadows writhe, before a door opened on the other side. It slammed shut with a crack like breaking bones.

"Miriam?" he called. "Miriam, is that you?"

Chris jogged along the corridor, trying to hold his gaze on that distant door. But the floor was as soft and pulpy as the walls, and he staggered against the corridor's tilt. Reaching the door, he grabbed the handle, yanked it open. It pulled away from the jamb with a glutinous sucking sound.

"Miriam?" he whispered and peered from the threshold.

The room was dark and small, lit only by a single candle flame that trembled in the corner. Bent over the candle, her enormous frame half-consumed by shadows, stooped Eve, her hands pressed up against her face in an attitude of prayer. Or so it seemed. She rocked softly, sobbing, repeating over and over her mantra of guilt. "I'm sorry I'm sorry I'm sorry I'm sorry."

Clutched to her forehead, Eve held a long metallic cylinder—some kind of prayer tube? It glinted dully in the candlelight.

Behind Chris, the laughter again; though closer this time, just over his shoulder. He glanced round just in time to see another door close, farther down the corridor. He turned from Eve and ran toward it. As his fingers reached for the handle, the everywhere drone and grind was burst by a loud but muffled crack, like a gunshot through a pillow. Eve's murmured incantation ceased. Chris pushed open the door, repulsed by the softness and warmth of the handle, and entered the next room.

It was small and sloped, with beams like the ribs of a whale arcing in and out of the sickly pink light. The room appeared empty, but then a shadow congealed, and Chris saw, huddled in a corner, a stooped figure. She had her back to him, her hands pressed to her face, as though weeping. For a moment Chris thought he was looking again at the hunched form of Eve, that he had left her room only to enter it again.

But it was not Eve.

Chris heard weeping. It sounded unreal, like a poorly recorded cassette tape looping in some other corner of the room.

"Miriam?"

At the sound of his voice, the figure cocked its head. Chris spoke her name again and stepped forward, then stumbled back with a gasp as she twisted impossibly upright, looking down on him from her full height. Her face was bleakly pale in the fitful pink glow. Her hair, ash blonde in life, was crow black and writhed in the stuttering light as though alive. She wore a robe of impenetrable dark—or perhaps she was robed in darkness itself, for she grew out of the shadows with no distinct beginning or end. Her lips, too, were black as the void and slightly parted and did not move when she spoke.

"Chris," she said. The voice came from behind him, from the side, from everywhere but that mouth. The words crackled and hissed. "My Chris. Come to me, my darling. Come."

Her fingers seemed impossibly long and bone-like as they reached for him through the flickering pink. Her shadow loomed among the rafters.

"Oh god," he said, and his voice sounded foolish and small. "Oh god, sweet god. Miriam."

He reached out toward her and closed his eyes.

14

Since the moment Callum first woke, he'd been in a kind of panic, a half-dream state in which the darkness was alive and filled with terrors. The emptiness of the cottage—his father's absence—was just an undercurrent, something of which he was only dimly aware. That awareness fueled his anxiety, but he was yet to fully confront it. The fact that Chris was missing was somehow less real than the shadows in the corner, the monster under the bed.

The gunshot, which had been stifled as though fired within a box, brought him sharply and at once into *this* reality. His father was out there somewhere. Out there somewhere a shot was fired. Rather than increase his fear, the dull crack from the barn seemed at once to transform it. The sound emboldened him, gave him purpose.

In the bedroom, Callum rummaged through the open suitcase for his clothes. He stripped off his night nappy and tossed it on the floor; the fact that it was dry did nothing to stop the flush of shame he always felt at having to wear it. He pulled on jeans, a t shirt and a gray Batman hoodie, zipped to his chin. He took the Maglite, slipped his penknife into a pocket, pulled on his Blundstone boots.

He searched the living room for something he could use for a weapon. Finding nothing in the kitchen drawers, he looked further into the lounge, grabbed an old and slightly bent iron poker from the blackened hearth. Something about the heft of the cool metal reassured him and, holding the poker like a sword, he flicked on the flashlight, lifted the latch on the front door and stepped out into the night.

It was easy to be brave inside. The cottage had become almost familiar, strewn as it was with his clothes and possessions, the handful of books and toys they'd brought with them to the beach. Though Chris was not there, the cottage still radiated the memory of him, and with it the promise, however faint, of security and protection. When Callum stepped beyond the gate, the enormity of that outside world overwhelmed him at once. The night sky curved above him, a boundless blackness pocked with cold starlight, vast and indifferent. A faint wind sucked at the pasture beyond the cottage, whispering and hissing, filling the air with swirls of white noise. The light from the cottage spilled only as far as the gravel drive, the outside edge of its protective circle. Beyond lay the hollow dark of the farmyard and, towering over all, the deeper dark of the barn.

Callum gripped the poker tighter. His hand holding the flashlight shook.

He shined his light up at the barn. As soon as the beam left the gravel, it disappeared, consumed by the barn's insatiable lack.

Gravel crunched underfoot. Callum willed himself closer, each step forward a struggle against his own terror. Even in the daytime, the hulking barn filled him with dread. Now, at night, it seemed alive, pulsing with malice. And yet the barn, he knew, was where he would find his father. Where else could he have gone? The ruinous old building had exerted a strange attraction over Chris since they got here, one Callum had observed but could not fathom. And the gunshot could only have come from inside.

So he pressed on in search of his father—in *need* of him—not once thinking about what he might actually find.

The closer he came to the barn, the harder it was to proceed. Decaying boards; a collapsed window frame; a faded sign above the crooked double doors. The flashlight picked out details that only deepened his fear of the building. The circle of light shrunk as he neared the doorway.

Callum listened. Only his breath, loud in his ears. The swish of wind in the grass. A metallic rattle from the empty pens.

"Daddy?" The word stuck in his throat. "Daddy?"

The door to the barn was ajar, just wide enough to slip through. The splintery edge caught on his hoodie and dragged the decaying wood loudly against the hard dirt. The flashlight jerked in his hand, its beam swallowed by the cavernous dark. Callum's mouth was dry. He could hardly breathe.

All was still in the barn, the outside sounds muted. There was a smell—not bad exactly, but . . . wrong. A rankness that transcended mere neglect. He strafed the floor, the walls, with the beam of his flashlight. The roving white disc revealed dust and debris, collapsed beams. A boot. Another.

Sick with dread, Callum held his light on the shape in the corner. He approached, steps heavy, thick, as though walking through treacle. Above the boots, a pair of work pants, the color deadened by the stark white of the flashlight. Above the pants a checked shirt. Above the shirt . . . He tried to swallow, but his tongue was swollen in his throat. Above the shirt, the face of the farmer, eyes fixed and blank, staring into the light. Her glasses were no longer on her face. The floor beneath her was dark and slick and shone as his hand holding the flashlight quivered. Beside her open hand, a metal tube like a lightsaber. In the center of her forehead, a black hole oozing red, a burn mark on either side.

Callum was breathing fast, panting almost. His stomach knotted, heart drumming in his ears. Yet even over the sounds of his own body, which seemed loud to him in the dull stillness of the barn, the murmurs from the shadows were close and clear. He jerked the light away from the body of the farmer, over toward the sound.

There stood his father, facing the wall, scrutinizing minutely some knot or warp in the ancient wood's grain.

"Daddy?" Callum moved toward his father cautiously, hairs prickling, voice stifled by the yawning dark. "Daddy?"

But his father did not turn around. He merely stood there, staring at the wall. And muttering.

Muttering.

15

"Miriam. Miriam. Miriam. Oh god, sweet god. Miriam."

The shadows curdled around him as her bony fingers caressed his cheek. The ghastly moon of her face softened, the black lips parted. Miriam gasped as she pulled Chris up toward her. Her grip around his neck was so tight, her embrace so filled with need that he feared his spine would break. He felt his feet lift from the ground.

The building was coming to life. The moment she touched him, the great, invisible gears began to grind—at once all around them and deep inside his head. A vast and hidden bellows began to wheeze and, somewhere—infinitely distant, infinitely close—the clang of metal on metal. The storehouse was changing, rearranging itself to make space for him.

Some quality in the weird pink light intensified. The room in which Miriam held him was not the same, yet it remained familiar. Chris breathed in sharply as he pulled his lips from hers, and the sound reverberated high and clear off peeling concrete walls. He had been here before. The writhing symbols like alien writing. The faraway ends of the chamber, engulfed in shadow. There was a gurgling sound, like the vomiting of pipes. Chris glanced down. The drain was backing up, black gunk rising beneath him.

Miriam's fingers tightened on his cheek and Chris felt her inside him, her fingers like roots burrowing beneath his skin. The black filth was up to his knees and still it rose. He felt it course through Miriam, pouring into him through her fingers.

He sighed and his eyes fluttered. He pressed his lips to hers and let himself be taken.

16

The fluting of magpies. A kookaburra's raucous mirth. Dawn colors filtered through tangles of wisteria, making the skylights glow. Steam hissed. Liquid bubbled. Paula turned the stainless-steel jug as milk frothed inside.

Already it was morning and she hadn't slept a wink.

The boy sat awkwardly on the leather couch. Gypsy Rose lay curled beside him, her head on his thigh. The boy patted her absently, staring at the book-covered walls—through them. Dark circles ringed his eyes, the lids puffy. He was obviously tired and yet he would not relax, sat stiffly, as if at any moment he might have to leap to his own defense. That same rigidity had settled over his face, locking it into an expression both somber and grim.

Paula could feel it herself. The set of her jaw. The swollen tingle in her mouth where she'd chewed and kept chewing her lips. The pell-mell tumbling of her heart.

As soon as she'd heard the shot, Paula had lumbered from the paddock down to the farmyard, Gypsy Rose trotting alert beside her. She'd headed straight for the barn—that dull report could only have come from one place. Even as she reached the half-open door, she reproached herself for not looking there first. She had avoided it out of fear and now . . .

She almost collapsed with relief when she saw the light in the barn. She spoke Eve's name from the doorway, tugged at the protesting wood to clear enough space for her to squeeze through. Gypsy Rose whimpered and remained at the threshold.

"Eve?" she said again. But even as she said it, knew it was not Eve.

Dust particles writhed in the stark blue-white of a flashlight beam, oppressed on all sides by the liquid dark inside the barn. The roving disc illuminated for an instant the man from that morning, the visitor to the cottage. The light jiggled and danced, faintly outlining the boy, his son, who dragged at the man's arm, pulling him away from the wall. There was something wrong with the man—he stumbled in a kind of daze, not all *there*.

The boy spoke first, a warning: "Don't come in." He swiveled the light toward the open door and Paula blinked, covered her eyes. "There's a body."

Paula's every muscle seemed to contract, tightening around the vacuum where her heart had been just a moment before. The word 'body' hollowed her out in an instant, and she felt sick and awake and numb and raw and surely she was dreaming but of course she knew she wasn't, knew she would find this, had been expecting it, long, she realized, before tonight. Her hands found her belly and pressed, clutched the unborn baby to her.

"I need to see," she had said. But now she regretted it, wished she had not seen. The thing that lay sprawled in the barn was *not* Eve; it must not replace her memories of the living Eve.

Paula stirred hot milk into the chocolate syrup, topped it off with two marshmallows, the familiar actions a balm that almost grounded her. She carried it over to the boy, but her hands were shaking and the saucer swam with spilled chocolate. He thanked her mechanically, sat gripping the cup, seemingly unaware of what he was holding. What was he thinking? Of his father, down at the cottage? Chris would be on the bed where they'd left him. The boy had tried to get him into a chair, but Chris's legs wouldn't bend and he teetered beside it as lifeless as a mannequin. Paula helped the boy usher his father into the bedroom, lowered him back onto the bed. They stood above him in silence, looking down at the catatonic man. The boy had reached for her hand and she had taken it.

"Drink up," she said, forcing into her words a certainty she did not feel. "I'll go through to the house and make up a bed. You need to sleep— we both do. Once we've had a good rest we'll know what to do . . . about everything."

He glanced up at her. And in his eyes she saw such exhaustion, such a depth of sadness she couldn't hold his gaze.

"You drink up," she said again, her composure crumbling. She had to leave now—this moment—or it would all fall apart. "It'll help—the marshmallows especially. I'll just be in the house. I won't be gone a moment."

Gypsy Rose padded after her as she left the café, crossed the deck to the farmhouse. Zorita was on lookout by the front door, a sentry so alert, so focused on her watch that she barely registered as they passed. While Paula loaded her arm with a clean sheet, pillowcase and duvet cover from the linen cupboard, the kelpie remained at her post, diligently waiting for the master who would never return.

The bed in the spare room did not need changing. The sheets had not been slept in, had only a faint dusty smell. But Paula changed them anyway, knowing it was only busywork. As long as she was awake, she needed something to occupy her—the baby, the boy, the dogs, even the washing up. Anything to distract her from the lump of granite in her chest.

When the bed was made, she sat on its edge with a sigh, her exhaustion bone deep. She realized belatedly that the boy might not want to sleep alone, that she should instead just invite him in to lay beside her. He was only a child after all. What, six? Seven at the most? Only a child and completely alone. As was she. Perhaps they would be a comfort to each other. She imagined them laying together, here in this bed, her arms around him, realizing as she did so that it was not for his comfort but her own longing to be held.

Eve.

She touched her belly again. Not entirely alone. This lumpen knobby thing would soon be outside of her, a separate and unique being, with his own body, his own mind. He would one day grow up into a boy just like the one downstairs. *No*, she thought, *not* just *like. I hope he never carries such a weight of sorrow.*

And then she thought, *I will carry it for him.*

The rock in her chest emitted a dull pulse and she closed her eyes, but tears would not come. It was too soon; she was still in shock. Eve's body still lay in the barn, would lay there until Paula finally pulled herself together enough to call the police. But then it would be real, and she was not ready for that.

She was not ready for the questions. The intrusion into their privacy, the quiet life they had tried to build for themselves here. Now it was just *her* life. Just her and the baby, and a farm they could not possibly tend alone.

Paula could feel her thoughts spiraling. What about the boy? What if Chris never woke up? Her mind flashed to an impossible future, one where she was mother to both—the baby, now a toddler, and the boy, his older adopted brother.

What had they been doing in the barn anyway? What did they have to do with Eve—with . . .

Paula jerked awake. She had no idea where she was, no sense of how long she had slept. She'd only closed her eyes for a moment, just long enough to rest them, and . . . Like something dredged from the bottom of the ocean, she felt the downward drag of sleep, puffing her eyes, pulling her back toward its depths.

With a groan she rolled over, pushed herself to sitting. It would be so easy to just lay back down, for her head to sink into the pillow, to fill again the impression her body had left on the newly made bed. But the boy, she was responsible for him. She'd told him she would only be a moment.

Zorita was still erect by the front door, more like a statue of a dog than a living thing. Gypsy Rose lay beside her, brows furrowed in a question, eyes on Zorita, one paw outstretched toward her companion.

Paula crossed the deck, squinting against the sun, disgusted by the feel of daytime on her skin. The exhaustion weighed heavily on her. The boy would be asleep, too, she knew, curled where she had left him.

But when she opened the door to the café, the couch was empty. The boy was gone.

17

Callum watched the movements of his father's lips. The hot chocolate—no longer hot—sat untouched on the bedside table. The marshmallows had half dissolved, pink and white blobs congealing as skin formed on the cooling brown milk. Chris hadn't touched it. Hadn't noticed, even. Callum had brought it down all the way from the farmhouse, stepping carefully, eyes locked on the rim of the cup careful not to spill a drop. He imagined the gift might stir the man from his catatonia, that he would sit up, thank Callum with a Father's Day smile, draw him into a warm and reassuring hug. And everything would go back the way it was.

But Chris had not even looked up. Had not in any way acknowledged the presence of his son.

Callum had been afraid at first that his father was angry, that he'd done something wrong, ruined something in the way he always did, and now Chris was mad, punishing him by pretending not to see him. And *wasn't* it his fault? Hadn't it all started with Chris's rage over the stupid walk? If Callum had been a good son, if he'd done what his daddy wanted, instead of sulking on the path, then maybe Chris would never have gotten so cross. Wouldn't have shouted the eff word. And then everything else, all . . . *this* . . . would never have happened.

Chris lay across the bed, rigid as a statue. He hadn't moved a muscle since Callum and the farm lady half led, half carried him in. He looked uncomfortable, with his feet jutting from the mattress. His arms were stiff at his sides, fingers crooked. Callum tried holding his hand, but the digits did not soften at his touch, and it was not the comfort he had hoped, was awful in fact, holding that snarled claw. Chris's head had not found the pillow, nor the mattress beneath. He held it forward as though propped from behind. The tendons in his neck were like cords of steel. His eyes bulged.

The sun was fully risen now and through the window Callum could see the pasture steam faintly, releasing the night's moisture back into the air. *Morning*, thought Callum. *Of course.* He left the cup of cold chocolate, left the bedroom. His father made no move, just lay there like a toppled statue.

Callum found the kettle in the kitchenette, unplugged it, held the spout under the tap. Setting the kettle to boil, he tore open one then two sachets of the complimentary Nescafé, emptied them into a mug. He took milk from the fridge, poured some onto the granules, drank the rest straight from the carton. He shivered. Even with his hoodie on, the room was cold and dim. The sunlight outside didn't seem to touch it. Through the far window he saw, beyond the drive, the dark edge of the barn. Callum shivered again, turned from the window, not wanting to see.

While the kettle rumbled and sighed, Callum knelt beside the ash-flecked hearth, pulled kindling and the last few sheets of newspaper from the log basket. He took the sheets, one by one, and crumpled them into loose balls, the way Chris had shown him yesterday. As he bundled and scrunched, he felt a blaze of anger erupt in his chest, tighten his throat. The barn. The horrid barn. As he stacked the kindling, then one log, another, he pictured the conflagration, the match touched to paper, the rising flame. He imagined the barn engulfed in fire, and he, with fists clenched, watching it burn. Perhaps, then, his daddy would wake.

Callum struck one match, then another, but each time the tiny flame fizzled. At last, he lit one right inside the grate and the flare as it sparked did ignite the newspaper. It smoldered, seams of orangey-red flickering along the paper's creases. And, for a moment, it looked as though it might catch, as though the wispy tongues of blueish, reddish flame would lift, gathering vitality as they devoured first the kindling, then the logs above. But though the sticks blackened and seemed ready to burn, the tenuous flame winked out and the room filled with smoke.

Callum knelt in the pall, chin boring into his chest. His shoulders slumped, shaking, throat so tight it hurt. Smoke and tears stung his eyes as he noiselessly wept.

A sniff. A snort. Callum wiped his nose on his palm, wiped his hand on his jeans, pushed himself to standing. The kettle had long since clicked off but the water was still warm and he poured it into the waiting cup. Even after he stirred it, though, the coffee didn't look good. It was too pale and the granules floated at the top, brown and blobby. But it smelled right, smelled like his father in the morning. The smell of the kitchen when he rose for school, or on Saturday mornings when he got up early to watch TV.

"I brought your coffee, Daddy." Callum placed the cup on the bedside table, next to the cold hot chocolate. "Daddy?"

But Chris did not respond.

"Daddy?"

Callum climbed onto the bed, curled against the rigid body. For a long while, he watched the lips move, then lifted his head to listen. Even with his ear right next to Chris's mouth he couldn't make out the words. They were just whispers, chaotic exhalations of warm air with a familiar unpleasant odor. He lay his head down on the man's chest, ignoring its erratic rise and fall. He clung to his father tightly, desperately, as if this embrace were all that tethered him to the world, as if to release his hold for even a moment would be to fall and never stop falling.

Acknowledgments

Thanks, first and foremost, to the tireless Tricia Reeks from Meerkat Press. This book would not exist without your commitment, your patience, and your endless dedication to both the craft and the hustle. Thanks for your belief in these stories, for making space in your insanely busy universe for true collaboration, and for being an all-round excellent human being.

Thanks to the publishers, editors and competition judges, who first saw in one or other of these stories a spark, and some connection with their vision. Shout outs in particular to Eric Secker, Sarah Read, Lee Murray, Sophie Yorkston, Keith Stevenson, Cameron Trost, Dirk Strasser, Michael Pryor, and Stephen Higgins.

The stories in this collection would not exist in the form you find them without the kind words and critiques of many fellow authors and fine friends. Thanks to the Carrington Critters, Bianca Nogrady, Steve Fraser and Amy St. Lawrence. Thanks to Andrew McKiernan, Jo Anderton, Cat Sparks, and Jason Crowe—and to the Sydney Shadows, for the love (and the shade). Thanks, too, to Kirsten Farrell for the sensitivity reads, and Halinka and Andrzej Orszulok (and, of course, Alan Baxter) for going *way* above and beyond to make the one Polish phrase in this book both beautifully poetic and actually make sense in the two languages. Lastly, thanks to Mike Lewis: silver lining to my blacker-than-black cloud.

Special thanks to Kaaron Warren and Aaron Dries, co-conspirators extraordinaire—for having my back, keeping me sane, and making me laugh till wine shoots out my nose. May the cat scratch ever at your door. And to Kaaron's dad, Victor Warren, for his deep consideration of the title story in this collection.

Boundless thanks to Rosie: first reader, reality checker, duprass lifer. And to my mum and dad: for tolerating a lifetime of my bullshit; for supporting my obsessions, whatever form they may have taken; and for that first notebook and the dream it recorded.

And greatest thanks of all to you, dear reader. For holding this book in your hands. For making it this far. For making space in your life and your mind for this weirdest and most wonderful of all communions—the magic that unfolds when one imagination meets another through the words on a page.

About the Author

J. Ashley Smith is a British–Australian author of dark fiction and co-host of the Let The Cat In podcast. His first book, *The Attic Tragedy*, won the Shirley Jackson Award. Other stories have won the Ditmar Award, Australian Shadows Award and Aurealis Award. He lives with his wife and two sons beneath an ominous mountain in the suburbs of North Canberra, gathering moth dust, tormented by the desolation of telegraph wires. You can find him at spooktapes.net, performing amazing experiments in electronic communication with the dead.

Did you enjoy this book?

If so, word-of-mouth recommendations and online reviews are critical to the success of any book, so we hope you'll tell your friends about it and consider leaving a review at your favorite bookseller's or library's website.

Visit us at www.meerkatpress.com for our full catalog.

Meerkat Press
Asheville